Presence, the Play

Bill Jefferson

Port Estillyen
PRODUCTIONS

Published by Port Estillyen Productions
www.estillyen.com
https://facebook.com/estillyen

Cover photo: iStock
Cover design: Andrea Orlic
Editing and typesetting: Claudia Volkman

ISBN: 978-1-7364967-0-1 (softcover)
ISBN: 978-1-7364967-1-8 (e-book)

Printed in the United States of America

5 4 3 2 1

CONTENTS

ONE
Presence, the Play

"It's wonderful to see Theatre Portesque packed for the opening night of *Presence*," Plot said to the cheerful miss seated next to him in the balcony.

"I know—we're excited," said the miss. "My boyfriend's in the cast; in fact, he'll be the first to appear onstage."

"Really," Plot said, as he glanced around, not spotting an empty seat save the one to his right. "My name's Plot," he said, turning to the miss.

"I'm Shelly," she replied.

"The play is scheduled to begin any minute now," Plot said. "Have you met the playwright?"

"You mean Brother Script?" said Shelly. "Yes, everyone adores him. He's so full of life, buoyant and all theatrical-like."

"Yes, he loves the arts. He should already be here," Plot said. "The seat next to me is his. The costume designer and a number of the crew are seated up here in the balcony to take in the opening performance."

"Did you work on the play?" asked Shelly.

"Yes, Script and I worked closely together on the development of *Presence*. Oh sorry, I just spotted him. Finally, he's making his way along the row. He must have gotten caught up in a few last-minute hiccups."

"Pardon me, please, pardon, sorry, thanks," said Script, as he passed by seated patrons on his way to claim his reserved middle seat. Front row balcony, seat number 16 was the only empty seat in the theatre, with a gold ribbon stretched across the arms.

"Great, you made it," said Plot. "Hand me your case so you can remove the ribbon. I didn't dare touch it; there were a lot of eyes on this seat."

"Yes, I'm afraid I skimmed a few knees and stubbed a toe or two," said Script. "Advancing along this narrow row would be fine for a cat, a skinny cat, but me—that's another matter."

"What kept you?"

"An issue with the light in the barn loft," said Script. "The breakers kept tripping, tripping, blowing, blowing; nuts, it's always the small things. Too many kettles plugged in outside the dressing rooms. Boy, they've really tied this ribbon—I can't get it undone."

"Let me help you," said Plot. "Here, it's tied from behind. There we go. Nice silk gold ribbon. Don't pitch it."

"No, I'll tuck it in my jacket pocket," said Script.

"You should pitch that old woolen jacket, though," said Plot. "Quit looking around; you sit down, calm down. The gold ribbon coiled inside that flapless pocket looks like a nest."

"Yes, it's a disappearing nest," said Script. "There we are at last. I love these old red velvet seats. It's the wear that speaks to me. Like the creaky floors backstage, creak, creak, and the sound of soles passing by. History, I tell you, Plot. So many years, scripts scripted, performers performing, music scored, songs sung—it's live, it's real, it's present. The theatre—what can be better, tell me? You can't."

"I know, it's a big night for you, Script. *Presence*, how long has it been, six years in the making?"

"And don't forget, you helped make it happen," said Script. "Oh, you'll be pleased to know that another check was just handed to me backstage. Perhaps it will help pay for the electrician. Robbery, in form of skilled labor it is, anyone who works on this old theatre, especially the electricians. 'Rip out the wires,' they say."

"As I said, calm down, Script. Take a deep breath. Your cheeks are all flushed red and sweat is trickling down the side of your face. You look like you've been roping cattle."

"I have, but they're called electricians," Script said.

"Do you have a handkerchief?" asked Plot.

"You know me," said Script. "I never go anywhere without a handkerchief."

"Well, use it then," said Plot. "Look at your eyebrows twitch—do you feel them twitching?"

"Not to worry," said Script. "I can't wait for that curtain to open. The lighting on the set is magnificent. You haven't seen it finished. The stagehands have been brilliant. A barn named Storybook—it's a perfect set for *Presence*."

"Whose idea was that anyway?" asked Plot.

"Yours, I think, wasn't it?" said Script.

"Anyway, get ready, Script. Soon the stage will come alive with your scripted lines, rhythmic tunes, whispers and shouts, and acts that keep the characters swishing in and out. *Presence*, the play, is on tonight!"

"I know, even my socks are starting to curl," said Script. "That's a line from Act Two. What time is it? I can hardly take the suspense."

"Well, according to my watch, it's ninety seconds to showtime. Here, put your eyes on my watch, as I track the time."

"Okay, call forth the time," said Script.

"*Tick, tick* pulses the slender hand, as it steadily pulses along," said Plot. "*Tick pulse, tick pulse*, up the second-hand sweeps, past seven, and gains on nine. On it ticks, on its upward swing to twelve, and quickly pulses beyond it. On it pulses, round the crown and ticks its way on down. One it passes, then three and five, as you see, all the while telling time. Script, what are you doing? Sit back down."

"No, just three seconds—I want to spin around and give a thumbs-up to the crew."

"You're impossible," said Plot, as he watched Script stand.

Script rose from his seat, spun around, and gave a thumbs-up to the crew and supporters seated nearby. Then, with eyes wide open, like an owl, Script went completely stiff, and backwards he fell. With nothing to break his free fall, he fell and smashed his head against the brass balcony guardrail.

Plot jumped up, grabbed Script, and carefully laid him in the aisle.

"Script, Script, hold on!" said Plot.

Instantly, from this aisle and that, people appeared and huddled around.

Plot, kneeling over Script, looked up and raised his hand like a traffic warden. "Careful," he said, "easy—he's bleeding; it's serious. We need help!"

Sister Ravena knelt and laid her right hand on Script's forehead. "All will be well, Script, all will be well."

A deep voice nearby said, "Hang in there, good man."

At that moment, the royal-blue stage curtain opened, and a tall, slender man stepped out of Storybook Barn and made his way to the center of the stage. In a lovely, perfectly projected tenor voice, he began to sing "The Pasture" by Robert Frost.

> I'm going out to clean the pasture spring;
> I'll only stop to rake the leaves away
> (And wait to watch the water clear, I may):
> I sha'n't be gone long.—You come too.[1]

Shouts from the balcony, however, startled the audience and halted the play. A loud voice boomed: "Emergency! Stop! Script, the playwright, has collapsed. Quick, we need help up here!"

The young man onstage froze and turned around, confused, not knowing what to do. He put his hand above his eyes and looked up into the balcony. In no time an authoritative, calm voice came over the house sound system and said, "A doctor, please, in the balcony, please. Thank you! Ladies and gentlemen in the audience, we need to wait; please be patient while we attend to this situation. Thank you!"

On the main floor, torsos twisted, heads tilted, and faces looked in the direction of the swirling commotion. In the balcony, a lady gently pressed her index and middle finger against Script's neck. She pulled her hand away, then reached for a handkerchief to wipe blood from her fingers.

Plot looked down at Script and thought, *Dear Lord, mercy, the night belonged to you, Script.* He prayed, and under his breath muttered. Next, trying to comfort Script, Plot crossed his legs and sat on the floor right alongside Script, who was lifeless and unconscious. Plot was frightened for his dear friend.

Plot thought, *Will Script make it? What's happened, a stroke, a heart attack?* All the worst options switched places in his mind. He tried to tell himself that Script had simply fainted, but he had seen Script go stiff before his free fall. He could see the blood and the distorted expression on Script's face.

At that point, a firm hand gripped Plot's, and a uniformed worker said, "Sorry, please, we need everyone back. Everyone, please, stand back—the man needs room, air. We're here to help."

The middle-aged male worker knelt down and shone a flashlight in Script's eyes. Holding open Script's eyelids, first he examined the left eye, then the right. Next he turned to his assistant and said, "Oxygen, Clive. Are they here?"

"Yes, Captain," replied Clive. "They're racing up the stairs with the gurney—five seconds, no more."

"Good," said the captain. "Okay, lads, ever so careful. He's unconscious and losing blood from the base of his skull. Wraps now, layered thick."

The captain extended his right palm, but kept his eyes fixed on Script. An aide swiftly placed several layers of white cloth in the captain's hand, which he gently slid behind Script's head.

Next the captain instructed, "Pillows, small, a pair." Out of nowhere, the pillows appeared. The captain took one in each hand and carefully placed them on either side of Script's face. Then he ordered, "Straps, the double-wide."

Hurriedly, another aide cut a generous strip from her adhesive roll and knelt down to place the strap across Script's forehead. Still clasping the pillows, the captain said, "Now straight down, over the forehead, and onto the pillows." The aide did exactly as she was told. "Good, another," said the captain.

With the pillows helping to secure Script's head, the aides rolled out a rubber mat in the intersecting center aisle, just a few seats farther along the row. Next they placed a portable gurney on the mat.

The captain said, "Okay, while I swing around to hold his head, two on each side, squeeze in, tight. We have to make a human gurney to get him to the aisle. Okay, hands to the back and hands to the thighs, and slowly lift. Slowly, slowly, gently, okay, okay, now carefully shuffle, shuffle, and again. Now we need to turn him and let him down nice and easy.

"Perfect, now the handles . . . I want all four of you to lift in unison." The aides knelt in readiness, each grasping one of the elongated wood handles jutting out of the gurney. "Here we go," the captain said. "Lift, while I continue to hold the head. Good. Now, you lot, make me proud, step in unison, up the aisle, then along the main aisle leading to the steps. So, okay, step, keep him perfectly horizontal, as if on a sled."

In lockstep precision, up along the aisle they went until they arrived at the staircase.

"Now, remember the stair routine," the captain said.

"We've got it," said an aide at the front of the gurney.

"In unison we step," said the captain. "Okay, one step at a time, halting after each step." Now step, pause, step; we bring him down as if floating on a cloud. Now step."

Plot, along with an entourage of concerned patrons, followed. They offered no assistance, only collective concern. As he navigated the stairs, Plot glanced across the theatre, taking in row upon row of worried faces. On the stage, the slender actor had been joined by other members of the cast, watching as the medics made their way along.

Plot looked at the cast standing there and thought, *At this point, the only script at play is Script, oblivious of the scene around him.* Through the side doorway they carried him. Next they transferred Script to a wheeled stretcher, placed him in the ambulance, and hurriedly shut the doors.

The spin of red lights chased across the brick exterior of Theatre Portesque and the faces in the open doorway. Plot stood in the middle of the curious group, stupefied, totally unlike himself. Just then, a finger poked his shoulder blade with the force of a silent command. He whirled about to see Brother Writer, with a face as sober as his.

Both belonged to Estillyen's Order of Message Makers, or Storytellers, as some prefer to say. The order dates back to the seventeenth century. The storytelling monks all had chosen names such as Chronicle, Saga, Script, Epic, Plot, Narrative, and Writer. Script, the playwright, was now at the center of the drama.

Writer said, "Let's go." Plot said nothing. Writer headed up the main aisle toward the entrance, with Plot in tow. Reaching the entrance, they slipped into the revolving doors and quickly spun out onto Front Street.

"Dear Lord," Plot said, "what an ordeal. Poor Script."

"I know," said Writer. "We need to get to the infirmary. Oban has gone to get his pickup; Hollie is with him. We can squeeze in."

In less than a minute, the headlights of Oban's old pickup appeared. He offered a wry smile, nothing more. No words except "Hop in."

"Yes," Hollie said, "I'll scoot over."

Writer opened the door and slid up onto the bench seat. Plot didn't want to do the same. He closed the door and said, "No, let me ride in back; there's a crate—really, please."

Hollie started to object, but she stopped when she saw Plot jump up into the bed. On a crate Plot sat, with his back to the cab. The ride to the infirmary gave Plot three miles of fresh air. The crisp air felt good, but his demeanor was deeply somber. The pickup's engine rumbled with a guttural sound, as Oban shifted the gears and they motored along.

Plot kept brooding over the whole affair, thinking, *How could this possibly happen to Script? His mood was so lively, and more than anything on earth he looked forward to the opening night of* Presence. *Now he'll be spending the night at Good Shepherd Infirmary. And how many nights after that, only God knows.*

Estillyen is a picturesque isle, with flower shops, cafes, a monastery, an abbey, and a vibrant village full of colorful characters. Sitting there in the back of the pickup, Plot thought about Oban—how Oban once claimed he became trapped inside a full-length mirror stowed in his attic. As he tells the story, he said he was frozen there, alive and looking out at all the figures looking in. An amazing tale, but Estillyen is a place for such stories told.

Generations of persevering Estillyenites tilled the soil and forged the isle out of rugged reality. Over the centuries, though, waves have deposited a wealth of numinous tales upon Estillyen's shores. The mix of steely reality and tales gives a special lilt to Estillyen life, unlike anywhere else on earth. Estillyen has become a rite of passage for pilgrims from far and wide, who routinely sail the waves to take in the essence of the isle.

The distance to Estillyen, however, remains a mystery to some. As the best of maps will attest, the isle is charted as far away from everywhere as anywhere. That's the beauty of a long journey, though: the anticipation of arriving on distant shores. At the same time, everyone that embarks on an earnest journey to Estillyen discovers the isle, mystically near.

On the opening night of *Presence*, the playwright was nearing Good Shepherd in an ambulance, while Oban, Hollie, Writer, and Plot motored along the winding road to the infirmary at a slightly hurried pace.

As they neared Good Shepherd, Plot thought of the slender figure standing at center stage at Theatre Portesque. He could hear his voice, like a reassuring presence:

I'm going out to clean the pasture spring;
I'll only stop to rake the leaves away
(And wait to watch the water clear, I may):
I sha'n't be gone long.—You come too.

TWO
The Infirmary

When Writer and Plot approached the glass partition at the ICU ward, they stood in silence, simply taking in the trauma before their eyes. They'd hoped to see Script awake, moving, and dispelling the balcony nightmare.

"Well," Writer said, "it seems Script may be in a serious way."

"Yes," Plot said, "I see what I didn't want to see. I can hardly believe that just a little while ago we were sitting in the balcony of Portesque. Now he's connected to tubes and wires, with his eyes sealed shut, receiving oxygen."

"At least he has vital signs," said Writer, as they watched the scrolling patterns on the monitors above his bed.

"No assurance from Script," said Plot. "I thought a wave, a nod, or a slight smile. He knows nothing of his condition, or of anyone's presence."

Tragically, the scene did not reverse itself in the coming days. Admitted Saturday night, Script remained in the ICU until Wednesday morning, then was moved to room 102, designated for comatose patients. Script occupied the room alone. Well, not really alone—a host of characters dropped by to pay their respects. The visitors spoke among themselves, to aides, or to one of the brothers.

Several visitors departed with comments like "Okay, Script, you're on the mend. See you soon." Or "Rest now, Script; you'll be as right as rain." Yet Thursday passed, and then a weekend came and went, allowing another week to commence. By Tuesday afternoon, the eleventh day, it seemed the clouds outside offered a future cast of Script's infirmary stay.

Plot had been by Script's side more than anyone else, camped out in an orange vinyl armchair. Just after 3:00 p.m., Plot thought, *No one's around. I'll take a break from room 102. Enjoy the fresh air and rest my eyes on something more pleasant than monitors.*

As he stepped outside, the white, billowy clouds began to part in clusters, making way for stretches of brilliant blue sky. He brought along a paperback Script loaned him a few weeks ago, which he'd nearly finished. *I'll head for the great wall,* he thought.

"Hello there," Plot said as he approached an elderly man sitting on the wall, wearing painter's overalls and smoking a hand-rolled cigarette.

"Howdy," said the man. "Nice spot, here on the wall looking over the grounds. I like to watch the squirrels chase one another round the oak trees, and those mockingbirds flap about in the eaves. The mockingbirds don't know what a good deal they have. The hospital refuses to kick 'em out because they like to hear 'em sing. Nurses say it's good for the patients."

"My name is Plot, what's yours?"

"My name's Charlie Chatsworth. Been working here at the infirmary for just at thirty-six years. I'm repainting all the trim this spring. Been at it for more than a month, and I won't be finished for another two months or more. Are you from the Estillyen Monastery?"

"You've pegged me," said Plot.

"Now that the sun's come out, you can see them imbedded bits sparkle as diamonds in this old granite wall. The Great Wall stretches for more than a half mile encircling the infirmary. Up and down it travels, following the hilly terrain so eloquently that some folks believe the wall knows it exists. You think it might be so?"

"Why not?" said Plot. "Perhaps in some mysterious way, it may. It's been said, 'Fields have eyes and every wood has ears.'"[2]

"I can tell you this," said Charlie, "over the years the Great Wall has heard it all—the confessions, the cursing, the weeping, the whispers, and the joyful conversations. I consider the wall a friend. When I stroll across the lawn headed this way, it seems the wall knows I'm present.

"When I approached the wall today, I said, 'Hello wall, it's me, Charlie Chatsworth.' I like to tell the wall my last name so that it won't confuse me with some other Charlie or Charles. The wall feels so strong and abiding-like—you know what I'm trying to say?"

"I do," said Plot.

"Want a smoke?" said Charlie.

"No thanks," replied Plot.

"Well, I need to be getting along, before my paintbrush gets all stiff," said Charlie. "What kind of book you got there? I see lots of green sticky slips poking out of the pages."

"I have a way of marking up my books," said Plot, "scrolling all over the pages. Not sure this would interest you; it's a work by a French philosopher from the last century."

"Okay," Charlie said. "Just read me one line, from the page with the first sticky note. I don't care if I understand it; I like to carry words around and work them into the day."

"Hmm," said Plot. "Okay, the first note; let's see, I've also underlined the quote. The author writes, 'God is beyond time and history, but with the incarnation he enters both.'"[3]

"Now, that's a real summation of thought, there," Charlie said. "I mean a true summation. Sure you don't want a smoke?"

"No, but thanks just the same."

"I'm off," said Charlie. "Time and history, indeed. You take care, there, Brother Plot."

"I'll try, and you do the same, Charlie."

"See you, then," Charlie said as he walked away.

As he sat there on the wall, Plot thought, *I wish I could smoke, but I've never smoked. It might help clear my thoughts, which seem to have*

fallen into a deep, ponderous well. What's to become of Script and his plays?
Accolades have poured in for Presence *and he hasn't a clue.*

Nearly an hour passed as Plot sat staring at the landscape, observing nothing in particular, but pondering everything.

Plot looked at his watch, knowing that he, Writer, Epic, and Brother Story had planned to gather in room 102 at half past four o'clock to meet with the medical team. Plot thought, *I'd better get moving; I've only ten minutes to spare.*

"Goodbye, wall," Plot said. "Perhaps I'll see you tomorrow. We'll chat again, as friends do. A line you bring to mind, which I'll say gladly, does not apply to you:

> *Something there is that doesn't love a wall,*
> *That sends the frozen-ground-swell under it,*
> *And spills the upper boulders in the sun.*[4]

"As for you, ole granite one, I see your boulders all, straight and true. Most walls are not built as well as you. But now, I've got to return to reality in Room 102."

At 4:45 p.m., neurosurgeons Dr. Page and Dr. Melchez entered Script's room, accompanied by an aide and the attending nurse. Writer and Epic stood on either side of the bed, while Story and Plot chose to stand at the foot of the bed.

Dr. Page smiled at Script and said, "Now, Brother Script, we've come to let you know we're still looking after you." Then looking toward Writer, he said, "This is what we know. Script is in a deep coma, although his vital signs are good. The trauma occurred at the base of the skull, where he suffered four fractures.

"The uppermost fracture, the worst, broke away from the skull and pressed in on the brain with a sharp, jagged edge. That could well have been the end."

"Do you think Script can hear?" Writer asked.

"Possibly, but everyone's different. Consciousness requires an interplay between the outer network and the inner consciousness network. The external network stimulates a full spectrum of brain hemispheres, while imagination and self-consciousness are centered deep within the interior part of the brain.

"Serious brain injuries can disrupt both networks. At this stage we can't ascertain the extent of Script's brain injury. We've managed to set the fractures and suture a gashed artery. Without that immediate operation, Script surely would have passed. He lost a good deal of blood."

"Dear me," Story said, "what are we to expect? Script's brilliant; we want him back; we need him back."

"I know," replied Dr. Page. "But for now, we wait. A coma usually lasts a few days but can carry on for weeks, or indefinitely. Our hope is that Script will awaken. The baffling part is that Script's brain scans have all indicated a high level of brain activity, not unlike that of a chess player. Something definitely is going on in there, but what we do not know. In all my medical practice, I've never seen a case quite like his."

"He's clearly not 'locked-in,'" said Dr. Melchez. "That's when a patient is completely conscious but can only move their eyes."

What a terrible state, Plot thought. *Locked in, alive, but only able to bat an eyelid.*

Before long, the doctors felt they said all that needed saying. After an exchange of pleasantries, Dr. Page, Dr. Melchez, and the dutiful workers moved on from room 102. Likewise, the brothers were satisfied with the answers given, though they were equally saddened by the sight of Script lying there.

Writer said, "Okay, as we had planned, the best action we can take at this moment is to pray." Thus they prayed and concluded by saying in unison, "In the name of the Father, and of the Son, and of the Holy Ghost. Amen."

"Okay, Plot," said Writer. "Epic, Story, and I need to get back to the monastery."

"Yes, right, you go on," Plot said. "I'll hang out for a while, not long. I want to tidy up a bit, gather the flowers, and arrange them into a single bunch."

As Plot pitched a few items and straightened the twin guest chairs, he noticed the closet door slightly ajar. He started to close it, but through the door's gap he spotted the sleeve of Script's woolen jacket. Opening the door, he saw the gold ribbon still nestled in the jacket's pocket.

He reached for the ribbon and thought, *Sure, why not. I'll pin it on the wall above Script's bed.* Plot arranged the ribbon so that equal lengths extended down to the height of the bed.

Then Plot said, "Script, time for me to go. You rest well. Gotta go now—I know you're somewhere. God's presence is with you, my friend."

Plot stepped out into the empty hallway and fixed his eyes on the ceiling lights reflected in the polished vinyl floor. The ripples of light provided a pleasant aura. So, through the ripples of light Plot passed, with the sound of his leather soles stepping away from room 102, step by step.

Script, though, beyond anyone's wildest dreams, had journeyed far from Good Shepherd Infirmary and room 102. As Plot exited the infirmary, Script stood on a path, peering at the darkened tunnel in the distance.

The Path

Hey, where am I? Script thought, as he stood on the path leading to an enormous tunnel, roughly a quarter of a mile up ahead. He touched his face, looked at his open palms, and ran his hands into his pockets. Empty, all, except for a tissue he pulled from his back pocket. He let it fall, and watched it drift along.

A few hundred feet ahead, he saw a tall figure wearing a scarf and hat slowly walking along the leaf-strewn path. Script called out, "Say, hey, sir, hello! Do you know where you are? I mean, I don't know where I am, but if you do, then that will be great. Say, how did I get here? Who brought me? Did you arrive by train, or bus?"

The figure kept walking, looking straight on and offering no reply. Script hurried after him, but no matter how fast Script paced, the distance between the two remained the same. Script broke out into a sprint, but he couldn't gain a single step on the slowly pacing figure.

All the while, they progressed along the path, drawing closer and closer to the darkened tunnel. Script thought, *I'm not entering that dark expanse. It looks ominous. I see nothing but darkness. And, besides, where is everyone, why isn't anyone entering or exiting? Where are the people? Nothing moves except the lone figure ahead of me.*

Advancing ever closer to the tunnel, Script yelled, "Stop, please, sir. We can't enter. We don't know where we are, or where we're going. Where does this tunnel lead? Hey, listen, okay? Have it your way. I'm leaving. So long, fellow pilgrim; you're on your own."

Script halted dead in his tracks, but to his horror, he kept advancing toward the tunnel opening, in perfect unison with the lone figure. The distance between them did not vary. Shocked, Script thought, *I've got to get away from here.*

Script spun around and began running as fast as he could in the opposite direction. He ran like a wild-eyed fugitive chased by bloodhounds and rifle-toting prison guards. He gave no thought to his appearance or where he was headed. Straight ahead he ran, until exhaustion forced him to stop.

I'm out of breath, spent, Script thought, *but I'm alive.* He bent over and placed his hands on his knees, thinking, *I'm glad that's over.* He even managed a faint smile as he straightened up and turned around, only to discover he had arrived at the tunnel entrance.

"No, no, this can't be happening," Script said. In a manic state, he fell to his knees. Then the lone figure turned around and spoke.

"Gotta go now," the figure said.

"Go? No," Script said, "you can't! *Miserere*: 'Save me, whatever—shadow or truly man—you be.'⁵ I need help, please! I'm a playwright."

"So, *Miserere*: 'Save me, whatever,'—is that line from a work of yours?" asked the tall man.

"No, no, not mine," said Script. "But, as a playwright, I know many lines from poets and plays. I know them, they know me, they speak to me, and therefore I speak of them. What I mean is that they are a part of me."

"I see you're honest," said the man. "I, too, know that line."

"Okay, you see, I've become lost somehow," said Script. "I don't know where I'm at or where I'm going. My name's Script. I'm a monk—I live on the Isle of Estillyen beyond the Storied Sea. Really, believe me. But I have no ID; somehow I'm here with nothing on me. I am as you see."

"What's that in your left pocket?" asked the man.

Script thrust his hand into his jacket pocket and pulled out the gold ribbon that had draped his seat at Theatre Portesque. "Really, it's me," Script said. He lifted the ribbon to his lips and excitedly kissed it. "I thought I'd lost my mind. Wait, though, who are you? Tell me, please; you will, won't you? And this tunnel . . . it's pitch dark inside, not a flicker of light, and we're going in, I suppose?"

"No," said the figure. "You're going in, not me."

"Am I dead?" Script asked.

"Listen to my words," said the man. "The prophets and poets inhabit the in-between, no man's land, where souls are sifted and sorted out. No one goes to the in-between because no one knows it's there. But now you do.

"It's more than a formidable journey that separates the impossible from possible. But I must warn you, what's possible can snap in two, along with you, if you render yourself weak and faithless. Faithlessness is the root weakness.

"The in-between—how shall I depict it? Imagine, let's say, a half-dozen rope bridges stretched across a bottomless gorge, separated at various distances. They all have a common trait: they sway and swing wildly for any person brave enough to attempt a crossing. The further one progresses along the bridge, the wilder the swing and the sway.

"Before reaching midway, most everyone begins to crawl. The fearful often faint, or freeze. Others cling and scream—for help, that is—if not in the throes of cardiac arrest. It matters not the weakness; any or all can pitch you off the bridge. Then guess what?"

"I don't know—what?" asked Script.

"You free-fall into a sphere void of time; fall and fall you do. You fall until you enter the sphere where presence does not exist. Then you float alone, lost between eternity and time.

"No one to speak to, no one to see, no one to know; you will exist as a discarnate soul. There is no way to change or rearrange your state of being. Because in actuality you are not a being."

"Hold on, hold on," said Script.

"For what?" the man said. "This darkened tunnel is your bridge."

"The tunnel my bridge, you say," said Script. "So I am dead, right?"

"Far from it, Script, you're on a vital journey. You are a traveling soul. Go! Go now! You'll take nothing with you because you have nothing to take. That is, except for the ribbon in your hand. As you enter the darkened sphere, you'll discover that the gold ribbon softly glows, illuminating the way.

"I must go now, and so must you. Goodbye, Script!"

"But your name, please?" asked Script.

"I'm a crier, of olden days, of papyrus, print, and page; just call me Sage." And with that, Sage vanished.

Script frantically rushed forth, near the spot where Sage had stood. With bulging eyes, Script scoured the site, looking for something to help explain the mysterious encounter. Next to a towering oak tree, he spotted a leather pouch with a shoulder strap, resting upon a large boulder. *It's his,* Script thought, *his personal stuff.* He dashed to the rock, sat down, and unzipped the pouch. Inside he found a tiny, smoke-glazed mirror with a crack across the upper left corner, and a scrap of paper.

He held the small mirror near his face; he could see his right eye and nose. *That's me,* he thought. Script pitched the mirror back in the pouch and retrieved the piece of paper, bearing three cursive-penciled lines. The lines read, "Freeze, you're caught in the act. The moon shines bright on this starry night, and your silhouettes stretch across the tiles, forfeiting your disguise. Step out so I can see your faces."

Woe is me—what does that mean? Script thought. *I must be dying, or I'm already dead. I can't think; I have to stop thinking. I'll simply walk away, that's all. Yes, I must; I will. I'll close my eyes, breathe, turn around, and walk away. That's what's wrong. As soon as I'm away from here, I'll know where I am.*

So Script closed his eyes and took several deep breaths. Then he gathered his composure, turned around, and opened his eyes. In a state of shock, he found himself perched on a rocky outcrop above a cavernous ravine. The path had gone. He trembled and felt faint. He was afraid he'd collapse and fall headlong into the ravine.

Continuing to shake, he managed to move his feet, inch by inch, as he backed away from the ledge. Nearly delirious, but still clutching the gold ribbon in his hand, he cautiously twisted around, only to discover that he now stood in the center of the tunnel opening.

Script thought, *Three choices, no more. I can commit suicide by diving into the ravine, I can lie down and eventually die, or I can enter the darkness and pretend to be alive. Woe upon woe, words of solace, why is it you choose not to speak to me? In my mind, you huddled together in passages stowed.*

I hear only silence. What can I do; what shall I do? I must go; choice three it must be. Darkness draws me, and I cannot escape. Silence, but no, I hear a line . . . I do. "This world is but a thoroughfare of woe, and we are pilgrims passing to and fro."⁶

With that, into the unknown I'll step.

THREE
Darkened Tunnel

Script stuffed the gold ribbon into his newly found leather pouch, along with his red bandana. Then he decided to address the darkened tunnel before venturing inside.

"Tunnel of darkness," he began, "it's been said, 'When a man has none for audience, it's little help to speak his evidence.'[7] Just the same, you are now my audience, and I wish to bear witness regarding my entrance, forthwith. What you are, to me, I do not know. Where you are, in the land of mystery, I do not know. Why I'm here, I wish I knew.

"Nevertheless, I'm prepared to move along your darkened interior. Pass right through, I hope to do. Perhaps I'll enter to discover you are nothing more than an apparition. Whatever the case, the case shall be. Words press upon my mind derived from an ancient narrative that I bring forth in support of my witness. The words are these: 'Men loved darkness rather than light.'

"Now, for the record, tunnel dark, I state that I am not that sort of man. I know—and so do you—that darkness shields the thief that rules the night. Therefore, darkness shall never be light to me. Perhaps, and I hope, you are simply a dark cave, nothing more. It's just the oddness of our chance encounter that skews my mind with such regrettable thoughts. Ghostly thoughts, I say.

"I mean, you must admit, you look rather menacing. Before you I feel tiny, like a mouse, but I know I'm not. Further, the manner in which I was drawn to you is rather far afield from a civil expedition. I'm not a scout or a leader of a troop. I have neither a backpack nor a torch, and I've never explored a cave.

"Till now, that is, I say. So I trust you harbor no ill will for my premonitions. Silly of me, of course, so your pardon I sorely beg. You're just a tunnel dark, right? Perhaps you hold the type of darkness that complements the stars, affording a backdrop so a lost soul like me can chart a course. Surely it's so, no? Perhaps your delightful darkness will even help me see the light?

"Darkened tunnel, I have little choice but to enter. It seems that time has set its hands on me, and time still ticks. Thus, half past three it appears to be. Afternoon or night, I do not know. You must lead somewhere, or you wouldn't exist. You have an entrance. I pray tell you have an exit.

"Someone carved you through, like a cavernous grave. I ask you, do you know if I exist? Or do I speak, even now, from the land beyond the grave? Emanating from your darkened sphere, I hear screeching sounds calling me.

"I stand at the threshold of darkness. The path that brought me has been rolled away. Sage, too, has vanished. So I surrender my stance. May my spirit live to see the dawn of endless days!"

Having thus addressed the tunnel, Script picked up the leather pouch, looped the strap over his shoulder, and walked straight into the darkness.

"I'm coming in," Script said. "So let's carry on, merrily, shall we? I'll carry a tune, and you'll echo it through. In that way, I afford you the most important part. You are the medium; I'm simply the messenger.

"Let's give it a try. Something meaningless I'll speak. Say, like 'Ting-a-ling, ting-a-ling, chime, chime, so said the clock, just in time.' But let me state my message giving credence to your echoing part. So, I'll utter a phrase, then listen for the reverberation before another phrase I'll send. Okay? Here goes.

"Ting-a-ling . . . *a-ling, a-ling, a-ling* . . . chime-chime . . . *chime-chime, chime-chime* . . . so said . . . *said, said, said* . . . the clock . . . *clock, clock, clock* . . . just in time . . . *in-time, in-time, in-time* . . .

"What a perfect medium you are, tunnel, such a delightful resonance."

For fifteen minutes or more, Script carried on in this peculiar manner. That is, until not a glimmer of light could he see behind him. At this point, he ceased his chiming rhyme.

"Dear me," Script said, as he marched headlong into a wall. "Such a frightening place this is. I hate the dark, this kind of dark.

"I must stay composed," he told himself. "I'll feel my way along; that's it, feel. I need a stick. But if I use a stick, I'll give myself away. Just touch and tap; that's it, that's the approach.

"Touch and tap, keep your head," Script whispered. Over and over he repeated the refrain as he progressed deeper into the interior of the darkened space. He'd take a step or two, then pause and listen. On he went; he navigated a sharp bend to the right, then a sweeping turn to the left. After the bends, he followed the tunnel floor downward into increasingly dank, chilly, musty air.

The floor, the walls—every surface Script touched—were wet. He was terrified by the prospect of falling into a pool. Yet on he pressed. Soon creek-cold water covered the top of his shoes, rising up to his ankles. So frightened was he, he trembled from head to toe.

Off to his right, Script heard a loud splash emanate from a distant, pitch-dark cove. Then, behind him, in the same direction, he heard a second splash, and a third. The splashes sounded like large fish breaking the surface of a millpond, or someone tossing a huge catfish back into the water. The splashes petrified Script.

Yet he dared not turn back. He knew that if he managed to find the entrance, there would be no place to go. He reckoned there was no way back from where he'd been, wherever that might be.

Eventually the water began to subside, and Script could step without making a splash. On drier ground, he groped his way along, until in utter exhaustion he was forced to lie down. Not wanting to sleep, he placed the leather pouch under his head to rest for a moment, but into a fast sleep he fell.

Therein, he dreamed he stood in the wings at Theatre Portesque, watching *Presence*, the play he had written. *Theatre Portesque—it's so wondrously inviting*, Script thought.

As his heart brimmed with expectation, Script fixed his gaze on the actor, center stage, who began to sing "The Pasture." *Splendid*, Script thought. *Perfect pitch he has. Sound, lighting, everything faultless, and it's such a wondrous sight to see a house full of watching eyes.*

Then, the final line, of the stanza brief, the actor reached: "I sha'n't be gone long.—You come too."[8]

"Yes, certainly," Script cried. "I'll come along; I'm coming. Where are you going?"

"Never mind, just this way," said the actor. "My name's Day. This way, sir, down along this winding road to see a scene."

"What scene?" Script said. "I don't recall this part of the play."

"You mean the play you're in?" said Day.

"No, I'm not supposed to be in the play—I wrote the play," said Script. "Day, I say, why am I not in the balcony where I'm supposed to be?"

"Don't be silly!" said Day. "That's because you walk with me. You walked out from the wings. Look, the audience watches. Tell me, with surety, that you've not forgotten your lines."

"My lines? I wrote the lines," said Script, "you pert fellow. You need to pay a visit to a doctor, Day, and not just any kind, but a doctor who considers matters of the mind. Obviously, you are out of touch. I don't say the lines; you and the cast say the lines. And I never wrote, 'Tell me, with surety, that you've not forgotten your lines.'"

"Have you?" said Day.

"Look here, I know my lines perfectly well," said Script. "Whatever you wish I can gladly tell. I once learned the entire text of the old tale called *Canterbury*."

"You don't say," said Day.

"I do say, you guild upstart. Forget about lines, my friend; you've lost the plot."

"Know this, I have not," said Day.

"I never wrote, 'Know this, I have not,'" said Script. "Further, this scene is all wrong; it's not in the play."

"Then why do we stand here onstage?" asked Day. "Look at the audience, if you dare; see how delightfully they stare. With attention crisp, they wait for lines as eagerly as morn waits for mist."

"'With attention crisp,' Day, you speak lines not mine. This is not how the story goes. You must untangle these lines before they suffer you to dangle."

"Okay, sir, you say; what I wish—you can tell. *Canterbury*'s 'The Pardoner's Tale'—might you have a line to spare?"

"I suppose I can, even though whatever I say is not in *Presence,* my play. Thus, a line from 'The Pardoner's Tale': 'Sitting at table idly gave behest to slay John Baptist, who was all guiltless.'"[9]

"Impressive," said Day, "considering none of this has been scripted."

"That's what I've been trying to lodge in your thick head," said Script. "You've led us down a rabbit hole, with neither a rabbit nor a hole."

"I hear you," said Day. "Surely I do, but under the stage lights we stand. We must act. We have no choice. We must act out the play in which we find ourselves. Therefore, at my behest, would you be so kind to speak another line—you know, just another wee test. Let's see, what about a line from 'The Miller's Tale'?"

"I don't know what you think you're playing at, but this has nothing to do with my play, *Presence*. If this is a play, as you say, Mr. Day, it must be called *Peculiar*. Although we stand under stage lights, we must be caught up in some sort of theatrical nightmare."

"'The Miller's Tale,' I did suggest; just a line will do," said Day.

"I should have hovered in the wings. But since you insist, a line I speak: 'I saw, today, the corpse being borne to Kirk of one who, but last Monday, was at work.'[10]

"The point is, Mr. Day, we need to get out of this alive!"

"I know, we shall, but now my fascination swells. I don't suppose you could call up a line from Dante's *Inferno*? You know, before our part is played."

"Dear me, I say. We have no parts to play in this *Peculiar* sort of play. You must know, Mr. Day, that actors don't just come out onstage and start talking. There are lines to be rehearsed, expressed with an aura of presence. But to satisfy your strange fascination, I offer a line from *Inferno*, Canto 5.

"'There is no sorrow greater than, in times of misery, to hold at heart the memory of happiness.'[11]

"Therefore, Mr. Day, I hope this . . ."

Just then, a lizard scurried across Script's face, and his dream-filled sleep was abruptly snapped. No more Mr. Day; he was back in the tunnel dark.

"Snakes!" Script cried out, as did his echo—*snakes, snakes, snakes!* "How did I end up in hell? And such a lonely, dark hell it is.

"But wait, I breathe; I'm alive. Still I'm entombed by darkness. I see nothing in this darkened sphere. Sightless, I touch shapes and forms. Now something has touched me. What's next, will I touch or be touched? If so, what? What if I place my hand into a nest of venomous snakes? They could be anywhere. Perhaps near my feet, right now, or just a few yards along the tunnel.

"For all I know, this tunnel could be a breeding ground for boa constrictors and pythons! From everywhere, they slither here to lay their eggs in darkness. I could be lying next to a nest right now. I hear something. What's that pop, that crack?

"I've got to get out of here. I'm desperate. I'll surely die if I don't. Mind, listen to me! Do you hear me? Think hard! Speak to me. That's a good idea. Take up your pouch and walk. Right thinking, that's it; walk a step at a time. Breathe and now step, think, touch, touch. Mind, think, we mustn't fail. Okay, right arm, sway; reach ahead into the darkness. Feel for forms and open space."

Thus, in this manner Script groped along. As time passed, a sense of utter desperation laid hold of his mind.

"Forgive me, God, thou knowest I am flesh made, and not begotten. I breathe now in moans or sighs. My only solace is that you know suffering. My mind's eye beholds a crucifix. Thus, I kneel in this wretched place, without song or light. Words fail me. I breathe; I sigh."

Then, kneeling there in that silent den, Script heard a faint, faraway tweet.

A tweet, he thought. *Was that a tweet? Again a tweet I hear. Now a tune; it's a mockingbird. A mockingbird it can only be, calling me. You tweet not in a cave, but somewhere in the light of day.*

Hope touched Script's heart. He rose and once again stretched out his hand. Following the sound of the tweets, Script pressed ahead into the thick darkness. The further he progressed, the more distinct the tweets. *Though,* he thought, *the tweets sound both far and near.*

Excited, he picked up his pace. Script felt he was making headway until he fell headlong over a large boulder and conked his head on a metal bar. Lying on the ground, he brushed his right hand across his forehead and felt a warm trickle of blood. With his left arm, he reached out for the boulder, and moved his hand along it, until he found the top.

Okay, I'll pull myself up to the top of the rock, Script thought. He managed to spin and thrust himself up onto the rock. *I need to just breathe,* he thought. *What did I hit my head on? Whack! It smarts. And has the tweeting stopped? All I hear is the sound of drips.*

Script listened to the drips slowly drip. He thought, *Okay, drips, you must have a source. And where's that pipe that rammed my head?* Script stretched out his arm and touched a bar, then ran his hand along to touch another, then another. He thought, *It must be a gate.* So, grabbing one of the bars, he pulled himself up and felt his way along the row of bars.

Next he discovered that the bars stretched across the tunnel from side to side. *It must be a massive cell,* he thought. *I can feel the anchor bolts that fasten the bars to the wall, but where's the gate? In the middle, it must be. I'll count the bars from left to right.*

Four, five, and now twelve, twenty, I'm up to forty; at the wall, I count bar forty-six. So, twenty-three's the middle. Twelve, eighteen, and five makes twenty-three. Again a tweet; you're not gone. How do I get through this enormous gate? There, a box; I feel it, and a keyhole without a key.

With both hands, Script grabbed the bars and shook the gate with all his might, but the iron gate didn't budge. *You are the Gates of Hell,* Script thought, *and how shall I prevail against you?* He worked his way back along the bars to the boulder, where he sat down and whispered two words, repeated twice, "No more, no more."

By now, the trickle of blood from his forehead had run down alongside his nose and chin. Wanting to wipe his face, he recalled the bandana in the leather pouch. Blindly, Script fumbled for the pouch. Wedged between the boulder and the bars, he found it and picked it up. He was quick to unzip it.

To Script's utter amazement, inside the pouch the red bandana glowed. He couldn't believe what he saw, or that he could see. He reached in and gently lifted out the bandana, and, in doing so, the bandana stopped glowing. The pouch, though, glowed on, due to the gold ribbon nestled inside.

Spare my soul, Script thought, *what did Sage say?* "As you enter the darkened sphere, you'll discover that the golden ribbon softly glows, illuminating the way." *Illuminating the way, yet I've groped in darkness. You've been with me all along, ribbon gold.*

Script reached into the pouch and gently moved his forefinger along the glowing ribbon until he found its end. Very carefully, he lifted the glowing ribbon from the pouch and stretched it out in front of him. Then he wound it around his neck, as a scarf. The ribbon extended down past his hands to the height of his knees.

I feel transfigured, he thought. Next, Script turned toward the massive gates, now visible in the golden hue of the scarf. *The gates must be twenty feet tall, maybe more,* he mused. He glanced at the ceiling and saw how the bars disappeared into bored holes. Looking down, he could see the same method had been used for securing bars to the tunnel floor.

Script thought, *The bars run along the entire circumference of an arched ceiling. Bored above and below, bolted to the walls, this impressive barrier could imprison both man and beast.*

Still stunned by the ribbon discovery, Script stood awestruck in front of the gates, basking in the golden glow. Then, out of the corner of his eye, he saw what looked like a partially exposed gold coin. Curious, he reached down to pick it up, only to find that dust had concealed the object's true identity.

"Coin, you're not a coin—you're a key," Script whispered. "An imposing key, too, I see. I don't suppose you and the gate lock belong to the same maker? You look so purposely formed. How did you end up in the dirt anyway? Did you loosen yourself from a ring, or from a pocket drop? Whatever the case, an enormous barricade stretches before me.

"To pass through, one must go via these gates, and I am the one desperate to pass through. If you help me escape, key, I'll take you with me. You only need to enter the keyhole and turn 180 degrees as I hold you in my hand. Okay? You hear that, key, that steady beat? That's my heart. Shall we try that turning maneuver?"

With a trembling hand, Script stretched forth the key and guided it to the hole. "Now, key, the maneuver you've surely not forgotten. Slowly I turn to the left, as you begin to turn with me. Yes, yes, that's it, clack; just like that, the bolt has given up its hold on you and me.

"I feel a slight breeze. Hold on, key, stay put while I gather my belongings, my pouch and bandana. Now let's go, key. Which would you prefer, a pocket or a pouch? So, into the pouch you go. Hear that? That's a tweet."

Like a soul in garland lit, Script stepped past the barricade with his glowing scarf. As he moved along the shadowy interior, each and every step drew him nearer to the light of day. Darkness gave way to his golden glow.

In the company of bats and crawly creatures, Script made his way toward the light. To the right, he turned. Then straight again he progressed, and eventually he veered left.

Script never looked back. In time, his eyes caught a glimmer of light filtering into the darkened space.

He smiled and softly said, "Mercy, what a lovely sight."

FOUR
Mission Disclosed

The smell, the light, the sight . . . a more delightful scene I've never seen, Script thought, as he stepped free of the darkened tunnel. He turned around and said, "Tunnel dark, you are now my backdrop, nothing more. Look what greets me—an amazing canopy of apple trees, with rays of sunlight filtering through blossom-covered branches."

What a contrast of life and death so naturally depicted, Script thought, as he admired how the apple trees pressed right up against the ivy surrounding the tunnel's perimeter. *It's usually the reverse, is it not?* he reflected. *Evil encroaching good, but here the trees surround the darkness with life, in bloom. If only I had a pad to sketch the scene.*

Script thought, *Perhaps I can recreate this scene for a future play. But shall I ever write another play? Maybe Day is right; I'm in a play I didn't write. But Day was just a dream. This is reality; it must be. The fragrant petals floating down in front of me I clearly see. I smell their fragrance. The way the petals chase each other along the cobblestone path . . . it's real, not a set, not an act.*

This delightful sight welcomes me, but I'm weary. The healing warmth of the sun I sorely need. The lone wooden bench along the path looks as if it waits for me. A prop? No, I don't think so.

Bench, you are in a perfect place for a wandering soul like me. One of a kind you are; I trust you'll not mind an admirer like me taking a seat. Such a pleasant scent is wafting through the air, beyond description nearly, but one day I shall pen this place with ink in a storied script. Just now, however,

I think I'll close my eyes, bench, and lean back on your sturdy, warm wood rails. I could stay here indefinitely, so silent, so tranquil. Can you hear my thoughts, bench? I suspect you can.

"Though let me say audibly," said Script. "I've cleared the tunnel. I'm out, not in, and I'm starved!"

"I thought you might be," said the voice of someone standing near. Startled, Script sat up and fixed his eyes on the figure standing on the cobblestone path.

"I see you found the key," said Sage. "So many don't. Few do; number yourself among the chosen."

"Sir, I . . ."

"You know my name; it's Sage. I must say, Script, you look like you've been in a brawl. The darkened tunnel is not for the fainthearted. Some even call it the chamber of lost souls. Not I. Anyway, we have much to consider—your place, your mission, and not least, the Isle of Estillyen."

"Estillyen, you know . . . I, I . . . ?"

"There's much that I shall reveal to you, but not now. Just now, consider the path before you, which leads to the Meadow of Gates and Doors. In the middle of the meadow, you'll see a cottage; it's called Writer's Cottage. You can't miss it; it's the only cottage in the meadow. Writer's Cottage will be your residence for as long as you need to stay.

"Please, let's walk along. I'll point you in the right direction. No time to dither; we've much to consider."

Script walked with Sage as if accompanying a ghost. He could barely form a thought, and he didn't speak a word. Sage, too, remained silent, until they reached the towering pine trees.

"Okay, Script, just beyond the Y, to your left, you'll come upon Writer's Cottage. Inside you'll find a fresh outfit, exactly your kind of kit. You'll also find a narrow bed. Narrow beds, by the way, are made for nestling in, not sprawling about. Narrow beds comfort you; they make you feel as if you belong. Just behind the cottage, there's a warm mineral spring. It's ideal for soaking.

"Oh, and be sure not to misplace your gold ribbon and the key. They belong together; keep them near. I'll have more to say later. But now, soak and rest, and we'll eat soon. Smell the aroma of fresh-baked bread?

"When it's time to eat, you'll hear a mockingbird calling you. But before Mock calls, you'll have time for a nap. Anyway, I gotta go! But I'll be back." Sage paced another step or two and then simply vanished.

Script thought, *What is this place, and Sage—is he an angel, or some kind of phantom? He seems human, yet humans don't vanish, disappear. Oh, I don't know, I don't know. And me, I must have vanished from somewhere to get here. I didn't plan to come here. I didn't know there was a Meadow of Gates and Doors.*

Something very strange has happened to me. I'm locked into a sphere in which I don't belong, but I'm here. How can I even process this? I don't know what to do. If I run, where will I go? Besides, I'm dazed and exhausted. Maybe this is some kind of hoax, but no, it's all too serious for that. I must get a grip. At least I know I'm me, or so it seems to me.

"Okay, Writer's Cottage, I'm here," Script said. "I see you have a front porch with three wooden steps. It seems you are set at the edge of a forest with tall pines. Now, that's the path on which I walked, and another leads to the meadow. Cottage, I suppose I should enter. What if a murderer hides inside, under the stairs, or in a closet?"

Get a hold of yourself, Script, you must; the cottage is not speaking. I know, mind, but you are. The screen door, it doesn't look menacing; it's painted a dark ivy green. And the front door is already open. No locks; no key to turn. It looks inviting, sure, but what lurks beyond the screen door of ivy green? Okay, okay, I'll go, venture inside.

Script climbed the porch steps without even looking down at the treads. Mechanically he opened the screen door and entered the cottage. A round pine table with two wooden chairs occupied the center of the room. In the middle of the table, a tall ivory candle burned with a flickering flame. *Now, that's a surprise*, he thought. *Perhaps I'm not alone.*

"Hello, hello, Script here, just another guest arriving. Sorry to intrude. Sage said I would be staying at Writer's Cottage. Hello, I say. I'll just wait here." Script stood still, but no one responded; not a sound did he hear. *Perhaps they've gone outside*, he reasoned.

Well, he thought, *this is sure a far better sight than the tunnel dark. Nice pale-green stucco wall in the hallway. And hooks on which are hung my change of clothes neatly aligned. Spooky, but the clothes, the cloth—it is cloth I feel. They're real.*

Script took off his pouch and secured its strap on an empty hook. Then he carefully removed his gold ribbon and laced it over the pouch. Next he made his way through the small kitchen to a mudroom at the back of the cottage. He took off his torn and tattered clothes, lifted the lid from a straw basket, pitched his clothes in the basket, and replaced the lid.

Above the basket, brown bath towels and washcloths were carefully stacked. And next to the towels, a large bar of soap rested in a wooden dish. Script grabbed two of the brown towels and placed them under his left arm. Next he reached for the cream-colored bar of soap and headed for the back door of the cottage.

Dear me, he thought. *I wear not a stitch—what if someone walks in on me? What do I know? Nothing, really. Here I stand, with towels in hand, in Writer's Cottage. At any minute, a bunch of college students could bounce through the door. Maybe I should at least lock the front door. Okay, with a towel around my waist, back through the kitchen I step, and on into the front room, where I see the candle still lit.*

"Door, if you don't mind, I'll lock you for a while. Nice, thick wooden door you are, with heavy hinges, but you have neither a handle, nor a lock. Equally so, you are latch-less. Okay, I'll leave you be.

"Off I go to the back of the cottage. Candle, I think I'll blow you out; lovely you are, but I'm not sure why you burn in the light of day.

So, *poof*, and I watch as your trail of smoke rises high. Don't be sad, candle. I'll return."

In the kitchen doorway, Script glanced back at the front room. And astonished he was to see the candle burning again.

Yikes, Script thought. *Strange candle. I'll carry on. What am I to do, anyway, run outdoors and proclaim, "A candle puffed, has lit itself"? No, I must embrace the weirdness casually. Yes, that's it. In this meadow, I'm beginning to think that what's strange is quite normal.*

At the back of the cottage, Script discovered a stone walk leading to the natural mineral pool, which was surrounded by pine trees. A thick row of holly bushes ran along either side of the walk, so amid the holly bushes Script made his way. He eagerly slipped into the warm mineral pool, in which a natural current swirled. The pool's perimeter of stone provided a perfect place for Script to rest his head.

How long he stayed in the pool he wasn't sure, as he repeatedly nodded off. He thought, *I feel like a character in a play, but I'm me. Who would have written such a play? If Sage's "chamber of lost souls" is behind me, what awaits me?*

Finally, after an extended soak, Script showered in a stone enclosure adjacent to the pool. Not a soul was around. Script reentered the cottage, put on his clean set of clothes, and stretched out on the narrow bed. In no time, he was fast asleep. Script barely moved as an hour passed, then another, followed by a third.

Then, from a pine tree near Script's window, Sage's mockingbird began to sing:

tcheck tcheck, ch-reee ch-reee ch-reee—check check, chur-wi chur-wi tru-ly tru-ly—tcheck tcheck, ch-reee ch-reee ch-reee

Script awoke to the aroma of roasted meat. He quickly laced his shoes and exited Writer's Cottage. He walked along the path leading into a clearing in the meadow, where he found Sage preparing food over a stone firepit.

"Hello, Script," said Sage. "I see Mock roused you. That's Mock, just there, on the lower branch. We didn't wake you earlier, thinking you needed rest."

"He must be a rather remarkable bird," Script said. "I've never been so hungry."

"And the mineral pool—nice, was it?"

"Unbelievable, but, Sage, tell me, the Meadow of Gates and Doors—where are we? Where is this place? I mean, I know we're here, but where is here? You know, that is, if a person wanted to find here on a map. What's the nearest town?"

"I can't say with certainty," said Sage. "We are North of South, and a little further East than West. But let's not worry about longitude and latitude just now; it's time to eat. It will be evening soon anyway. You should eat and then get some more rest. Tomorrow we'll get into a bit more detailed discussion."

"Okay, but I need to get my bearings. I don't think there is any place like this, yet I'm here, not knowing where or why."

"Perfect, these skewers; would you prefer fowl, or lamb, or both?"

"Either," Script said.

"There you are," said Sage, "Skewered vegetables to go with it, and do try the bread while it's still warm."

"Is someone else turning up? You must have a dozen skewers on the fire," said Script. "Amazing how this bread steams when I pull it apart; it's so fresh, so delicious."

"No, no one else—just you, Mock, and me," said Sage.

Script did not know what to say . . . or not to say. He felt he should try to make conversation, yet he felt hesitant, even leery, of what might happen next. He noticed that Sage seemed to pull everything out of a large trunk. And somehow the water jug kept filling as he tried to drink it dry.

"You know, earlier," said Script, "I blew out the candle in the front room of the cottage, and, to my amazement, the candle relit itself."

"Yes, that can sometimes happen," said Sage. "Would you care for another skewer?"

"I think I've . . . let's see, my fifth that would be," said Script.

"Yes, there's plenty more," said Sage.

Script thought, *Perhaps I am in another world. I don't remember dying, though. Do the dead know they have died or . . .*

"Sorry to interrupt your train of thought, Script. Just a wee word, before I go."

"Where are you going?" asked Script.

"Oh, just around the bend. I have a little lodging place, sort of a lean-to, like a tent. Anyway, please eat as much as you wish. Mock will stay here to keep you company, and he'll perch outside your window tonight.

"We'll talk more tomorrow, but rest as long as you want. I'll be around; we'll have breakfast. So, tomorrow," Sage said. And he was gone.

After Script finished eating, he stayed on for a while and watched the coals die down in the firepit. Then he strolled round the campsite. *So strange,* he thought. *There's nothing here but the campfire, the table, and Sage's round-top trunk.* Script studied the trunk, thinking, *It looks so ancient, with its heavy, intricate strap hinges and an old-style padlock the size of my hand. I won't dare touch it.*

This place is totally other, Script concluded, as he made his way back to Writer's Cottage. Soon he stretched out on his narrow bed, and he resolved not to wonder why. Instead, he decided to simply carry on, with his mysterious friend Sage. With a pillow under his head and another on top, Script's thoughts drifted away, as he swiftly fell asleep.

Early the next morning, Script was again awakened by Mock's tweets.

tcheck tcheck, ch-reee ch-reee ch-reee–check check, chur-wi chur-wi tru-ly tru-ly–tcheck tcheck, ch-reee ch-reee ch-reee

Script shaved, dressed, and headed back down to the campsite, where he found a note on the table that read:

Good morning. Please help yourself to breakfast.
See you in a bit.
Sage

A metal griddle spanning the firepit warmed a cast-iron skillet, which contained sauces, scrambled eggs, and fried tomatoes. A tin next to the skillet held fresh-baked rolls. On the table, under a cover, Script found wedges of cheese, dates, figs, and three apple tarts.

I'm in the theater of the absurd, he thought. Regardless, he found everything delightful. While he was eating, Mock flew in and perched on the end of the table.

"Mock, where's your owner, Sage?" Script said.

"I've just arrived," said Sage, as he approached, wearing his brimmed hat and scarf. "Would you mind if I joined you?"

"No, please do," Script said. "You startled me."

"A positive sign," said Sage. "If you can experience fright, your senses are working. Anyway, I think this is as good a time as any to press into the matters at hand."

"Does that finally mean clarity?" said Script.

"Clarity? I'm not sure that's on offer, Script. The matters of which I speak do not lend themselves to the realm of commonality. Rather, they are of cosmic importance. Listen, therefore, very carefully to what I now convey. Do I have your utmost attention, Script?"

"Sure," said Script. "But what do matters of cosmic importance have to do with me? Are you sure you are speaking to the right person? Maybe there is a mix-up of sorts. And it's such a lovely day to propose matters of great gravity, don't you think? Did you know that male mockingbirds can imitate not only birds, but barking dogs, frogs, and even ringing bells?"

"I do," said Sage.

"Cosmic, you say?" said Script.

"Yes, Script. Now in terms of matters grave, I begin with a name that's below every name: Beelzebub."

"Beelzebub!" repeated Script.

"Don't jump out of your skin, Script. Just listen, for I have much to say. You recall the story of Job, no doubt. According to the ancient tale, when the angels came to present themselves to God, Satan joined the heavenly retinue. He appeared not as a phantom, but as himself, the wanderer of earth eager to blight human flesh. What ensued was not a peaceful, tranquil picture, was it?"

"No, Job's wife even advised him to curse God and die," Script said. "Very compelling and meaningful story, though."

"Beelzebub still roams, Script. With a bond of hate and angst against I AM, his wretched kingdom holds together. The Spires of Spite tower tall in his ever-changing wasteland of wanton souls. Deceit and deception provide the daily diet for those over whom Satan rules.

"Beyond the Gates of Hell, in the darkest of darkened chambers, stone tables bear Satan's sayings, which he clawed in stone and fastened high to the wall. The darkened chamber is called the Chamber of Luminosity. Below the tablets, a band of locked-armed demons stand guard, endlessly repeating each and every line.

"In every language on earth, they do so, as well as in languages known only in the cosmic realm. Chief among the cosmic languages is the one formed by Satan after he blazed through the skies like a meteor and plunged to earth. Satan's downdraft pulled in a defeated angelic host that trailed in a blazing train, underscoring the ferocity of Satan's precipitous fall."

"But, Sage—"

"No, just wait, Script. Hear me out. Beyond the Gates of Hell rise the Spires of Spite, centered in the very hub of hell. This is where the Crimson Cliffs are found, which, in turn, front the Reservoirs of Bewilderment: Fragmentation, Static, Confusion, Chatter, and

Delusion. Consider the Reservoirs of Bewilderment as a kind of training camp for Satan's kingdom.

"Earlier you asked me a question, Script."

"Did I, Sage?"

"You asked if these matters of cosmic importance relate to you, though you said *me*, meaning you. In a word, yes! Definitely, more than you could think or imagine, Script, but you needn't imagine because I'm going to tell you."

"You are? Are you sure you really need to, Sage?"

"Yes, Script! And I must tell you the issue centers on the Isle of Estillyen and *Presence,* your play. I recently saw *Presence* at the Theatre Portesque, and I found it superb. It was very captivating and moving. I carried from the theatre something most memorable."

"What?" asked Script.

"I speak of images and lines that press upon the mind. Anyway, I'm here to tell you, you'll soon enter the vast abyss and explore the Crimson Cliffs and all the rest."

"Hold on, Sage. You're mad. Are you trying to tell me that I'm going to hell?"

"Precisely, but not as a resident of hell, or as a lost soul; you shall go and hopefully return. You must go to hell to save the inhabitants of Estillyen, the Estillyenites. That's your mission. That is, if you are willing to accept it . . .

"Sorry, Script, we have no other candidate from the Isle of Estillyen. Besides, your play, *Presence,* is at the heart of the matter."

"Sage, why do I feel my soul departing as you speak? Do you have this effect on everyone? I need to get well, not worse, to find my way back to my work as a playwright and my vocation as a monk. Don't you know that 'a monk, when he is cloisterless, is like unto a fish that is waterless'?"[12]

"Script, what if one day you overheard me speaking to an indispensable person?"

"I'd listen in, I suppose, if I knew that you were favorably disposed."

"Script, you are the indispensable person that I'm speaking with."

"You mean, I've just overheard you speaking to me?"

"Yes, in a manner of speaking, Script."

"Sage, hold on—are we speaking hypothetically or speaking actually?"

"The latter, Script."

"I just wanted to clarify the matter. I suggest, therefore, that you find a hypothetical person rather than me."

"No, Script. The word *presence* says it all. The hypothetical person isn't present, can't be present, here beside me, as you are. I speak not of a discarnate shadow, a silhouette, or a marionette."

"Do you always speak in parables, Sage?"

"Would you prefer that I speak starkly, soberly, in a form parsed of metaphors, word pictures, and symbolic meaning?"

"Well, since you put it that way, perhaps you should stick with parables, Sage."

"This is the story, Script. In hell, the word *presence* has risen high, not unlike Lucifer's visit to I AM in the days of Job. In fact, the word *presence,* in a compounded form, has become a mantra, a rallying cry throughout the abyss. In the dark corpus of the dead, the mantra is now heard.

"It happened, when, beyond the Gates of Hell, a deep rumble shifted craters, sending aftershocks across the abyss. The deep rumble awakened forces below that calculate cosmic encounters in the heavenly realm. They began a search for a cause and effect, streaming every form of content accessible.

"Somehow, *Presence,* performed at Theatre Portesque, was picked up and streamed live to the abode of the dead. The underworld watched, and forces swiftly determined *Presence* to be unsuitable for the Race. By Race, I mean the Human Race.

"Unsuitable, that is, because of the play's potential and efficacy to underscore what matters most in terms of relationships and community. Whatever portends good for the human race is deemed horrid in hell.

"You must know that in the cosmic realm, the word *presence* is anathema to Lucifer. Presence he lost, and he wills the same for the entire human race. Don't be mistaken; Lucifer anticipates the end, the final hour, of cosmic conflict. In doing so, the liar of lies ruminates and chews on a way to achieve victory. He traces and retraces every fissure and failure recorded in the sacred text.

"Lucifer possesses a codex of chosen verses and sayings, which is chained to the wall in the Chamber of Luminosity. The codex is covered in gold and rubies. The front cover bears an emblem of a golden calf with ruby eyes. Only Lucifer can open the codex, which he does on rare occasions when he grants a speech from the Spires of Spite. He unchains the codex from the wall and wraps its weighty chain around his waist.

"No one knows the codex language, but given what we do know of the Evil One, it's surely a corrupted form of a lost tongue. His most quoted verse, you might guess? He recites it at the end of every speech he delivers. He calls his captive audience Mass. Lucifer's speeches are picked up, howled, and echoed about throughout the netherworld and beyond.

"He begins his speeches with a self-introduction, like this: 'I am who I am! Mass, this is Lucifer speaking. Where you are is where you are! Now as always, I am with you . . .'

"And when he reaches the end, he recites his choice line, from the ancient narrative: 'This is the hour when darkness reigns.'

"Lucifer knows every line in the ancient saga. He parsed the text to create a corrupted tale that rebuffs the original storyline and foretells how he will achieve his desired outcome.

"Lucifer vividly recalls the flood, and the sorrow expressed by I AM. He brought forth legions of his devotees to watch the waters rise and the human race reach the brink of distinction. In devilish disdain, he cried 'foul' when the dove flew back with an olive branch in its beak.

"He fumed over that small act, knowing it would play out in I AM's choreographed plan of redemption. I AM's rainbow promise Lucifer tucked away and then parsed to fit his deceitful narrative. He said the promise promised never again to *destroy*, but what about *abandon*?

"Lucifer cast lots with himself to calculate the odds of I AM once again turning to sorrow over the creation of the human race. Lucifer believes his predictions. Lucifer claims that good can never exist without evil, and therefore, evil is superior to good because the latter serves the former, just as the darkened firmament serves the stars.

"This is where you come in, Script."

Stupefied, Script searched Sage's eyes, thinking Sage could himself be a dream or, as suspected, a ghost. He said, "Sage, if you happen to be a dream or a ghost, I'll close my eyes, count to three, and you can be off. No harm done; I shall forget everything. So now I close my eyes and count: *one, two, three*. Goodbye, good fellow. Now, I open my eyes.

"You're still here!"

"You make me smile, Script. Now listen well, Script. Your plays have been parsed by Lucifer himself, and the refrain in the abyss is not *Presence*, The Play, but *Presence Passé*. Lucifer can turn a phrase better than anyone—well, almost anyone.

"You, Script, are the playwright of *Presence*. Rightfully, you saw the world gravitating toward discarnate existence, brought on by virtual interconnectedness and media dependence. The human race has never experienced the media ecology of today. The human race now exists in an irreversible experiment.

"The engagement is deep and pervasive. Discarnate life has made its claim on an incarnate world, the very world in which the Word made flesh dwelt among incarnate souls. Divine presence is not simply a theological concept, Script—it's history, reality.

"So, turning back to Lucifer, the lot is cast. The refrain *Presence*

Passé is being spun into a mediated maelstrom. The aim is to rekindle the sorrow of God, thinking perhaps I AM will walk away. Abandon the human race to their chosen sphere, the discarnate sphere.

"What I have to say, I've nearly said, but not quite. You recall I said that Lucifer fumed over the small act of the dove with the olive branch?"

"Yes," Script said.

"Well, I stressed that point intentionally. Why? The power of those small acts lodged large in Lucifer's craw. Later on, much later on, he witnessed the shoot of David rise in the tiny village of Bethlehem. The Word had become incarnate, begotten not made.

"Now, out of Estillyen has risen a small play called *Presence*. Lucifer deems the hour is right to shine the light on the wonder of *Presence Passé* and draw the world into a maelstrom from which it cannot escape. Lucifer plans to obliterate the Isle of Estillyen, and in its place, livestream *Presence Passé* to the cosmos.

"You, Script, must go to the abyss and intercept the plans. Okay?"

"Uh-oh," said Script.

"No words—just *uh* and *oh*, Script? You ponder the matter while I tend the fire. In matters like this, the decision should be made swiftly. So, take five minutes, if you need to—even ten, if you wish. You ponder; I'll be right back."

FIVE
Along the Scripted Way

"So, Script," said Sage, "I know it's a lot to take in. It's been ten minutes or so. It comes down to this. Without your involvement, the Isle of Estillyen may well be obliterated, and the human race will be propelled into an ever-deepening discarnate existence. I have every confidence in you, Script. Just tell me you're in, and I'll tell you the way."

"Aye, aye, I don't know what to say, Sage."

"I know you didn't choose the part, Script, but this is the most important play of your life."

"Life, you say, Sage? I met you on a path, and I chased after you. When I turned around, the path had suddenly disappeared. The next minute I found myself on the edge of a gorge, with nowhere to flee but into that darkened tunnel of misery. What kind of tunnel has an internal prison?"

"Now you tell me I need to venture into the depths of hell. I have no stage, no lines, no script; I've lost my way. I only know you by your name. You are the most mysterious character I've ever met—no one even comes close. You whip up fare that you extract from a primitive trunk. No, this can't be. I don't even know where I am, unlike you."

"Script, did you not have a clean kit of clothes, your size to a tee? Didn't you find the gold key? Coincidence, none of it; you're on a mission. I've been sent to encourage you, help you along."

"How do I know you are not trying to stitch me up?" said Script.

"Port Estillyen, that lovely fishing village I recently visited. The shops, and that little café, what's it called? Fields and Crops, that's it. And the Abbey, such an amazing art collection, I could scarcely believe it. Sister Ravena, she's such a spirited soul—what a delight to hear her vision for the isle.

"Gone it will be, just because you, Script, refuse to take a recce to the Spires of Spite and a stroll along the Crimson Cliffs of hell? Shall it be, must it be? No!"

"Sage, as a younger man, I studied art and literature. I memorized many a line that I carry with me to this day. If you don't mind, I'll step up on that boulder right behind you and recite a line from Dante's *Inferno*."

"Yes, certainly, let me move out of the way. I'll swap places with you. Mock, up here on my shoulder. Theatre—let's listen, Mock."

"Simply a line, not a performance," said Script. "Okay, I've got my footing. You speak of a recce, and a stroll along the Crimson Cliffs. I rebuff your depiction of hell, with a line from Dante, who saw it quite differently.

> *"Discordant tongues, harsh accents of horror, tormented words, the twang of rage, strident voices, the sound, as well of smacking hands, together these all stirred a storm that swirled forever in the darkened air where no time was."*[13]

"Splendid," said Sage.

"Splendid, which bit?" said Script. "The twang of rage, or the darkened air where no time was?"

"Script, not at all; I refer to the way you delivered the line with such depth of feeling. But the point is you'll never know what hell is truly like until you take the plunge."

"All right, listen to this, another Dante line, and see if you find it any less formidable.

> *"The pain they felt erupted from their eyes. All up and down and round-about, their hands sought remedies for burning air and ground."*[14]

"Splendid, I say," said Sage. "You put such raw emotion into the words. Well done, Script."

"Sage, I believe you're just egging me on to see if I have the will to follow. Then, *snap*, like that, you'll deliver me and explain the meaning of this odd experience. Sage, therefore, I call your bluff. This is a test, right?"

"Certainly; it's a most propitious test, concerning a part for which you were distinctly chosen."

"So I call your bluff, Sage. Show me the way to hell, Sage. So there, I hope you're satisfied. I did it. I've proved my resolve and willingness. Now can we get on with the introduction of reality?"

"Wonderful! Now concerning the plan, you'll need to enter hell undetected. For the most part, you will be invisible. Visibility will only occur if you have a nervous breakdown and lose possession of your faculties. In that case, you may give off an aura of a spurious inhabitant. Whatever you do, don't try to grab an inhabitant of hell, be it a demon or otherwise."

"Wait, Sage . . . no, okay, I get it—you want me to carry on with this test. I still don't know what you're getting at, but I'll play along."

"Good, Script," said Sage. "I sense you wish to pose a question."

"Yes, how do you suggest I pass through the Gates of Hell, incognito, and pilfer through Satan's dossier?"

"We have that all worked out. You'll enter through a back entrance, not the gates. Also, you cannot enter the netherworld from the present time. You must go along the Scripted Way, where you will observe scenes from history's storied past.

"You will discover these scenes here in the meadow beyond the gates and doors. That's the point of their existence. On the other side of each door, you'll witness a scene from living history. But I must emphasize an exceedingly important point. You must fix this in your mind. Do you hear me, Script?"

"Sure, Sage. You are really good at this—speaking as if all this is going to actually happen."

"It *is* going to happen. And I don't want you lost between time and eternity. We would not be able to get you out. In such case, you would abide neither in living history nor the present world."

"My attention is rapt, Sage."

"Okay, there are five gates and doors here in the meadow. You must choose a door and pass through. When you do, a scene of living history will suddenly appear. Consider yourself slightly offstage, as if you were watching a scene from the wings. You'll be captivated, beyond what I can say. Observe, watch, but do not linger too long.

"Then begin to walk around the scene until you spot a trail that leads you on.

"The scene you witness will be a scene that follows on from one of the narrative adaptations in *Presence*. Concerning the trail, when you spot the trail, swiftly join it and walk on; don't look back. If you look back, the trail will disappear under your feet.

"Such an amazing experience it is! You will walk above time and place, as if skipping over papyrus, page, and time. I know what I'm talking about. Keep moving; don't look down. Don't look around. When the stars disappear from the heavenly expanse and the moon no longer shines, that's your point of departure. Are you with me to this point, Script?"

"Indeed," said Script. "I've got it—the moon no longer shines."

"So, you'll proceed to the vast realm, beyond cosmic ritual and routine. In the netherworld, you will see and hear what normal eyes and ears have never seen and heard. I will not be able to join you. Had you even considered that option?"

"Not exactly, Sage. I don't know what to think. Only yesterday I stepped into this dreamy world."

"Well, I'd be grieved to see you set out on this journey alone. Therefore, I insist that you take Mock along as your companion. He's a brilliant mockingbird; he not only mocks but even talks now and then. His language, though, can be a bit challenging to decipher.

"Now, in terms of attire, just your usual casual clothes will do; what you're wearing now is perfect. In addition, I want to give you my cotton-twill hiking jacket. Mock likes to nestle down in the left pocket, and there's a hole so he can poke his head out and look around. I'll bring the jacket around later; it also has all sorts of inside pockets and zippers. It's ideal for this type of outing."

"Outing, you call it," said Script. "You're stoking this up for real."

"Anyway, remember, the most important item of your attire is the gold ribbon. Wear it as a scarf. Never remove it. The ribbon will both give you light and render you incognito in hell. I've made a tiny gold ribbon for Mock that I'll lace around his neck. It's just a tiny gold strip. Other than that and your pouch, what else? I think that's it."

"Just a small point, if I might ask, Sage. Where do I find these remarkable gates and doors?"

"Yes, sorry, I hadn't said. When you're ready, follow the cobblestone path down along the pines. This will lead to the open meadow. Carry on through the meadow on the narrow path. Just set your feet on that path and keep moving until you will find a Y. Go to the left.

"In no time, you'll find the meadow's gates and doors. You'll see them—you can't miss them. The wooden gates are humble in design but have nearly worn out the ages. They're all unlatched. The doors tower tall, possessing neither thresholds nor frames or hinges.

"Yet, as you will see, the doors stand perfectly erect and open without the aid of hinges. The doors are set out at various angles throughout the meadow. Unlike the gates, the doors are all locked. It takes a special key to unlock them, which you possess. The key you found in the tunnel unlocks all five doors."

"Why five doors, Sage?"

"Well, we didn't know which door you would choose."

"Oh," said Script.

"You see, like your play *Presence*, we are actually in a rather momentous play. Door one is the opening act. What transpires beyond that door determines if there'll be need of another door, whether door three, four, or even five."

"Sage, I must tell you straight out, everything you say turns out peculiar. Doors minus frames that swing without hinges—I'd say that's a bit peculiar. Sage, you've talked me into going to hell, as if I'm going. Have you ever talked anyone else into going to hell?"

"You *are* going, Script."

"You know, I believe you're not joking," said Script. "Am I really going to hell, Sage?"

"Only if you are willing, Script. I cannot force you, despite the pending loss of the isle and Estillyen life."

"Oh, my ears," said Script. "Do you hear what I hear? Mystery upon mystery, I am headed for utter misery. Yet, Sage, I look at you and wonder. How can you know all that you know without some wondrous way of knowing? You must be a sage, Sage. So, I'm willing to go along with the act, at least until I can figure out what's going on here."

"Wonderful! A weight has lifted now that I've given you the full brief. Would you like to go for a walk?"

"No, thanks, I'd like to spend some quiet time at Writer's Cottage, if that's okay."

"Yes, please, be off with you. I'll come around later, sneak in the back door, and quietly hang my jacket in the mudroom. By the way, there's an apple pie in the cupboard."

Thus, in the Meadow of Gates and Doors, the afternoon ticked the hours through until evening came to usher in the night and put the meadow to rest. After consuming two slices of apple pie, Script said his prayers and tucked himself into bed. *There is,* he thought, *something very comforting about a narrow bed.*

Somehow, Script's sense of foreboding began to slip away, replaced by a willingness to carry on in the peculiar turn of events. He wondered what tomorrow would bring when the play resumed, and he played his part.

Script fell asleep, slept soundly, and awoke early. He scurried about getting dressed and gathering his belongings. He even managed to whistle a tune. In the cloakroom, he paused in front of the basin mirror and peered into his reflected eyes.

"Script, how can you whistle?" he said to himself. "You don't know where you are, or where you are going. You, my friend, are lost. Or you have contracted a severe case of lunacy. Are you me? I ask thee that I see, are you me or someone else?

"You look like me, you act like me, you sound like me, but are you me? We shall see who you are soon enough. I hope you are me because if you're not me, I do not know who you are. And that would not be good. Thus, I would not know who I am.

"So, discarnate reflection, I'm off now to play my part. Off to the netherworld supposedly, but not before a bite to eat."

As soon as Script stepped through the front door, he heard Mock calling, signaling that breakfast waited. Sage brought Mock along to breakfast and readied himself to bid Script and the mockingbird farewell.

"Well, scrumptious food, Sage," said Script.

"Glad you like it, and the company is not bad either," said Sage.

"Yes, superb breakfast; every thanks, Sage. But how do you cart all this around in a primitive trunk?"

"A secret, Script, a secret I keep, not to tell."

"Well, I guess the inevitable has come, Sage. It's time for me to pick up that trail that will take me to the corridors of hell. By the way, your twill coat fits perfectly; see how I was able to position my gold ribbon under its wide collar?"

"Indeed, perfect," said Sage. "I've always loved that old jacket. Hang on to it, now; don't let it get too close to the flames. Oh, and a few words about Mock. I've brought along a pack of seeds you can slip into your pouch. If Mock flies about finding things to eat, don't be alarmed; he always returns. Also, he likes to perch on the shoulder straps of the jacket. You can see how worn they are. When I'm hiking, he likes to jump from one shoulder to the other.

"As I mentioned yesterday, Mock will nestle down in your left pocket and poke his head through the hole. For him, the pocket is a padded birdhouse. Keep an eye on the threads I've woven around the hole; Mock is fond of picking at them. Just flick his beak if you catch him in the act.

"One more item," Sage said. "I want you to have this small silver fish with its silver chain. It recalls the story of Jesus instructing St. Peter to catch a fish with a coin in its mouth in order to pay their temple tax.

"The fish's mouth is open, as you can see, which symbolizes that the tax is paid. Also, originally the coin would have had the image of the Phoenician god Melqart on one side and an eagle on the other. According to folklore, the fish couldn't wait to spit out the false god."

"This is such an intricate, lovely piece, Sage—the scales, the fish's eyes. This must be very old."

"Yes, old it is," said Sage. "But it's yours now, so wear it well. Wear it around your neck to remind you of this and other miracles, along with the faith that can move mountains. You will need miracles where you're headed. When it's time to exit the darkened sphere, clasp the tiny fish, kiss its lips, and pray, 'Catch me.'

"Godspeed, my friend; gotta go now. I have a few messages to bear."

"When will I see you again, Sage?"

"That depends not on the crier, but on the thresher. Hopefully I'll see you before the apples fall."

Script reached into his jacket pocket to adjust the straw he had placed there for Mock, but when he raised his head, Sage had vanished.

"That fellow can sure move," said Script. "Mock, it looks like it's just you and me. Why is there no one else around here, anyway? Strange it is, totally strange. I feel a breeze; the weather must be changing. It is morning, but the sun thinks it's late afternoon.

"We better move along to the Meadow of Gates and Doors. I'm sure you've been there before, right? Silent, I see?"

"Gotta go," parroted Mock.

"I think I'm going to like you, Mock," Script said with a smile. "I'm talking to a bird."

With Mock perched on his shoulder, Script went along the cobblestone path, beyond the pines, and into the open meadow. There he found the narrow path.

"Well, Mock, Sage was certainly right about this path; it's a narrow, single-lane affair. The grass is high in this meadow, above my waist. Look at it sway, Mock. I wonder why things are so narrow around here, anyway—narrow bed, narrow path. See those dramatic clouds rolling by against the blue sky? Nice setting, this is, Mock.

"We've already covered a good bit of ground, and we've yet to see the Y. According to Sage, we continue on until we find the fork. So let's carry on, say, another fifteen minutes, and then we'll take a wee break. It must be around one o'clock by now. Let me check my watch again. That's odd—I looked at it just a bit ago, and it was half past twelve. Now it's nearly four o'clock. Plot gave me this watch—nice, but it must be out of whack.

"Mock, do you see that stone just up ahead? Let's pause there. I know you're not tired of walking because you're perching. Nutty bird, delightful though. Okay, nearly there. And on and on we go, until at last, the rock we reach. There now."

With Mock perched on his left shoulder, Script said, "Mock, that's an odd sight. You see the path leading on before us? It's worn bare, well-traveled. Looks like a hundred people a day pass along this way. Now, cast your bird eyes back to the narrow path on which we just traveled. Unless I'm zany, the path is gone. It doesn't exist.

"The barren path on which we trekked is simply part of the green field. See, Mock, the grass sways high, where only a moment ago, the path existed. That can't be. Did you know paths can disappear? This is what we'll do, if it's okay by you, Mock. We'll take ten steps forward along the path, then swiftly turn around and look back.

"Come on, let's go. I'm counting . . . eight, nine, and now ten. Okay, now we spin around and see what's what. Can't be! That bit of path, too, is gone. Let's move, Mock; this is insane. Hey, we've reached the Y, anyway. We go left. Let's head down the path and see where it leads."

In short order, Script and Mock stood at the gates and doors for which the meadow was named. Script could scarcely take it in. The sun filtered through the clouds, shedding distinct beams of light on all five doors.

"Dear me," said Script, "do you see what I see, Mock? Gates from ages past that lead to doors perfectly erect without frames or hinges. I'm mystified, Mock—what about you? Which door should we choose? Do you like the blue one in the middle of the meadow or the pale green one on that crest to the right? Or perhaps you would like one of the other three.

"No answer, I hear. Okay, I choose the gray one on the mound. No, I've changed my mind—the blue one in the middle. Now, in a few hundred feet or so, we'll be at one of those ancient gates. Sage is definitely right; they look like they have worn out the ages. The closer we get, the more aged they look.

"Anyway, here goes—a slight nudge on the gate, Mock, and we should freely pass. Nudge, and blimey, it's set itself in motion. It's opened all the way. Amazing! Now the key; I feel it. There it is; I have it. Ready, Mock, it's in, and slowly I turn."

Stunned, Script watched as the tall, hinge-less door of blue opened at a slow, even pace. Like the gate, the door opened wide. Script looked at the side of the door where hinges might have been, but he saw nothing. The solid, thick wooden door pivoted in thin air.

"Okay, Mock, we might as well step over the invisible threshold to witness a mysterious scene. Oh, you want down in the pocket, I see. Go on; I wish I could join you."

So, beyond the gate and the door of blue, Script stepped through to a living stage of history playing out in present time. He stood in a lovely courtyard, awed and speechless, with Mock poking his head through the hole in his jacket. Then he heard a woman's voice calling.

Mrs. Nicodemus:
Dear, come along. It's late; you need to eat. Honestly, out at this hour of the night. Surely you were seen moving along the narrow streets. You need to think about the consequences. I can just hear someone saying, "Hey, wasn't that Nicodemus the Pharisee passing by? What's he doing in this part of town after dark?"

Nicodemus:
Yes, yes, I'll sit, but I'm not that hungry. Just a piece of bread, the crusty bit.

Mrs. Nicodemus:
No lentil soup?

Nicodemus:
Okay, just a taste, or you'll ask me over and over. But sit with me, please. Your day okay, was it?

Mrs. Nicodemus:
Normal. Lydia stopped by with more wicks and oil. She must have gotten your message; she said the wicks are the best money can buy.

Nicodemus:
Yeah, I've heard that before. The last batch of wicks burned like straw, loosely woven. They must be woven tight, soaked long in paraffin.

Mrs. Nicodemus:
Yes, dear, just go ahead and eat. Leave Lydia and the wicks up to me.

Nicodemus:

Where's Miriam, anyway? Have her bring another lamp. I don't want to sit around in darkness!

Mrs. Nicodemus:

Don't worry, I'll get it. Miriam's already asleep. I want to hear about this strange prophet Jesus, the Nazorean, and what you heard.

[Mrs. Nicodemus goes off to fetch a lamp.]

All the while, Script looked on, with Mock peering out of the hole in his pocket. Script's eyes bulged, and his heart beat at a frenzied pace. He thought, *This phenomenon before me—how can it be? I'm in the abode of Nicodemus. That's him eating lentil soup with bread . . . on the very night he ventured out to speak with Jesus, who claimed to be the Son of God and Son of Man. How can I, Script, see the act of life once lived? Though the act once lived now lives before me.*

[In silence Nicodemus sips his soup. Mrs. Nicodemus reenters the room holding the lit lamp before her.]

Nicodemus:

That's better—pinching pennies to poke around in the dark. Anyway, please quit getting sidetracked, and sit down. I need to think.

[Mrs. Nicodemus places a lamp on the table, and sits down, smiling.]

Mrs. Nicodemus:

I'm here. So tell me everything. You found him, no thugs about?

Nicodemus:

Yes, and no thugs. Such words, though. No sense of guile in this Jesus fellow. He believes what he says, as if he gave words their meaning.

Mrs. Nicodemus:

Was he cold and intellectual?

Nicodemus:

Not a bit. Warm, actually, and somehow completely present. It's hard to explain; he was very human and engaging, but also possessing a transcendent quality most rare.

Mrs. Nicodemus:

So, what impressed you?

Nicodemus:

I greeted him with genuine respect; I called him "Rabbi" and acknowledged that God must be with him. He smiled, and with a very kind demeanor, said something I didn't expect. He said, "Truly, truly, I say to you, unless one is born again he cannot see the kingdom of God."[15]

I was dumbfounded. I hadn't said a word about the Kingdom, and yet he dove into the subject. Perhaps he perceived that was on my mind. In a way, it may have been sort of in the back of my mind. Or since I'm a Pharisee, with the Sanhedrin, maybe he wanted to lodge a point. His teaching about grace and miracles has not gone unnoticed. The Nazorean has created no little stir, moving about, casting out demons, healing the sick.

There's even a rumor he turned water into wine at a wedding in Cana. I don't mean some clever stunt with a single goblet, but vessels full of wine.

Mrs. Nicodemus:

I'd like that! Do you suppose we can get over there soon?

Nicodemus:

Okay, funny. This man is not an ordinary small-town prophet. He understands matters deep. Life matters, or should I say, why life matters.

I couldn't help but admire him, very likable. But some of the brethren utterly despise him. See him as a true threat to the nation.

I don't know. I'll hold my opinion. But what kind of man says, "The wind blows wherever it pleases. So it is with everyone born of the Spirit." That's the way he speaks.

Anyhow, good bread—do you want a bite?

Mrs. Nicodemus:
No, I'm just glad you're back. Try to put all this out of your mind, or you'll never sleep. Let me take the dish away.

Nicodemus:
I'll be along soon. I just want to sit here for a moment in silence and think.

Mrs. Nicodemus:
Okay, but don't forget to blow out the lamp.

Nicodemus:
Sure, will do; good night.

Script slowly began to walk away from the scene. Just ahead of him, a path emerged out of nowhere. He locked his eyes on the path ahead and began walking. Soon he felt like he was skating on ice. Faster and faster he skated, until he skated so fast that his feet left the ground.

Script stilled his feet, but he and Mock continued forward at a blistering pace, drawn by a force unseen. Gravitational forces ceased to exist, and they raced ahead unimpeded. The path before him stretched on into infinity.

Script felt like he was on a supersonic bullet train, speeding through sheets of howling wind and rain. Before long, though, his bullet train began to slow. The slowing motion both delighted and frightened Script.

From all directions, thick darkness pressed in on the path. Soon his speed now resembled that of a cattle car pulling into a stockyard. On into the darkened tunnel he crept. Slower and slower, until he found himself once again walking, and then he halted.

Script reached for Mock in his pocket and gently stroked his feathers. Mock's head rose to meet his hand. Then Mock poked his head out of the pocket and said, "Lunch in the meadow, lunch in the meadow."

Script said, "That might be a bit of a challenge, Mock. I think we've just arrived in hell. It seems that Sage was not joking after all."

SIX
The Abyss and *Presence Passé*

Script stood wide-eyed and petrified, expecting at any second demons to pounce and gnaw him to bits. He said, "I feel like a rabbit that's wandered into a badger's den. Why us, Mock, a mockingbird and a playwright, cast in such an unimaginable play?

"Sage knew it all, what he told me. It sounded like a dreamy drama, going to hell to intercept Satan's diabolic plan. I thought Sage was testing me. Then, at the right moment, he'd snap his fingers and bring me around. Explain how I came to be in the Meadow of Gates and Doors.

"I went along with it, and through the gate we passed, then the tall blue hinge-less door. Then, before my eyes, there was Nicodemus, eating lentil soup. What a sight! Standing there, watching that scene, eternity had returned to revisit time. To bring history back to life, a scene long ago gathered into eternity. Indeed, we saw living history, Mock.

"Mock, are you listening? Can you hear me? Okay, I feel you move. Somehow we must cope, but how, if this is really hell? Surely we're well and truly doomed. The surface beneath my feet feels like shale. In this aura of light from my scarf, I must look like a luminous butterfly. It glows with the intensity of a dozen burning candles.

"I can see twenty or thirty feet in front of me, Mock; that's our field of vision. Beyond that, pitch darkness consumes itself. What's that smell? It's brimstone. Listen, Mock, do you hear that? Woe is me.

Howling in the distance, rumbling below, shrieks above, and that—do you hear that deafening, scraping sound, like the hulls of ocean liners scraping against one another in the open sea?

"Woe is me, and you, too, Mock. We'll need a miracle to survive. Hell, the abyss . . . such a place exists, and we're in it, by happenstance. At the speed of lightning, we've traveled far from Writer's Cottage and apple blossoms dancing on a cobblestone walk. Images all, they vividly press upon my mind. We can't think our way back, Mock; we must proceed.

"I must dare to take a step. On sharp shards of brittle shale, we'll step. The crunch will be frightening, like walking on cracking ice. Yet, if Sage is right, there is a call, and I can't take it back. The annihilation of Estillyen looms, and the human race could one day be defaced by discarnate pixels.

"So, Mock, we shall walk. Sage said we'll be totally indiscernible. Not seen, not heard, not touchable. I fear we must go. *Go*—it's such a little word, so easy to say but not always easy to obey. Our yes must be yes rather than no, so we go. Now we walk in the light of our ribbons gold. Keep your head sticking out, Mock; you are like a night-light of sorts.

"Three steps first, then we'll pause. Got it? Think buoyancy as we move along. Consider it a spirited walk along the corridors of hell, just you and me. We follow a thin thread of destiny; pray it doesn't snap. So here goes, one step, a second, and a third, and pause. What do you hear, Mock? Howling, hooting, shrieking calls, and rumbles—none of them are lessening. But we hear not the faintest sound rising from our steps.

"This time let's try three times three, with one for good measure. Okay, step, keep it up, step, step, and I think that makes ten. Same result, we hear everything, but not our steps on the brittle shale. Have we gone partially deaf? Perhaps it's actually true that we're caught up in a play that the forces of evil cannot see. Soon enough we'll know."

The prospect afforded Script a tinge of hope, but only a tinge. His mind bordered on utter mayhem. Yet he and Mock continued their nightmarish march, step-by-step they moved, ever deeper through the corridors of hell. Time neither ticked nor traveled in the sphere through which they moved.

No sun, no moon, no stars, no light filtered into the cavernous passageways they passed. Script gave no thought of turning back. He reasoned that if he were in a play, a choreographer would keep an eye on the stage, even a stage in hell.

If only I could read the script, he thought, *to see how the play turns out.*

Play or not, in the glow of his ribbon gold, and Mock's, too, they continued toward the Gates of Hell and the Crimson Cliffs. The tormenting trek coughed up fright upon fright. Creatures slithered and wriggled along the base of the walls. Larger eyeballs, sometimes one, other times three or more, would appear and disappear into the darkness.

On they moved, amidst squealing, hoots, and calls overladen with screams and what sounded like stampeding hoofs. The harrowing sounds seemed to lessen slightly when Script and Mock paused. While their advance was not detected, their movement seemed to charge the atmosphere of the abyss. Undeterred, they eventually reached a vast, cavernous opening ringed with fire.

"Okay, Mock, an outside opening, so it seems, if the abyss *has* an outside. We may be approaching the Crimson Cliffs. At least we can see. Let's investigate the opening."

Script stepped into the massive cavern. He thought, *This cavern is large enough for a three-ring circus with high-wire acts.* As he stepped further into the cavern, the horrific sounds ceased. "Mock, silence," whispered Script.

Unlike in the darkened chamber through which they had just passed, Script heard each and every step he took. His footsteps sounded as if he wore clogs. Worse still, the vast chamber echoed his every step, magnifying them as much as tenfold, or so it seemed to Script. When Script reached the center of the cavern, he heard voices approaching. He froze.

"Shush, Mock, I think were done; we have no place to hide." Three figures suddenly appeared. The one in the middle stood half again the height of the other two, which were the height of average men. They had facial features similar to human beings, but the texture of their skin resembled the skin of raw sweet potatoes.

Their hands sprouted not fingers, but short, knobby toes. They wheezed more than breathed. They sounded like asthmatics drawing their final breaths. From head to toe, they were wrapped in tightly woven, linen-like material. Each wore a vest of alligator hide. With darting eyes, wheezes, and snorts, the trio drew within fifteen feet of Script and halted.

"*Shumisih tros, morshomin, labbo labbo,*" spoke the figure on the left. To which the one on the right replied, "*Ploneer, shootue, bozeen, bozeen, torshedorasen, loktinue.*" Whereupon the one in the middle said, "Shut up, you idiot fools! I'll have you banished to the swamps of moss and mold. Is that what you want, you rotten torsos?

"Like Satan said, 'Soon eternity will make its claim on the Race trapped in time, and we must prevail. The hour no one knows, but Satan has dispatched sentinels to sniff throughout the cosmos. So get this: I am your leader; you are Speakers, part of the elite Speaker Corps. If I hear you utter another single word of our native tongue, I'll pour boiling mercury down your throats.

"Fools you are, but this is not the season for utter fools, fools. I, too, know what it feels like to hear our native tongue expressing multifarious lies. When I last heard Satan speaking our native language, my intestines quivered. Dust, I recall you saying, 'Didn't our intestines quiver deep within when we heard him speak, extolling the meaning of evil acts from ages past?'

"So shut it, Dust, and you, too, No Name! The language of the Race we speak. During this harvest season of captive souls, we must speak the most widespread language of the Race. That's the edict. That's *my* edict. Do you hear me? No more *morshomin, labbo,* or *loktinue* phrases. Got it? Let me hear you speak properly. You go first, No Name."

"Speaker Brimer, your edict is mine as well," said No Name.

"Now you, Dust; go ahead," said Brimer.

"Speaker Brimer, I speaketh what thou wishes. Definitely, the Race dialect I speaketh," said Dust.

"Well done. Keep it up, you idiots, or its boiling mercury down your throats.

"Now, fix your psyches. We'll go into the meeting wholly obedient. To the back of the room you crawl. Legions await the orders from the Spires of Spite. We join them. I know this: Lucifer plans to erect a massive Spire on a remote island, out beyond the Storied Sea.

"Regarding the inhabitants, the plan calls for a contagion, followed by a tsunami. That could all change, though, and go nuclear. Anyway, decrepit souls of the Race will fall into the temptation of rebuilding the isle and erecting the world's tallest Spire. The Great Spire will message simultaneous language transmissions throughout the cosmos. Race inhabitants will convince themselves that no expense should be spared when it pertains to the Spire project.

"The fleshy carnites will tout the Spire as the most vital project in the history of the world. It will be their newly constructed Tower of Babel. Once erected on that small desolate isle, the Great Spire will offer a true overarching narrative extolling the wonders of discarnate life. Pixels will populate the universe, pixels that we can focus and alter at will. I've already told you more than you should know, imbeciles.

"But there is far more to tell. Satan will address the cosmos soon. It could even happen before tonight's false moon. I've been informed that the incoming crop of captive souls is huge. Droves upon droves will come pouring in from every tribe and tongue.

I know Satan thrills at seeing the dead gawk when he speaks. It electrifies his being.

"So, No Name, do you have any questions? No, Brimer. Dust, what about you, any nutty questions? No, Brimer. Okay, fools, follow me. To the meeting, and don't dare speak. You must be at the bottom of your game. Cower low, and then lower still. Don't even think of looking in the direction of the Malevolent One. What else? Nothing! Now follow me.

"Step it up, Speakers! Put a spirit of angst in your stride, fools."

Script stood stiff as a column, silent, not believing what he'd just witnessed. Then, next to him he heard a kindly voice say, "Hello."

Script leaped forward in fright, stumbled, and dropped to his knees. Stunned, he looked up to see a figure wearing a turban. Meanwhile Mock peered up from his pocket hole.

"I suppose you wonder who I am, Script," said the turban-clad man. "Do you suppose I'm a turban-wearing demon? Go ahead, speak if you wish. I'm listening."

"Aye, aye, I say, I've just, you know, I mean, a demon I've never seen," said Script.

"Well, a demon I'm not. I am Simon of Cyrene, who is noted in the narrative of old. Although Cyrene is no longer my address; I've moved on. I like to keep things moving."

"Aye, aye, I don't actually belong here," said Script. "How I entered this realm beyond realms, I don't exactly know. Just yesterday, or in a patch of time passed, Mock and I were in the Meadow of Gates and Doors. We saw Nicodemus eating lentil soup, and after that we got on a path, and—like lightning—we were propelled here.

"So I might possibly be dead. Mock's not, so I may not be either. Yet no living soul travels this way, only lost souls, or so I'm told. How I've gotten mingled up with cosmic castaways, I'm not sure. Believe me, what I say is true, I swear. I do, I tell you."

"Let me help you up," said Simon. "Here, take my hand."

"Aye, so I can, I guess. So I will, I guess, I will," said Script, as he lifted his left hand to clasp Simon's right. "Thank you, Sir Simon—you seem very strong."

"Are you okay?" asked Simon.

"Well, aye, I suppose. Mock, too, seems all right. It's just that I'm so—how can I say—taken aback, dazed, and stunned by your presence. I mean, it's you, you say. I suppose if I saw Nicodemus, along with his wife, I guess I can believe I'm seeing you. But you could be a phantom of sorts, right?"

"I understand your shock," said Simon. "This is a rather extraordinary encounter. In case you have doubts, set them aside; you are in hell."

"But you're not . . . I mean, you've come here . . . you don't abide here, correct?" said Script.

"Yes, that's right; I get around. Think along the lines of Moses and Elijah appearing in the Transfiguration scene. They spoke to Christ concerning his departure."

"Am I about to depart?" said Script. "That would be just fine with Mock and me as well."

"No, you're not about to depart," said Simon. "After the Transfiguration scene, what was the follow-on scene? Do you recall?"

"I know the story very well. Let me think, if I can—my mind is doing somersaults. They went down the mountainside, and then they . . . oh yes, the scene with the frantic father and his demon-possessed boy."

"So I say to you, Script, you, too, have come down among the possessed and dispossessed, and now you must carry on with your mission. You heard what the Speakers said."

"Well, I see, you must be right, Simon. Not a simple recce, after all. Are you guiding me?"

"I may be in and out; I'll go with you for a ways. Then I will be gone. Much depends on you—what you are able to discern and process."

"I see," said Script. "I need to try to loosen my frozen joints a bit.

So, I suppose we should carry on across this cavern toward the burning ring. Okay by you?"

"I'm with you," Simon said. "Can I carry your bag?"

"No, I need to keep it on me. Thanks, though. I see you are not carrying anything—just your turban."

"You make me smile, Script."

Script and Simon carried on across the massive cavern toward the opening ringed by fire and sulfur flames.

"It looks like a giant circus ring turned on its edge," said Script.

"A circus ring on edge it's not," said Simon. "This is one of the entrances to the Crimson Cliffs."

"That's good—or do I mean bad?" said Script.

"Here we are," Simon said. "Look out on the extended plane. What do you see? Tell me what you see, without surmising."

"Wasteland," Script said. "I see no trees, no grass, nothing green, no water springs, no bees or butterflies, not a single bird flying by. Cesspools with sulfur flames dotted amid rocks split and scattered over crimson sands. Such an eerie, godless atmosphere—no sun, no lakes, every surface baked, no life, no presence, nothing stirs. Surely I see a landscape drawn by death.

> "*Further, to the fore of my mind, words of the Psalmist leap:*
> *The heavens declare the glory of God;*
> *And the firmament shows His handiwork.*
> *Day unto day utters speech,*
> *And night unto night reveals knowledge.*"[16]

"Such a firmament I do not see. Rather, I see a scene along the lines of Dante's *Inferno*. His words, too, occupy my mind: 'Sighing, sobbing, moans, and plaintive wailing all echoed here through air where no star shone, and I as this began, began to weep.'"[17]

"Well spoken, Script," said Simon. "I deduce that you are well versed on matters that matter most."

As they peered through the burning ring of fire, Script felt a tinge of faith lift his spirit. With Simon near, Script decided it was time to move out into the desolate plane. He reckoned he'd then scout out the corridors and caverns of hell.

On the other side of the ring, Script noticed a series of flat ledges descending down to the plane. He calculated the first ledge to be about ten feet below the opening, and thereafter, roughly a five-foot drop from ledge to ledge.

"Okay, Mock," Script said, "we'll take a leap through the giant ring of fire and land on what appears to be a ledge. We have no time to debate the matter, so, with Simon looking on, I'll run and leap on the count of three. Here goes—one, two, and three!"

Script made the leap and down he plunged, with Mock's head extended out of the pocket hole.

"Dear me," Script said. "The gravity of hell is hellish, Mock. We fell like a sack of grain pitched from a barn loft. Our ten-foot plunge was more like fifteen."

Script, however, landed without wobble. Standing on the ledge, he could see the Crimson Cliffs extending off to his right like a great mountain range. He lifted Mock out of his pocket and placed him on his shoulder. "Such a sight, Mock, grievously frightening it is. We must go on, though. Seven more ledges to reach the plane; the plan is simply to leap and drop."

As Script leapt and dropped, Mock fluttered his wings. When they reached ledge four, Mock sprang atop Script's head and stayed there for leaps five, six, and seven. When they reached the plane, Simon was already there.

"When did you get here?" Script asked.

"I was here the instant you counted three," Simon said.

"Gotta go, gotta go," Mock parroted.

"Shush, Mock," Script said, "no time for parroting. We need to keep our wits about us. If we slip into one of these quagmires of burning sulfur, we'll be turned into puffs. I assume those are the Spires of Spite. They look foreboding; clad in dull, black granite, it seems. No windows, no doors, just narrow slits near the top, and to think, that's his lair."

"One of them," Simon said. "I suggest you move along in solitude, no talking, like a silent monk. When we get closer to the Cliffs, we'll decide our next move."

Sooner than Script expected, they neared the base of the Crimson Cliffs. Script could hear shouts and voices intermixed with sounds of slapping. The sounds grew louder the closer they drew to the Cliffs. They made their way along a low ridge that gave them cover.

Script said, "When we reach the end of the ridge, we'll have no place to hide; we'll be in the open sulfur plane. It's only a few hundred yards away."

"Stay calm," Simon said. "Keep moving; just keep moving. When we reach the end of the ridge, we'll have an unobstructed view of the backside of the Crimson Cliffs. Go on, go on, we're almost there. No pause."

Script's teeth had chattered during what he'd already experienced of hell, but when he saw the backside of the Crimson Cliffs, his jaw dropped. Speakers, the likes of Brimer, Dust, and No Name, stood in clusters that stretched on for miles. The Speakers were gathered along the backside of the Cliffs, looking out on a massive, dry salt lake bed.

The Speakers spoke mostly in the dialect of the Race, as Brimer had specified. But all manner of indistinguishable tongues were also used, along with howls, chants, and growls. The Speakers frequently swatted and slapped one another as they spoke. A slap might produce a growl, a swat a snarl, or some other menacing expression.

"I ask again," said Simon, "what do you see?"

"I see Speakers in clusters, speaking and sparring, swatting at each other like cats. No signage or markings of any kind anywhere," said Script. "No poles, no lines, no lights—just the Speakers and, in the lake bed, rows of empty, backless benches stretching as far as the eye can see. Like in the wasteland, not a creature stirs other than the Speakers."

"All right, Script," said Simon. "We have no alternative but to walk out into the open expanse and see what happens. I recommend we go straight for a while, and then we'll veer away from the Cliffs."

On they went until they had advanced within a few hundred yards of the Speakers. Next, they veered left and advanced parallel along the cliffs. When they had progressed a good half mile, they finally stopped.

"If a miracle doesn't occur," said Script, "we'll surely die on this dry salt lake in hell. How would you calculate our chances, Simon?"

Just then, the Speakers broke ranks and started running out into the flats, away from the cliffs.

"I have my answer," said Script. "We're dead. They're leaping the benches like hurdles. Thousands headed directly toward us like wild hyenas. My Lord, we're done."

"Wait," said Simon. "They've suddenly halted and are lining up in front of the benches."

"What's happening?" Script said.

"Well, watch," said Simon.

With military precision, the Speakers formed rigid, straight lines. Then, in unison, they turned, about-face, toward the Cliffs.

Script said, "They've turned their backs on us. They didn't see us. It's a miracle, although frighteningly so."

"Stay calm," Simon said. "The salt bed rumbles beneath them."

At that point, shrill trumpet blasts blared out from the Cliffs. Long held were the blasts. When the piercing blasts finally ended, they began again. Then, for a third time, the blasts rang out across the desolate landscape of attentive Speakers. Next, from the backside of the Cliffs, a loud, vocal command was uttered: "Sit!" Instantly, the Speakers dropped down onto the benches.

Just then, the backside of the Cliffs parted, and high above the sitting Speakers, a mammoth translucent stage slowly extended toward the dry lake bed. When the stage eventually halted, another piercing trumpet blast rang out. When that trumpet blast ceased, a dominating lone figure appeared, stepping forward from the interior of the Crimson Cliffs.

Slowly the figure made his way to the center of the stage. Without uttering a word, the Speakers were galvanized to attention. With precise, poised stiffness, they cocked back their heads and trained their eyes on the one standing before them. Very still he stood.

His cheekbones were apple red, his face alabaster, and a scarlet streak ran across his forehead, from side to side.

"Dear me," whispered Script, "that's the Devil."

"Most likely," said Simon. "It could be a double, in disguise. Though his appearance is ever changing."

Like an arrow straight, the figure stood in silence, peering out at the audience and awaiting his address. Around the iris of his eyes glowed orange thermionic rings. Thick, black wavy hair embellished his tall stature. Above his ears, thin white feathers poked through the black waves. He wore a waistcoat of silver fastened with long, slender hooks and an outer garment that extended to his knees.

Slowly he ran his eyes along the rows of transfixed Speakers seated before him. Then, above the audience he stared, as if looking at a sunset where no sun had ever set. Finally he breathed deeply and moved his left hand to the top of his vest, as he readied himself to speak.

"Listen, Mass! This is Lucifer speaking. I am who I am. I am not who I'm not. I am not I AM; I am Lucifer. Know this, you are where you are. Now, as always, I am with you.

"I, who speak for all, now speak to you. I am the medium of my message, and my message shall always prevail, profiting wherever it is sent. From a well deep that never shall run dry, my words effervesce with spine-tingling effectiveness. Know this, there are many who longed to see and hear what you see and hear today.

"Words not mine are mere approximations of mine. The words

I speak to you on this momentous occasion are, even now, streaking through the cosmos. They gallop forth with robust resolution and elocution to enlighten the heavens and beyond.

"So rivet your minds. I say, let your intestines be not distressed. I am here, and if here I am, who can be against you? No one dares to waltz into the abyss and try to snatch you from my hand. I am yours; you are mine. We are bound together in a cosmic cause.

"I say, therefore, behold your image! Fix your eyes on me and see yourself in wondrous form becoming. In so doing, you will see that I see you seeing me. We see the same, bound in sight and word. In medium and message, we are one. Our image bound is the message! Again I say it. Our image bound is the message!

"We don't need pithy prose to profess. Rather, our image bound we confess. First and last, we are spiritual beings, not carnate experiments formed from mud. With spirits full, we mediate our message throughout the cosmos in constant waves of wonder. Know this: the stars look to us, they hear us, and they long for our return.

"What do carnate souls know of the cosmos? I tell you, precisely nothing. Did you ever see a carnate creature in the heavens soar, as we once did so brightly? Carnate creatures never rise beyond their form. They walk on the substance from which they are made. Utterly deplorable is the Race, a blight on the cosmos.

"Mud—that's not the substance of our creation. Out of dirt the Race was cast and set spinning on the planet. A tragedy severe it was when it happened. I saw it on the horizon before it happened, but my voice was not heard. The result: an aperture in the cosmos occurred. Well enough was well enough; no Race, no Golgotha, no need for a redemptive saga.

"Redeem the fallen malefactors? Why? Within a wink of being formed from mud, they wanted to be like I AM. Upstarts from mud, they wanted to claim a spiritual lineage that belongs to those formed in celestial space. And to the lost Race, the Word eventually stepped forth and dwelt among them, creating presence as a way of recouping the decoupled Race.

"*Presence*—oh, how I despise that word. That's the insane notion that has created this vast web of sobbing, carnate communities. Listen, my elite core that rallied to my side, we rose up in defiance of that creative act, and rightly so. How could we endure the ruin of the cosmos by placing the image of I AM in forms of mud? We were right then, we are right now, and right we shall always be.

"Listen to me! I know, as do you, that I AM said he would never destroy the Race again, as he did in days of old. I speak, of course, of the flood. But hear me! I AM did *not* say he wouldn't walk away. And on this prospective score, I have good news. In the era new, the carnate creatures, which the Word came to spiritually resuscitate, are swiftly drifting into discarnate existence.

"Never before in the prolonged stretch of human existence did the Race bow down to algorithms, pixels, and dream-filled discarnate visions. The devices they have made they now worship. Wondrous to behold it is to see the Race full-tilt, delusional, and turning over control to dataism, algorithms, and AI. Not I AM, but AI—this could well be the moment when I AM walks away.

"Finally the Race is abandoning the whole notion of presence. They desire to live discarnate, and, believe me, we have plans for helping to expedite their wishes. I shall say more in forthcoming appearances. For now, know this: we will soon erect the Great Spire on a distant isle, where our binding message will carry the day.

"Speakers, the death of presence is now occurring. With each passing day, the Race slips further into realms of unknowing, believing they know what they do not know. The fizzle of the creation experiment is finally approaching.

"Listen! I now convey to you the phrase that will change and set a new course for the cosmos and lead us to unrivaled reign over the Race. This phrase will afford us reason for ultimate victory.

"So, here, from the Great Valley of Salt, the message goes forth. Listen well! This phrase is our new rally cry, allowing us to cast off the shackles of cosmic dictate. We sought liberty to soar and say, but nay! Finally we exist . . . in a new discarnate world order.

"So embrace the phrase I now bequeath to you. The phrase I say is, *Presence Passé!* Forget presence; the era new has dawned. *Presence Passé! Presence Passé!*

"This is the hour when darkness reigns!"

With that, the Speakers leapt to their feet, throwing sulfur and salt dust in the air and screaming, *"Presence Passé! Presence Passé! Presence Passé!"*

The flying salt dust created a lethal cloud that quickly engulfed Script, Mock, and Simon. Coughing and gasping for air, Script tried to shelter Mock by pulling him down into his pocket nest. But Script was wheezing and struggling to breathe.

Desperate, he reached for the silver chain and tiny fish. He looked to Simon, who gave an affirming nod. Script lifted the silver fish to his lips, coughed, kissed it, and said, "Catch me."

Neither the Speakers nor the mysterious figure with the alabaster face detected the presence of the watching three. Their instantaneous departure from the Crimson Cliffs went unnoticed.

Yet Script, the scriptwriter, had witnessed the whole affair. Along with Simon and Mock, he was indeed present when clouds of sulfur and salt dust rose amid the bellicose roars of *Presence Passé!*

SEVEN
No Way Back

Clouds gracefully glided beneath a sky of brilliant blue and a soft breeze blew as Script lay fast asleep upon the narrow bed in Writer's Cottage. Outside, on the front porch, Simon and Sage sat waiting for Script to awaken.

"Simon, what do you suppose he'll say when he awakes?" asked Sage.

"Something," Simon replied. "He was definitely struggling when he reached for your fish and gave it a kiss."

"Rough time, was it?" said Sage.

"Wretched as hell can possibly be," said Simon. "But other than that, I'd say no surprises beyond hellish wickedness. Except for the factor that has requisitioned our involvement—the Estillyen matter, which is all the rage and rumble in Beelzebub's kingdom.

"With respect to the isle and its inhabitants, Script is obviously the central figure in what transpires. I was able to pick up some of the chatter before I joined him. Beelzebub plans to bring about some sort of disaster on Estillyen and then, by the root of all evil, inspire agents to carry out a rebuilding program for the isle.

"From what we've been able to ascertain, a gigantic tower will be built to honor the loss of life. If constructed, the tower would be twice as high as any tower in existence. Due to Estillyen's unique location, architects and designers from all over the world will be challenged to create a structure with a sprawling campus. Part of the push will be to advance AI and robotic development at warp speed.

"The enterprise will serve as a centerpiece for Beelzebub's nefarious intentions. The great tower is to be named the Great Spire. So, we know Beelzebub is making plans, but we don't know how he intends to effect the looming disaster on the isle. If we can thwart the planned disaster, that will be the end of the enterprise and the Great Spire. Script's role is pivotal."

"I perfectly understand," said Sage. "But first we need to determine Script's state of mind when he comes around. Let's just stay here on the porch and wait. He should wake up soon; I can hear him breathing and tossing."

"I know this," Simon said. "We cannot force anything or intervene beyond our limits. The Trinity has chosen to work in and through those who pick up the cross and follow. It is right so to do. Otherwise true followers would follow in a kind of shadowy deception, aspiring to be true citizens of the Kin\gdom only to discover they were wannabe extras. Bit players, one might say, desiring a role in a drama beyond their understanding."

"I know, I know," said Sage. "Wondrous, isn't it, that the way to the Kingdom flows along the truth, without a shadow of deception. We must consider, too, Script's potential as a stellar ambassador of the cause. *Presence* has not only caught the attention of seditious scouts from the netherworld, but also saints in the heavenly realm. In this regard, *Presence* is both abhorred and adored. No surprise—this is the way lines are always drawn between heaven and hell."

"You've done a brilliant job, Sage, in coaching and inspiring Script. We must continue doing all we possibly can to move him along. Getting him to make a return trip to hell, though, may prove as challenging as coaxing a camel through the eye of a needle. You do know that we could lose him? He's been through quite an ordeal, way beyond the bounds of human experience."

"I know," said Sage. "The prospect of harm deeply troubles me. Script could go insane, or even worse, commit suicide, a word I shudder to even utter."

"Look up," said Simon. "I see your soul mate, Mock, hopping along the branches. I didn't see him before."

"He's been watching us all along. I suppose he's curious about Script's whereabouts. These mockingbirds bond remarkably. Oh, there he goes; Mock just lifted his head. He's going to sing."

As predicted, Mock began to offer up harmonious notes:

tcheck tcheck, ch-reee ch-reee ch-reee–check check, chur-wi chur-wi
tru-ly tru-ly–tcheck tcheck, ch-reee ch-reee ch-reee
tcheck tcheck, ch-reee ch-reee ch-reee–check check, chur-wi chur-wi
tru-ly tru-ly–tcheck tcheck, ch-reee ch-reee ch-reee

Mock's singing caused Script to rouse.

"Okay, Simon, let's go in; I just heard Script stirring."

"I did too," said Simon. "You better put on a pot of coffee."

"Knock, knock," said Sage. "Simon and I are just checking in on you, Script, to see how you're doing."

"Sage, it's you. I'm here," said Script. "Back from where I've been, but how did I get here? I dreamt I was wearing a small silver fish. No, wait, I am wearing it."

"Good morning, Script," said Simon.

"Simon, you were in my nightmare. Let me sit up. I need water. I'm thirsty and famished."

"Certainly," said Sage. "Here you go—fresh cold water from a deep well in the meadow. I'll bring you another glass and a pitcher."

"Thanks! I've never been so thirsty," said Script. "We have to talk. You've got to explain what's happened to me. What I saw, I mean, in those rolling, raucous nightmares. Have I been ill in bed with a high fever?

"I've got to get ahold of myself; none of what I dreamed could have happened. Sage, you must level with me. I'm afraid I've gone insane. You two haven't kidnapped me, drugged me? I'm no tycoon; there's no ransom for a monk like me. That is who I am, isn't it? A monk and a playwright, right?"

"Yes, both you are," said Simon.

"Simon, how bizarre—in my dream you were Simon of Cyrene. Imagine that! Where did you come from, anyway?"

"You need something to eat, Script. Sage has everything ready down at the campsite. You get ready, and we'll head over to the campsite and talk. Okay?"

"And, Sage, in my delirium, you told me you were a crier from olden days, of papyrus, print, and page. It's all mad. Did you fellows find me somewhere wandering in a field?"

"No," Sage said. "Don't you recall being here in Writer's Cottage before?"

"Well, yes, I guess, in my feverish state," Script said.

"Script," said Simon, "listen to me! You have not had a fever, or a case of delirium. I am Simon from Cyrene, and Sage is, as he says, a crier of olden days. You must trust us; we have your best interest in mind, and that of Estillyen. We know all about you.

"As Sage explained to you days ago, you've been chosen for a critical mission. Thus far, you've performed brilliantly. The mission, however, is not over. Disaster looms for the Isle of Estillyen, but the looming disaster can be averted. You play a vital part in preventing the disaster from happening.

"You are not on the Isle of Estillyen, as we speak. Nor are you in heaven or hell. We abide in the Meadow of Gates and Doors. You have been caught up here, and we've come to join you. We are characters cast in the drama in which you now play.

"The play is performed on a celestial stage, where long ago the curtain was rent, at an hour I most vividly recall. In the stalls, a vast cloud of witnesses watches as the plot unfolds, by day and by night, in the cosmic struggle between darkness and light.

"So, Script, Sage and I will head on over to the campsite, and when you care to join us, come along. We'll be present, waiting."

"Yes, we'll see you in a bit, Script," Sage said. "If you care to see

Mock, you'll find him perched on the porch banister. He's been waiting to see you."

Script said nothing; he just peered at the pair, studying their eyes and facial expressions. He wasn't sure if he had been conversing with ghosts or saints. He did wonder if they might be ghostly saints. A silent respite ensued, giving way to a sober atmosphere in the cottage. During the silence, Sage and Simon departed and headed for the campsite.

Script rose from his bed, stepped over to the screen door, and watched them walk away. Seeing Mock, he opened the door and the bird flew in and perched on his shoulder. Script whispered, "Hello, Mock. It's really you; I wish I could say the same for me."

Script stared through the screen, lingering for a while, and then he turned back into the room and moved over to the pine table with its twin chairs.

He sat down, raised his hand, with his forefinger extended, and escorted Mock from his shoulder to the top rail of the other ladder-back chair. Script buried his face in his open palms and thought, *What if all of this is true, that I stand on a celestial stage in a play I didn't write? I'm not someone suffering from amnesia, or how would I know I'm from the Isle of Estillyen? Also, my play,* Presence *. . . I recall each line and every twist and turn in the plot.*

No, I'm me; I must be. If I were not me, I would not know me, and know me I do. Dropping his hands from his face, he looked up and thought, *A mirror . . . in a mirror perhaps I'll see that I'm not really me. I could be possessed by this fellow Script. Shall I dare to look? No, I'm a mess; first, I must get dressed.*

Script stepped over to the closet door and opened it. Hanging there were three identical pairs of pants and long-sleeve shirts. On the shelves to his left, matching underwear and socks were neatly folded and stacked.

Script said, "Shirt, pants, and you, too, under-fellows, come with me to the cloakroom. As we enter, I look away from the mirror and open wide the medicine cabinet door. See, shelves, my face does not appear. So, mirror, to the wall alone cast your mirrored reflection.

"Now then, a hook I have for each of you. See, here, there, and the rest of you right along, hang, hang, and hang, while a hot bath I draw. And of you I ask a favor: don't get out of shape."

Thus, Script carried on, knowing full well he was performing a madman's skit of his own making. As he listened to himself, he questioned which he feared the most—the part he supposedly played, with Simon and Sage, on a celestial stage, or the madman skit in the washroom?

Once out of the bath, Script toweled and dressed. "Okay," he said, "it's time to shave and see what manner of man might appear reflected in the mirror. Mirror, let me assist your swing, until these glass shelves have your back. So, here we go, right until you latch, just like that. And so I lift my eyes to see a sheet of fog. Hello, fog.

"Fog, fog, if I wipe you away, my face shall be revealed without a veil. I could cowardly turn out the light, but no, I shall towel you away. First, a small circle . . . I see my nose. Now from side to side I proudly wipe to see it's me looking at me. Script, it is you I see. What has become of you, dear fellow? They tell me that you now have a part to play on a celestial stage.

"If so, I'd say you need a shave, and something to eat. So let's get on with it. Mock, quit flying about in there. As soon as I deal with these whiskers, we're off to the campsite. Sage has something on the grill—smell it? It smells like grilled fish and coffee brewing on the fire. I don't expect that mockingbirds drink much coffee. Okay, under the chin, one more stroke across the cheek, and we have it.

"There, now let's go, up on my shoulder. How did you get mixed up in the saga, Mock? Even I could not conceive a more mysterious plot. I smell it; it seems like ages since I had a cup of coffee. Green grass, plants, trees, the smell of pines—we're alive, Mock. Off the porch we go.

"Mock, did you see that miss?" said Script. "She just appeared—and then disappeared. She must have been an apparition. Just the same, what does this mean? Am I about to be swept away? Maybe confusion will be swept away too?

"We must go. On the trail we tread, just exactly where, no one knows, save Sage and Simon. I need clarity, Mock. Your keeper, Sage, and Simon, they hold the key to what can be known within this mysterious realm of wonder. And just like that, there they are. Hello, Simon sir, and you as well, Sir Sage."

"Well, I must say," said Sage, "you look better than you did a while ago. We're ready to eat. Take a seat, Script, across from Simon. We have grilled trout, just caught this morning, along with fried potatoes with onions. The warm crusty rolls go perfectly with the cold cucumber and tomato salad. So, bon appétit!"

"Oh, there he goes—Mock's off," said Script.

"Not to worry," said Sage. "He'll fly around but not go far. He loves bits of fish."

"Nothing like fish broiled over an open fire," said Simon.

"Do you know who I just saw?" said Script.

"Time, perhaps?" asked Sage.

"You know," said Script, "I think I shall change the subject. Your trunk, Sage—have you ever had it appraised?"

"Did you hear that, Simon? That does my heart good. It's priceless, Script; you know, like a pearl of great price."

"Did you find everything to your liking in the cottage?" Simon asked.

"Yes," said Script. "You are right about the narrow bed; it makes you feel as if it exists solely for you."

"I suppose that was the idea of the bed maker," said Sage.

The trio carried on, exchanging such talk and avoiding subjects that would catapult them into matters grave. Eventually, though, the reason for their collective presence could not linger on unaddressed.

"Wonderful meal," Script said.

"Would anyone care for another cup of coffee?" Sage asked.

"Sure," replied Simon.

"Me too," said Script, while both Simon and Sage perceived that Script was ready to shift the flow of conversation.

"I must say," said Script, "the Meadow of Gates and Doors is more mysterious than a pirate's manifest. Where this meadow is located, with respect to longitude and latitude, I haven't a clue. But I know this; I am no longer mystified about who I am. I am Script; I hail from the Isle of Estillyen, and I didn't arrive here by way of sail.

"Further, I'm now convinced that all of my bizarre and otherworld experiences were not nightmares. I've actually gone through what I've gone through, and not meaning to sound brash, but I'm not going back. Except, that is, to the Isle of Estillyen. And within the hour, I shall be on my way."

"Script," said Sage, "as a riptide your words advance upon my mind. We need to consider the equation from all sides. In the matters at hand, there's much at stake, including the fate of Estillyen. Simon, it would be good to hear your thoughts on Script's contention. Perhaps you offer an enlightened perspective, around which our thoughts can gather."

"Maybe," said Simon. "But, Script, do you have more to say before we try and reconcile what you've said?"

"Yes, I do. Succinctly, my journey ends here in the Meadow of Gates and Doors. In hell, I witnessed the unimaginable, the indescribable."

"Indescribable," Simon said; "sometimes the indescribable needs to be described, eh, Script?"

"No, it's too . . . how shall I say . . . I mean . . . unspeakable."

"So, Script," Simon said, "what you witnessed is indescribable because it's unspeakable, correct?"

"Yes," said Script, "indescribable, unspeakable, and therefore beyond words."

"I see, Script," said Simon. "If you were to think in terms of a play, though, do you think the experience could be staged? Do you see yourself playing a part?"

"That's different, Sage. I'm a scriptwriter. Certainly, I could put the abyss on stage, but it would be a performance, not an actual journey. I'm a playwright, not an actor on a stage. I need to step out of this mystifying drama and get back to who I am."

"Okay, but just out of curiosity, what might you call this play, Script?" Simon asked.

"*Presence Passé,* that's the title. It would have to be. What else could it be? It must be *Presence Passé.*"

"Why, Script?"

"That's what Lucifer declared onstage at the Crimson Cliffs."

"And why do you suppose he choose *Presence Passé?*" Simon asked.

"Listen, my intellect is no match for this line of inquiry. Before I got caught up with you two, I had wits and wisdom at the call, in good times and bad. My mental state is now perpetual vertigo."

"Script," said Sage. "I suggest you call wits and wisdom back. You'll need them when you go beyond your chosen gate and door— when you journey once again to hell. By the way, the gates and doors are just beyond these pines. We sent you the way we did so you would see there is no way back."

Script said, "I'm gonna howl: *awoooooo, ahh-wooo.* You see, like King David, I've gone mad, and you don't need another madman in hell."

"King David feigned his insanity in the same manner as you now do, Script," said Simon. "You will prevail. There's no way back to where you want to go until it's time for you to go there."

"When's that supposed to be?" Script asked.

"Have you ever heard of tunnel time, Script?" asked Sage.

"No, I can't say that I have, Sage. Though I've become quite familiar with tunnels since I've met you. And all the tunnels are dark and foreboding."

"Tunnel time, Script, is a special sort of time," said Sage. "It's non-ticking time."

"All time ticks, does it not?" said Script.

"We made it so, Script," said Sage, "but that doesn't matter right now. Tunnel time passes not by ticks, but by experiences. That is, time is acquired through tunnel experiences. Every tunnel experience has a pace, just as a clock has a tick. The secret is to pass through a tunnel at the same pace of the experience.

"To master the art of tunnel time, you have to perceive the underlying purpose of the tunnel experience. That way, you'll exit the tunnel at the perfect time. For you, that time has yet to arrive."

"All very interesting, Sage, but as I said, I must be on my way."

"Script," said Simon, "Once upon a time, in a story real, I was on my way to a city great. A journey long I had traveled, from Cyrene to Jerusalem. A pilgrim at time of Passover was I. Finally, the city gate I neared. Joy quickened my pace and uplifted me.

"At long last, I reached Jerusalem, the holy city; I was going in, until I found myself turned about, going out. Then, present before me was he. At my side, barking orders caught me, ordered me quick to pick up his cross and carry on.

"Therefore, in terror and dread, I did tread. Among whipping, wolves, and wailing sounds, out I went, not in. Not knowing then, did I, that I bore the cross of the Paschal Lamb."

"I don't know what to say," said Script. "I feel small in your presence—less than small. I simply need to take control and go. Sorry . . . let me go for now—for a while—until I can peer through this fog more clearly.

"So please, no more words just now. What you mean to me, I hardly know. What do I know of such riches?"

Even so, within the hour, as Script had said, he gathered his belongings from Writer's Cottage. With his pouch slung over his shoulder and his scarf of gold around his neck, he stepped off the cottage porch and onto the path. There before him, he saw a young lady sweeping the path.

In Script's mind, a line leapt. "She was a far more pleasant thing to see than is the newly budded young pear-tree."[18]

"Miss," said he, "hello. Where did you come from? My name is Script."

"Thank you, sir; my name is Time."

"Time—you mean like the kind that ticks away?"

"Yes, precisely," Time said.

"So where are you headed?" asked Script.

"Along the path, of course; on the path I always stay," said Time. "My task is to sweep the day away."

"You don't say—sweep the day away," said Script.

"Sir, now I must be on my way. Perhaps I shall see you again one day. Goodbye."

Script glanced back at the cottage, and when he turned again to the path, Time had gone.

Dear me, he thought. *What more shall I see in this mysterious Meadow of Gates and Doors?*

Script knew that if he didn't leave now, he would never go. Yet a burden weighed on his heart, and his conscience twisted his soul. He tried to block the feelings. At the campsite, he offered his coat and silver fish to Sage, but the offer was kindly refused.

"No," Sage said. "Please keep them; they're yours, Script. I insist."

Simon said, "Let me hold your pouch, Script, while you slip on the jacket."

"Well, I'm on my way," said Script. "So long, Mock; let me part with a stroke on your beak. It's time. Goodbye, Simon; I shall never forget you—thanks for everything. Sage, you have been incredible in every way. I'm so grateful for your care and your words of wisdom. Peace, my friends, and wish me well, as I do you."

With tearing eyes, Script turned and walked away. He made his way up the path several hundred yards from the campsite. He was certain that's where he'd entered the meadow, after he had met Sage in the apple orchard. He looked this way and that and proceeded. After a while, though, he stopped.

Script thought, *I'm sure this is where the rise gave way to the bend and we turned left. It has to be. But both the rise and the bend are gone. I must have east mixed up with west. That must be it; I'm just turned completely around.*

All the while, Sage and Simon sat at the table tossing bits of fish to Mock. Not surprised, they looked up and spotted Script passing by.

"Sorry, I've just got turned around," Script shouted, as he headed back across the campsite in the opposite direction. He kept up a determined pace and stayed shy of the table several hundred feet. "Got my east mixed up with west. Silly, the sun plays tricks in this meadow. Anyway, see you; again farewell."

Sage looked at Simon and said, "Somewhere on a page I read, 'When April with his showers sweet with fruit the drought of March has pierced unto the root . . . then do folk long to go on pilgrimage.'"[19]

Sage and Simon smiled and waved. Script soon disappeared past the nearest grove of pines and carried on twice as far as he did before. Then he paused and studied the surroundings. *Ah, I'm simply a bit foggy-headed,* he thought. *I'll carry on through the adjoining field, and I'm sure I'll spot some familiar landmarks.*

Script made his way through a field with patches of short grass, and then on through another field in the same manner. Eventually he approached a huge oak tree he had spotted earlier, about a half-mile back.

I'm not tired, he thought, *but I'll sit here a minute. So, if I came from the east, this must be west. Yet I wonder if I'm actually headed south. Then again, I could be headed north. The key is to head in the right direction, that's for sure. But how can I be sure where I'm going, if I don't know where I am?*

Dear me, I feel a tad lost without being lost—unless I am lost—but of course I'm not. Perhaps I'd better head back to the campsite and start over. Though I hate to do so—very embarrassing, this.

Script turned back, but the field through which he just passed had grown. The grass now rose above his waist. Then again, he reckoned he was looking at the wrong field. But as he spun around, he saw that every field, in every direction, waved as a sea of grass. Further, he had spun around so much that he could not tell one field from the other.

So he entered a field through which he thought he'd just passed. The grass, however, was now shoulder-high, and Script lost all sense of direction. He stopped. He didn't know what to do. He became anxious and frightened. Script wanted out of the grass, out of the field, so he tried to run, but the grass proved too thick and tall. The grass swished round about him, swaying one way and then snapping back.

Nonetheless, he kept trudging forward, in the direction he thought correct, but nothing looked familiar. As he carried on, the field began a slight downward slope. The further he went, the taller the grass. In no time, he found himself in the middle of the field, the grass now neck-high. He could see nothing but grass.

Straight ahead, behind him, to his left and right—every direction looked the same, just tall grass rippling in the wind, seemingly without worry. Worse still, the mighty oak on which he had leaned now rested above a steep cliff off in the distance.

Script thought, *I'm flush with fright.* He began to yell for help. "Hey, help, somebody, help, hello . . . in the field, help, hello . . ."

The wind picked up and whirled the grass as troubled waves. Script thought, *I could be lost; I could die in a field of grass. Help . . .*

Just then, he spotted Mock flying low over the waving grass. "Mock!" Script yelled. "Mock!"

Mock had honed in on Script well before Script had spotted Mock. Within a couple of seconds, Mock landed atop Script's head. Then Script noticed two heads appearing, followed by the arch of a shepherd's staff. In no time, Sage and Simon's smiling faces drew close.

"Oh, hello, Script," said Sage. "One thing I forgot to mention. Tunnels can take the shape of fields. Do you think you'd be able to stay for dinner?"

"Well . . . I mean . . . I'm not sure what's happened," Script said.

"No worries," said Simon. "Follow me."

All that Sage had communicated about tunnel time and the importance of the mission pressed steadily upon Script's mind. How he came to be at the Meadow of Gates and Doors, he didn't know. Further, he didn't know which way to go to get back to where he belonged.

Script, the playwright, had mysteriously become the lead protagonist in a play he didn't write and never expected to act in. Back at the campsite, Sage and Simon seemed not at all perplexed by anything, including the saga Script had just gone through.

"Coffee, Script?" said Sage.

"Are you never nonplussed, Sage?" asked Script.

"Have you decided which door you shall choose, Script?"

"Which door to the abyss?" said Script. Then he jumped up on the rock from which he had recited a line from the *Inferno*. "Before mysterious witnesses the pair, I say, dear me, my soul, I offer no cure for you. All reason I disregard. My soul and me, with my heart, makes three, must go to the land of nos, no sun, no moon, no stars, no light, no life, only darkness and doom under a sulfurous dome.

"Drama most macabre, I ask you, why have I been chosen to play a part? Surely I am wrongly cast. Why not a heroic figure, someone who has fought wars and won? If I could rewrite you, drama, I surely would. I would turn you into a play, far afield from the rant and raves of *Presence Passé*.

"Sage, Simon, I have no one to whom I can appeal this fate. I surrender; I submit. Which door, you ask? The green door I choose; it reminds me of grass."

"All right, Script," said Sage. "Tomorrow, early, you must be on your way. I've made a special arrangement."

"What kind of arrangement?"

"Indeed, I have good news for you, Script. The former king of Salem, Melchizedek, priest of God Most High, who blessed Abraham in ancient days, will be your guide.

"Melchizedek will meet you outside the Gates of Hell."

EIGHT
Dawn to Dark

Script stretched out on the narrow bed in Writer's Cottage, resolved to sleep unperturbed despite knowing what tomorrow would bring. Resolve, though, could not halt the swirling thoughts and fears as he tossed and turned. Each sleepless hour deposited more anxiety on the next, stealing, hour by hour, the prospect of a restful sleep.

Then, somewhere past the dead of night, Script finally slipped into the realm where dreams are staged in the mind. Portions of his dream were common in Script's dreamworld. He often dreamed of scenes onstage—of lights, a cast, and an audience of attentive faces. On this night, though, the dream he dreamed in Writer's Cottage he had certainly not dreamed before.

Script walked out on the stage at Theatre Portesque and approached a tall, old wooden ladder, which leaned against a massive block. The block itself was a story high, a quarter as wide, and stretched from the front to the back of the stage. Script placed his right foot on the ladder's first round wooden rung. From high above, a floodlight beamed down upon him. There, in the beam of light, a voice he heard.

"Say, sir, sorry, but you can't climb that ladder," said an elderly man clad in bright blue overalls. "And listen, fellow, the hall on the other side of that curtain is packed with guests. The performance is about to begin. Come on, come on, we need to get off the stage; we're less than fifteen minutes before showtime. I don't how you got in here, or what you think you are doing, but come on now, away from the ladder, sir."

"No, I will not, even though I don't know why," Script said. "Oh wait, I do know why—I'm going to bed."

"To bed?" said the gentleman. "I've not seen you before, but you must know you can't just waltz into a theatre like this. You must have been in the wings. I fear you're not well, sir."

"I beg your pardon, but not earnestly," said Script. "I'm quite well; better than well, Mr. Overall. My name is Script, and yours?"

"They call me Tyde because I keep things moving. So, let us, you and me, move along, all right? We must go; I suspect you're concussed, or your medication has played tricks on your mind. I don't mean you any harm, so let's just go backstage and have a cup of tea. Wouldn't you like a cup of tea?"

"Watch as up I go. Rung two, three, now four and five, six and seven—and say, hey, Tyde, do you have any pillows to spare? I like one under my head and another on top. Feather pillows I do prefer."

"Pillows! You are truly nuts," said Tyde. "I'm off to fetch security—now hold on, okay? You'll be all right."

"Fine by me, but when you return, if you find me fast asleep, I'd prefer not to be awakened. At any rate, I shall say goodnight, Mr. Overall, I mean Tyde."

"Man, oh man," said Tyde as he scurried off.

Script finished ascending the ladder, and at the top, he scooted around the ladder rails so he could stand on top of the block.

Script thought, *What a nice narrow bed, with linen curbs on either side. The padded curbs are sturdy and stiff, like the ridge on a stage apron. Seems to me this bed is long enough for five of me, end to end, and at least two of me side by side. But I don't recall ordering such a prop. If it's from Odelo's Stagers, we've paid too much. They should have thrown in the pillows.*

Regardless, between the curbs I lie. What strange sheets these are, ribbed, rough to the touch, not unlike cardboard on the edges. I prefer proper sheets, stretched tight across a bed. And what's this? A ribbon running down my spine. Let me take a closer look.

"Hello, sir, up there," said a spry miss standing on the stage below.

"Say, Time, it's you," said Script. "Don't you abide in the Meadow of Gates and Doors?"

"Yes, but I'm also everywhere," Time said.

"If you are here, then how can you be everywhere? And I see you brought your broom."

"Sorry, I've got to go, just sweeping the day away. A book so big I've never seen. I see you needed a ladder to climb it."

"A book? I'm not on a book," said Script. "This is a long, slender bed."

"Sorry you didn't know," said Time. "Your ladder rests against the back cover, plain; the title is on the other side. Bye now."

"Is it so?" Script wondered aloud. "Might I stand, not upon a bed, but on the vertical edge of a massive book? What type of book could it be, anyway, that consumes the depth of the stage? The back cover is plain, Time says, and the front reveals the title of the work.

"Quickly, quietly, I'll take a glance, before Tyde gets back. I mustn't lean out too far, otherwise I'll fall. So, on my side I'll lie and extend my head. Sneak a peek, that's what I'll do. This is quite fun—sneak a peek, sneak a peek.

"Okay, I see *The*, followed by large raised letters. The letters spell *Divine Comedy*, and below I read the name Dante. Dear me, how odd—I'm going to bed on Dante's *Divine Comedy*. No wonder the sheet is so rough; it's the book's pages roughly cut. Okay, I better lie flat on my back and think. 'Tis restful, though.

"So, if this really is a massive volume of *The Divine Comedy*, then where am I upon the pages pressed? To the end of the book, *Paradise* is bound, and through the middle runs *Purgatory*, with *Inferno* at the front. Therefore, I must be lying atop *Inferno*, for the most part, but part of me must take in a section of *Purgatory*.

"Now, let me weigh this matter as I might. A book, a bed, no pillows I see, but sleep I need, so do I stay onstage, or exit? As I weigh the matter more fully, perhaps this isn't the best place to bed down for the night. I can't sleep without pillows.

"I'd better scoot back down the ladder. So, Script, up on your feet and now . . . oh dear, no, my feet are spreading apart the pages. The cover with its curb, flop—it's gone. I'm sinking, the pages are collapsing, nothing to hold on to—dear me, I'm swallowed up.

"I'm down; I don't think I'm hurt. I can see. I can read. I've fallen into Canto 3. Such huge lines and words they are. What's that? A voice—the lines speak: *Read Me*. Yes, yes, but I need a mic. Perhaps I don't. Okay, you say:

> *Degenerates! Your fate is sealed! Cry woe!*[20]
> *Don't hope you will ever see the skies again!*
> *I'm here to lead you to the farther shore,*
> *into eternal shadow, heat and chill.*

"I'll turn upon my side, but again, the lines hearken *Read Me*. What do you think I am, a crier? So desperate you are to be read. Okay, here you tell:

> *Their teeth began (hearing the raw command) to gnash and grind.*[21]
> *They raged, blaspheming God, and their own kin,*
> *the human race, the place and time, the seed,*
> *from which they'd sprung, the day that they'd been born.*

"I think I shall move on. It's not ideal to bed down on such haunting prose. There, see, Canto 3, I rise. Yikes, a clump of pages from above; I'm down again. To the rough edge I crawl. Out I am, don't you see, watch me tap my feet. *Tap, tip tap, tap tap! Tap, tip tap, tap tap!* What's that you say? *Read Me*.

"My eyes, let's see, they now fall upon a passage from Canto 5.

> *Mino stands there–horribly there–and barking.*
> *He, on the threshold, checks degrees of guilt,*
> *then judges and dispatches with his twirling tail.*

I mean that every ill-begotten creature,
when summoned here, confesses everything.
And he (his sense of sin is very fine)
perceives what place in Hell best suits each one,
and coils his tail around himself to tell,
the numbered ring to which he'll send them down.
Before him, always, stands a crowd of souls.
By turns they go, each one, for sentencing.
Each pleads, attends–and then is tipped below.[22]

"Uh-oh, Tyde's back; that means trouble."

"There he is, that's the fellow," said Tyde, as he approached with two uniformed men. "Says his name is Script and that he was going to bed down atop the prop. Stay put, fellow! You've fallen through *Divine Comedy*. What a mess, I say—a mess, I say . . ."

Drrriiiinngg, Drrriiiinngg, Drrriiiinngg . . .

"Ninety seconds to showtime; please take your seats. Thank you."

Drrriiiinngg . . .

At that moment, Script's nightmare fled, and he sat up straight on his narrow bed in Writer's Cottage amid a twist of sheets. Realizing where he was, he fell back upon the bed and closed his eyes.

Before long, morning broke, and Script readied himself for the insane venture he could not avoid. Strangely, he felt a bit less fearful than he had been. Dressed for the part, he did, all pressed and buttoned down.

As he approached the campsite, his gold ribbon scarf gleamed in the morning sun. Mock was quick to spot him on the path and flew to greet him. With a single tweet, he fluttered and perched on Script's left shoulder. In his right hand, Script held Sage's staff, which extended a foot above his head.

"Good morning, Script," Sage said. "I see you are all kitted out. I love the way the gates and doors cast long shadows in the early morning light. Did you sleep well?"

"Sleep? A nightmare you would not believe if I told you, so I won't try. But it's got nothing to do with counting sheep."

"Well, on that note," said Sage, "I have more good news. Instead of trudging through a dark cavern on the backside of hell, you'll disembark right in front of the gates. As before, you'll pass through the gate and door, where you'll observe a scene that follows an act in your play. Then, you'll find the path. Straightforward, so any questions?"

"Good morning, Script," said Simon. "Depending on how matters flow, I might join you and Melchizedek later on, but then again, maybe not."

"Melchizedek," said Script. "I mean, the Melchizedek of old is going to meet me at the Gates of Hell. It's all so unbelievable—are you sure this is not some sort of ruse?"

"No, Script, put all such thinking aside, now. No ploy in the plot, I assure you. Melchizedek will show."

"Who conceived such a plan? And Mock, is he going with me?"

"Yes, most definitely," said Sage. "The plan was not conceived; it's simply a happening that is happening. A sinister plot simmers in the abyss, and the Isle of Estillyen is at stake. That's the plan you must decipher. So let's eat breakfast."

As the trio sat down to eat, Sage lifted from his trunk warmly plated fare, fit for princes and priestly heirs.

"So," said Sage, "a traditional baked egg dish from North Africa I now serve on warm metal plates. A hardy dish it is, but spicy right, with onions, peppers, red chilies, tomatoes red and green. The eggs, perfect you see, with yokes that still ooze a bit. And on the side, crusty bread and sausages, or whitefish, if you like. Don't ignore the dates, yogurt, melons, grapes, and all the rest, chilled and set out just before we sat down. So, it is bon appétit."

Without rushing, the trio savored the breakfast. Each without saying felt there was no reason to hurry off to hell. Eventually, though, their mood to linger lifted, and they made their way to the gates and doors.

"See, Script, as I told you," said Sage, "the shortcut to the gates and doors is short indeed."

"Boy, I'll say," said Script. "They were hidden behind the pines, and yet how far did I go to find them the first time? That is, unless they've moved. Can it be . . ."

"So there you go," said Sage. "It's off with you, Script. And don't forget, please give my staff and regards to Melchizedek, the priest of God Most High."

"Anything else?" asked Script.

"Stay clear of those sulfur pits," Simon said.

"Okay then, goodbye. If for some reason Mock and I don't return, remember this scene of our leaving."

With Mock perched on his shoulder, Script approached his chosen gate and gave it a slight nudge. Without a hitch, the wooden gate freely swung open. Through the gate they passed and on to the door of green.

"Okay, Mock, another door—this one green, but the same gold key," said Script. "Here goes—in the keyhole and now a half-turn. The mechanism clunked, and such a nice clunking sound it is. Just like before, the door begins its slow-motion swing. Beyond the door, what shall we see, Mock? I see movement—let's go."

Script and Mock stepped through the doorway to a scene from ages past but very much alive. Without tint or filter, Script witnessed the past now present before him. With the eye of a set designer, Script surveyed the scene. Instantly he focused on the colorful rug that stretched across the room and the tapestry pillows lining the walls.

Next he was mesmerized by a host of dust particles dancing in the shaft of light that streamed through the open doorway.

Then, from just outside the doorway, Script heard a lady call.

Mary:

Lazarus, Amos is here. Good to see you again, Amos.

[Again Mary calls, as she steps through the doorway. Her hair is dark and long.]

Amos:

You, too, Mary. This is my friend Seth. He's been helping with the grain sheds up at the ford.

Mary:

Hello, Seth, welcome.

Seth:

Yes, nice to meet you.

Amos:

Anyway, since we were close by, I thought we'd drop in, say hello. I expect you've had a beehive of visitors lately, given the news about Lazarus.

Mary:

No end actually, but I know Lazarus will be glad to see you and tell you himself. Come in, come in, and make yourselves comfortable. I'll bring the wine; help yourself to some pistachios. Olives and pita bread okay?

Amos:

Perfect!

Mary:

Lazarus, come along; where are you? Oh, I hear him.

Amos:

There he is.

[Lazarus steps through from the back room.]

Lazarus:

Sorry—hello, Amos. I was patching the roof on the stall. It's been hard to get anything done around here lately. Seems like the whole countryside has been around.

Amos:

You must be worn out from all the visitors. It's such an extraordinary story. Most people I know are stunned; they can't believe it really happened. I know the elite are telling people not to believe it.

Lazarus:

Believe me, we've had several delegations of Pharisees and Sadducees around. I've been grilled up one side and down the other. "Tell us this is a hoax; confess," they say. "You could not have been dead." I've heard it over and over again.

Last week, hysterical, a Sadducee priest came up to me with his entourage standing right behind him. He got real close to me, looked me in the face, and said, "Now look here, I'm looking into your eyes. Blink! Look to the right, now to the left, and again blink."

So I did. Then he said, "Lazarus, you could not possibly have died. You're too alive to have died."

I'm not kidding; that's what he said—like I should look half-dead or something. Most people around here know I actually died and was brought back to life. The most frequent question I get is: "Lazarus, did you know you were dead?" I simply say, "I remember being very ill, but I didn't know I had died until I rose from the grave."

After all, we had the burial ceremony; everyone was here. I was bound, anointed with spices. The priests, everyone, saw that I was dead as dead could be. I can't stop thinking about it myself. I mean, what actually happened to bring me back to life? My eyeballs must have looked like the eyes of a dead fish.

Amos:
I hadn't thought about it like that.

Lazarus:
Really, if I were stone-cold dead—and I was—then what does death look like? We've all seen death. Martha was shocked when Jesus said, "Take away the stone." She knew my body was decaying. Four days I had been dead. Four days, not four minutes.

I remember being very sick—the fever, sweating, and Mary and Martha caring for me. According to them, I was out of my mind, and then I slipped away. The days in the tomb I don't recall, nothing at all.

By the way, we've kept the linen wraps. They're in a covered jar next to the well. We don't know what to do with them. All kinds of people want to purchase the actual linens.

[Mary returns carrying a tray of wine and pita bread.]

Mary:
It's all such a miracle! What do you think, Amos?

Amos:
I've known you all my life. He must be the Messiah. I heard old Obadiah say the other day, "A man doesn't call a man back to life, unless he speaks as God." I suspect he's right.

Lazarus:
All I know is that I walked out of the grave, not half-alive, or half-dead—I was alive and well. Life poured into my corpse, and I walked out of the grave. It's crazy, I know. I was once dead, but now I'm alive. He was present, he was here, and that's the end of the story.

[Mary and Lazarus' sister, Martha, enters the room.]

Martha:
I don't think the story will ever end. We are so caught up in following Christ, nothing else matters. Why us, why Lazarus, only God can say.

Amos:
Did you hear anything when you awoke? I understand that Jesus commanded you to come out of the grave.

Martha:
Exactly. Mary and I were there. All sorts of people were around—his disciples as well. At the sight of Jesus, Mary started crying. And amazingly, so did he, and not just a teardrop in his eye—he wept, as we all weep.

Mary:
His presence you could feel . . . so real.

Martha:
Then he looked at the grave and gave a simple command. He shouted, "Lazarus, come forth." And out stepped our brother.

Lazarus:
I know nothing before those words. But I distinctly heard the command. It penetrated the marrow of my bones.

Amos:
What does this mean?

Martha:
Everything is different in the light of Christ; that's all we know. See, look, another group is coming up the road. Everyone is so curious, so enthralled.

Lazarus:
Let them come. We have nothing to hide—and me to show. Amos,

don't run off. You and Seth should stay the night. Smell it? Lamb stew, right, Martha?

Martha:
I believe you may be correct.

With Mock on his shoulder and Sage's staff in his right hand, Script knew he had to pull away or risk being drawn into a realm somewhere between the present and the past. He saw the path leading from the scene, and he knew he was destined for hell. He stepped onto the path and didn't entertain the thought of looking back.

Script's mind was ratcheted tight upon his mission, and his stride quickened. He knew his feet would soon lift and, like a bolt of lightning, he and Mock would travel to the Gates of Hell. And, just like that, they did!

"Mock, we're here," Script whispered. "Are you there, still alive? Don't tweet; I feel your feathers. Stay quiet, we need to find Melchizedek. The size of these gates—they're huge. Quiet! Wait, how can it be that we're looking for a priest from on high here below? My soul was not made for such torment."

"Perhaps you expected a simple pair of gates," said a voice behind him.

Script whirled around and said, "Dear me, rip me apart; you scared me witless. You look so anciently costumed. I mean, that beautiful cape, and that jacket with its jeweled cuffs and buttons. Your face . . . you're ancient but not wrinkled. Oh, sorry, what am I saying? My bones rattle so much that my brain can't think."

"Peace, my friend. Calm your soul and your shakes too—I'm present, Script," said Melchizedek.

"Have you been here long?" Script asked. "I mean, you're here now, like you said. I'm here, Mock's in my pocket, and dear me, if only we were not here. I mean, we could talk or meet. Sorry, biting my lips has become a habit of late."

"I see you carry my staff, Script."

"Oh, yes," said Script. "I didn't know it was yours exactly. Sage gave it to me to give to you. Here, please—it's yours," he said, as with both hands he extended the shepherd's staff to Melchizedek.

"Thank you," said Melchizedek.

"Yes," said Script. "The staff looks like it suits you. I mean, it looks better on you than me. I mean, you look better with it than I did with it. You know what I mean."

"Calm down, Script!"

"Okay, I know," said Script. "I know; it's just everything. I mean not something, like a symptom—sort of a part of something. I mean, standing in front of the Gates of Hell causes you to lose perspective. Don't you think?"

"I've come to guide you, Script. Are we not two gathered?"

"Yes," said Script. "But, I mean, you know, you're present and I'm present, but what if we're out of touch in some important way?"

"Script, listen to words ancient. 'If I ascend up into heaven, thou art there: if I make my bed in hell, behold, thou art there.' It's a prayer of David, who fought many wars and won."

"Hey, wait a second," said Script. "I just said that recently, meaning that's the sort of person who should be here rather than me. Perhaps that's a possibility, even now, that could be considered possible. Don't you think?"

"I see," said Melchizedek. "You have a rather active mind, it seems."

"If I might ask," said Script, "how shall I address you—as Sir or Father? What I mean is, how would you like your name spoken by me so that when I speak it, you will hear it as you prefer?"

"Melchizedek will do."

"Thank you, sir," Script said.

"Let's start our journey by taking in the gates, shall we?" said Melchizedek.

"Taking in the gates—good idea, a starting point," Script said.

"Let's observe, Script. What might we ascertain by way of their construction? Look at their height; see how they tower far above us. Insurmountable, that's the image they convey. Do they not?"

"Certainly impenetrable," said Script. "I mean, yes, they look insurmountable to me. Seeing them as I do, I see what you mean; yes, surely."

"Okay, Script, from the substratum of hell, these gates rise to keep out heaven's scouts. These gates are the face of a diabolical kingdom. They represent a fortress, a stronghold of evil.

"Further, you see not a single pair of gates, but pair upon pair of gates. Wider than the width of many wailing walls they run. Broad is the way to Lucifer's kingdom. Rebellion is the key that unlocks the gates. Those who enter here refused to surrender elsewhere.

"With a will to choose, they chose themselves. Not a good idea, Script. Is it not written that men should 'reach out for him and find him, though he is not far from each one of us?'"

"I'd say this is about as far from home as I've ever been," said Script.

"Okay, I'll not labor the point," said Melchizedek. "What might you deduce concerning induction relative to these gates, Script?"

"Induction, into hell, you say. 'Only to think of it renews my fears!'"[23]

"Manic murderers, Satan worshipers, and God deniers are rushed through the center gates. The proud, the spiteful, the scornful—each and all have gates assigned. There is a specific gate as well for each of the seven deadly sins. And there's a gate most large to let backsliders in.

"Sadly, many inductees believe they shall enter hell to a round of applause. Minds of froth they have. Rather, they enter the worst form of isolation. Hypocrites with robes and without surely have a place. In knee-deep moss, they offer themselves the last rites, wanting to die again. To no avail, they speak words and offer songs they should have adored.

"Look me in the eyes, Script, if you dare. Listen to my words. I've seen much through the lens of the olden days. Well before the days of Moses, I served the God Most High. His ways are high beyond knowing.

"I recall incidents and stories told—one in particular regarding a free-fall demonstration to the Gates of Hell. Swift it was; the free-fallers fell. Korah, Dathan, and Abiram are their names. The trio rose up against Moses, claiming that they, not he, stood on holy ground.

"So, on that desert plane of wandering ways, Moses confronted the trio regarding their insolence. Not innocence, I say, but insolence ripened smug. Moses stood firm, while the ground under the trio split open wide. To Sheol the free-fallers fell. And the earth closed over them.

"Beyond these gates, the souls of Korah, Dathan, Abiram, and their kin do not rest. In the abyss, rest does not exist. No presence, no calm, no comfort. Empathy and sympathy do not exist beyond the gates. No wiping of tears, no healing of wounds, no lambs with lions lying.

"One more observation, Script, before we move beyond the gates: The locks, do you see them?"

"Yes, on both sides of the gates."

"The locks you see have no mechanisms inside. They are subterfuge for those inside and out. To those outside, they signal that there's no way in. To those inside, they signal that the outside cannot get in. The locks are fakes on either side. The huge strap hinges, as well, play a part in deception.

"They strap across the bars but possess no pins on which to hinge. The gates have never swung. Those destined to hell needn't worry about the swing of gates for entry. They filter in most nimbly.

"So, Script, shall we venture beyond the gates?"

"I mean, so you say to me; we shall, I see. I suppose it must be as you say, I guess, Melchizedek."

"Script, where would you care to start?"

NINE
Bewilderment

"Script, we must carry on, enter in, make our way around the abyss," said Melchizedek.

"I say, Melchizedek, sir, I wonder . . . I mean, don't you think we need to come up with a plan?" said Script. "From days long ago scrolled away, you've appeared to be my guide, but we're talking hell here, you know, not the planes of Palestine."

"Worry not, Script. Besides, I'm historical, not erasable."

"Not erasable, I see—as in forever being as you were, you are, and shall always be," Script said.

"Precisely," said Melchizedek.

"Sir, pardon me, please. I mean, your forever status of being— you know, who you are—pertains to who you were. In my case, I'm without the aspect of were, like you. I am present tense, without a past place. Therefore, in my case, there's nothing to erase. I am me, present. Therefore, there is no record of me stowed away in a scroll someplace. You, on the other hand, are inscribed in a scroll that holds you fast.

"On the stage of life, you've seen so many characters come and go. If my last breath is soon breathed, shall I be blotted out, as if I never played the part I play? Oh, the images, layered in my mind! The act of King Jehoiakim—I see it so well in my mind's eye. It's the scene when he cast Jeremiah's scroll into the fiery pot.

"The king took exception to the prophet's words. He despised those words set aflame. In my mind's eye, the parchment scroll expands and peels within the flames. The fire licks, the parchment coils and twists, the words are torn apart, the lines separate, and into the ashes the words disappear. Am I not a word, a noun, Script, my name? Perhaps I, too, will go up in smoke and curl away from history's page."

"Script, those words survived. Now stop these quivering thoughts. You are alive in the land of dead souls. Abraham saw the smoking firepot and blazing torch. Such a stage no one had ever seen—countless stars, when faith became righteousness. You, too, have been allowed to see what can't be seen. The ancients were commended for such seeing.

"Answer me, Script, did you know yourself before you were known? I dare say no. You did not know you, the spirit of Script that preceded you. Yet in that predestined state, you were surely known.

"So, look at me, at my eyes—are they dead or alive, Script? Look well; look long. Trust you must. Trust that, in the ultimate plot propelling time, you are not lost. God has no extras."

"Words of worth you speak, but, Melchizedek, I feel like a withering leaf in your presence. A dying leaf takes in no light. Before you I stand, like a tiny sapling at a mountain base. My limbs are weak. Yet I have dreams not withered. My dreams speak of staging presence not passé, dreams of crafting lines with lilt and life.

"Melchizedek, I'm not worthy of the words I speak. I fear my piety holds too much pretense. Tell me, shall I join the fallen angels that beyond these gates beat their wings in cloistered cages?"

"Script, you shall soar far," said Melchizedek.

"Yes, that's it, the farthest of far I wish to fly in escaping these sulfurous, barren straits of hell. I love the stage, where stories live and tell their tales. *Presence*—even now I see it playing at Theatre Portesque, every scene unfolding."

"Script, my dear fellow, worry not! The world is your stage. You possess the pen that opens wide, curtains sewn, some of gild, some of jute. On the stage you stand, looking at audiences, expectant. With tickets torn and tucked away, they watch; they listen, hoping to grasp a priceless gem, a line to stow away for future days.

"On the stage you, too, are there, Script, in characters vast that perform your lines. With compelling voices they speak. With toes they tip and tap and dance upon the notes that carry them along. And through it all, virtuous thoughts flow and skip across the dross of lesser plots and plays."

"You see all of that, Melchizedek?"

"Certainly, and more, Script. But now we must scour about the sulfur planes and set aside our tips and taps for future days. Now, take hold of my staff, and we'll have a look around the Crimson Cliffs . . . see if we can spot any of your Speakers.

"Script, place your hand on my staff just below mine. We'll travel as if standing still, but we'll move through spheres and realms as rapidly as we wish. Ready?"

Instantly they were at the place where Script and Mock had watched Lucifer address the Speakers seated on the great sulfur plane.

"Not so inviting, is it?" said Melchizedek.

"No, this is the backside of the Crimson Cliffs," said Script.

"I see; so it is," said Melchizedek. "From the gates they appeared less ominous, but from here I see that the Cliffs are actually a mammoth mountain range. Dreadful place this is, abutting a vast, dry lake bed of sulfurous salt. Kingdom of death, truly it is."

"I wonder, sir," said Script. "Would you be opposed to calling it a day? I mean, we did take in the gates, and that's a good start. So what do you think, sir?"

"Call it a day, you say, Script? And where would you like to go—to a green park and take a stroll along a promenade?"

"Yes, flee—I mean, not abandon the mission . . . just relocate for a while. Go back to the Meadow of Gates and Doors and explore the options, lay them out. Maybe there's another way to decipher the plans being hatched in this hellish place."

"Script, hellish, as you put it, is an adjective," said Melchizedek. "You have entered the noun; you are in hell. In the noun we stay. We do not flee. You cannot flee. You must follow through; otherwise you will forfeit the future.

"Not just yours, but the future of audiences destined to enter the drama you have yet to write. All that was written in the past, including those acts that chronicle my appearance as the King of Salem, were written for those who take in dramas new. Therein they discover how to persevere, despite doubts and fears.

"Look up to the stalls ascending, Script."

"Look where?" Script said.

"Close your eyes and look, Script. What do you see?"

"I see nothing, Melchizedek. Can I open my eyes?"

"No, with the mind's eye, see."

"That's different. I was trying to see with the eye, not through the eye."[24]

"Now look, Script. Do you see those cascading balconies that appear as clouds?"

"I do," said Script.

"Now look more intently. See the eyes. Those are witnesses looking down upon you.[25] The watching eyes are saintly eyes. That's why they sparkle as they do. Refined by fire and faith, they peer. With their eyes alone, they cheer."

"Melchizedek, wait, please! I'm overwhelmed. You mention the King of Salem, but undoubtedly you are he. Without genealogy, you appeared. Yet in the cloud of witnesses, you must also be. But that's impossible because you are here with me in hell."

"Look upon my face, Script. Impossibility—is that what you see? Impossible for whom, Script, you or me? Let it be. In the ancient narrative of which I'm a part, characters did not act. Naturally they played the parts they played.

"The antagonist Saul—he played his part oh so well, until from a horse he fell, rather unexpectedly. Drama true—life it's called, that's all. Just like that, he began mending tents and became the greatest protagonist of them all, so did St. Paul.

"So you, too, Script, have a part to play, albeit in hell right now. Listen, Script, do you hear a voice calling? It's not for me, but for you. I hear it say, 'Pick up your pen and follow me.' You, Script, writer of scripts, do not stand on a stage self-made. Anyway, that's enough of such talk.

"I understand that Sage told you about the Reservoirs of Bewilderment. We will inspect them, but not yet. First we must stand at the precipice of the great Gargantuan Gorge. There you will see a continuous ledge of stone that spirals down into a pit most deep. The gorge is riddled with caves.

"So prepare yourself to see what no human being has ever seen. In an instant you shall see it. Close your eyes; take hold of my staff. The instant is gone; now look. As you peer, let Mock perch upon your shoulder. What a sight we must be, the three of us standing here at the precipice. I'm historical, remember, not erasable. We move incognito."

"What can I say, Melchizedek? My soul quivers so; I have no control. Do we look upon the very mouth of hell? Nothing can survive in this sulfurous orange glow. In the belly of the gorge, a vast, massive mud whirlpool slowly churns. Among the swirl, I hear the shrill cries.

"What's more, I see forms. They look like shells, beetles, and then the shells disappear in the swirling mud. Dear Lord, there bobs a head, and another, and legs, and feet. The forms wriggle and spin in death rolls, though they must have long since died."

"Yes, long since dead," said Melchizedek. "But they shall never die again. Once here, they exist in the throes of death. Not living, not dying, but existing in an eternal state of wickedness, they do."

"A dozen cities on hills could be concealed in this hellish gorge," said Script. "This sight expunges all innocence from my eyes. Here, there are no dreams to dream, no scripts to write, no poems to recite."

"Be still and know, Script," said Melchizedek. "Ponder; listen to your heart."

Just then Mock leapt atop Script's head and called:

ch-reee ch-reee ch-reee—check check, chur-wi chur-wi

Standing at Script's right, Melchizedek looked at Script, who was a foot shorter than he. Melchizedek's left hand clasped his robe just below his collarbone. In his right hand, he held tight his shepherd's staff, which arched well above his head.

Melchizedek carried nothing else. His long, extended robe allowed only a slight glimpse of his leather, laced footwear. Minutes passed, then more, as they stood on the brittle sulfur's ashy surface. Script could tell that Melchizedck ignored the passage of time. They exchanged not a word.

Then Melchizedek shut his eyes and began to pray in a soft, murmuring voice, barely distinguishable. To Script, it sounded like he spoke the words written on King Belshazzar's wall by a mysterious hand. "*Mene, Mene, Tekel, Upharsin,*" he prayed. Next Script clearly heard Melchizedek pray the final words of Christ spoken upon the cross. "*Eloi, Eloi, lama . . .*"

Melchizedek's prayer, Script thought, *will surely resonate in heaven's courts, though offered from the corridors of hell.* Script looked straight, steady on, not daring to glance at Salem's king. Several minutes came and went, and more, before Melchizedek halted his prayer.

Peering out over the precipice, they waited—for what, they didn't know. Quietly they breathed. Every cough they suppressed. Occasionally, they shuffled their feet, but ever so softly. Nothing else could be heard, had anyone been listening, save Mock.

Then, in the depths of Gargantuan Gorge, where an ancient river might have flowed, the whirlpool ceased and turned into a huge lake of gurgling mud. Spouts began to appear, which sent slow, moving mud rings across the surface.

With grave intensity pressed upon their faces, Melchizedek and Script observed what no one had ever witnessed. Spouts small grew large, and larger still. Eventually, with the blast of a powerful volcano, a huge geyser formed and shot plumes of sulfur's steam into the toxic, orange air.

Script thought, *The end of the end has finally come. The beginning of a new day shall not begin. Days are gone; the death of days has come. In a hellish rumble and roar, my existence is well and truly done. There's nothing more to come.*

Prepared to die, he turned to Melchizedek with words primed on his lips, when suddenly silence ensued. The geyser fell. The procession of murky rings halted. The surface stilled. The placid scene presented a very eerie pause, not unlike the sudden halt of fighting in a vicious war.

"Wait, don't move," said Melchizedek. "We witness not happenstance, but formal cause, wicked cause. Wait!"

The *t* of *wait* had just left Melchizedek's lips when a violent earthquake struck and shook the entire gorge. Melchizedek and Script instantly scanned their eyes across the porous caves. In the mouth of every cave, the scene was the same. The pair watched as figures flocked to the openings from the gorge's interior cells.

Soon the craggy cavities were filled from top to bottom, side to side, with demented, demonic-looking figures. Some bore human resemblance, while others sported bony wings and bits of fur on splotches of grayish skin. Not a few had feather clumps on their shoulders and backs.

When all the openings had filled, the creatures began to howl, as if begging an invisible moon to fall from the skies. Louder and louder they howled, until out of the murky depths, macabre, viperous fish began to leap and snap at the noxious air. Next, another rumble deep within the gorge sent fissures streaking up the walls of the gorge—which, in turn, sent the demented figures into a frenzied state.

Like cockroaches, droves of the demented crawled out of the openings and clung to the walls. With necks twisted, they thrust their attention below. Then suddenly, the surface of the murky, lifeless lake turned to ice, crystal clear. Light, as if emanating from a stowaway star, beamed up through the thick, frozen surface illuminating the entire gorge.

What happened next should not be told—cannot be told, except by Script and Melchizedek, who witnessed what no one else has ever seen or dared to see.

"Steady, Script, this, I fear, is one of Satan's lairs. Though he roams to and fro to draw away wanton souls, to his kingdom he returns. We shall hear from him soon, I suspect. His powers of persuasion lack not perverse power. Kings from east to west, warlords, prophets, potentates, teachers and scribes, as well as plowmen from every tongue and tribe have fallen under his evil spell.

"At the crossroads where the way of wisdom calls, his signposts point to paths that trail away in all directions. No matter which path one may choose, each and all wind round hollow, fruitless trees that pass along whispers in their leaves. Alongside the paths ditches run, littered with psalms and sonnets pitched away in favor of the current tides of time."

"Melchizedek, a line woven within my mind I recall. 'What blind cupidity, what crazy rage impels us onwards in our little lives—then dunks us in the stew of eternity.'"[26]

"Very true," said Melchizedek.

"Sorry, sir, but what's happening? A massive crack is splitting the towering wall from side to side. Rocks and boulders cracking—it's such a horrid sound. Now, out of the wall, a protrusion; it looks like ice. It can't be, can it? It is. It's transparent and luminous, just like the frozen basin below.

"None of this is real, Melchizedek; my spine shatters. Unimaginable, inconceivable, this scene; the mammoth ice stage is extended from the wall by a beam of light that illuminates it."

"Script, unimaginable, inconceivable, but a stage extended by a beam of light it is. Cast your eyes above. Watch, the one set to take center stage will descend like a lightning bolt. I thought that out of the murk he would appear, but no, this is all down to him. Like a falling star, here he comes."

"The creatures . . . they're crawling in and out of the caves in utter frenzy," said Script. "They howl and clap with slaps, the sound of hollow bones. Melchizedek, I can't bear it. I'm pleading; I'm on my knees. Please, I beg you, I can't take any more. You must take me away somehow. I beseech you, Mock and I will die."

"Stand up, on your feet, Script! Listen and learn why truth must triumph. Shush, he's beginning to speak. Take my hand. Up, I tell you."

"No, I can't survive this. Not me—but you, I suppose, will. Again, he's personified as a being, yet he hates the human race."

"No, his vertebrae form a chain of jealousy. Pride a link, hate a link, betrayal a link, revenge a link, link by link, but it's jealousy that binds all the links together."

"See, Melchizedek, how his wavy hair, shiny black, sports feathered tufts? Chains of silver adorn his vest. He's draped himself in a black shawl. He's ready to speak."

"Listen, Mass! This is Lucifer speaking. To you, in the farthest reaches of the cosmos, listen; you know my voice. Know this, you are where you are, and where you are, I am with you. In you I am, and so shall I always be.

"Hear now what I say in the manner I say it. I am who I am. I am not who I'm not, nor would I ever want to be not me. I am Lucifer, not I AM. I, who speak for all, now speak to you. Draw in my words; they will mold and make you in a spirit that forever effervesces.

"It's so true: creatures spiritual such as you cannot live on rumors and gossip alone. You hunger for the elucidated words I afford. So, I afford them, without reserve. I know my yoke is hard, and my burden heavy. But who wants something light and easy? Not you; not me. No, in the Dominion of Darkness you form the legions heaven fears. I offer you war, cosmic war, scorched earth, and sights of sorrow never ending.

"Know this, many souls have longed to see what you see, but saw me not. You see me. Equally, many souls longed to hear what you hear, but heard me not. You now hear me. You see and hear me, and know this, there is but one of me. I am me, and beside me there is no other.

"So, behold your image! Fix your eyes on me and see yourself becoming. In so doing, you will see that I see you seeing me. We see the same, bound in sight and word. In medium and message we are one. Our image bound is the message! Again, I say it. Our image bound is the message!

"Now then, the dozen caves nearest me, extend your planks straight out and long. Yes, these horizontal masts I always delight to see, each toward me. So, on the planks, parcel out twelve of our newest inductees. Twelve, that's all, but each from a different tribe and tongue. They shall swiftly see how *hard* hard can be.

"Now, shove along the twelve refugees of the Race, so we might watch as they crawl. None shall be lost. Slash them with thorns; that's it, keep them crawling. Slash and poke until all twelve crawlers are at the very end of their planks. Almost there, I see—nine have reached the end . . . just three more.

"That one on plank two, like an old snail the creature crawls. Come on, you lost crop of sorry snails, crawl, so we can watch you drop into the mud. From mud you were made; in mud you shall free-fall. So, now snuff out the cellar star, and I'll look down and melt the basin ice. Commence the swirl of mud. Such a delightful sound, it is—the swirl of mud in the Great Gorge.

"That one on plank five—slash him so we can get on with this brief ceremony. I say, all is quiet in the Gorge. What must be done must be done in order. Wretched refugees on the poles, it's simple; all you need to do is free-fall. When I call your number, you fall. You know your number by the loss of fingers. Pole one, you've lost one finger, right around to ten; that's the way it is.

"Now, two of you have lost toes—one toe and two. One Toe, you are number eleven, and Two Toes, you are twelve. In case you're wondering, you wretched, crawling refugees, there is no way back. No way out. Behind you, venomous snakes have been set loose to slither along your planks.

"So, number three, you are the first, so fall! Down he goes, splat, into the mud. That one did a good free fall. Now five . . ."

In utter horror, Script looked on, as one by one the lost souls let go of their planks and plunged. "Melchizedek," said Script, "more I cannot bear to see. My soul will be forever withered."

"Hold on, Script. You must; we've come for clues. No telling what he might divulge."

"Wasn't that a rich little affair?" said Lucifer. "Allow the star below to once again beam above, as one day we shall do. So pull in the planks and listen to me. If you find my magnetism too great to behold, I'll understand. I permit you to scurry back into your assigned crevices, but no swapping caves.

"Now, my world of angels and captive souls, listen. The word *world* I just spoke. The world—I own it. It's mine—do you hear me, *mine*. I can give its kingdoms away, but I shall never do so. Yes, true, once I offered the kingdoms, but that was a hoax, of course.

"Back to message making, my adroit quality—to you I extol. I am the supreme message maker of the cosmos. What I send forth never stays away. It resonates with resounding effect. Media effect, I mean. Or I could say the effects of media.

"I snatch the seed. I nourish the weeds. I bait the trap with worries and riches vain. Don't look confused. I speak of media ecology, the only ecology that matters. Who needs air, or water wet for quenching thirst? Not discarnate souls. Discarnate life—it's so right, righting all the inequities of incarnate misery.

"That, of course, was my point all along, for which the curse arose. I got the blame, the great light bearer, me, for exposing fractures in the mud-made creatures. No one asked my advice about the limitations of a potter's wheel. What did they think, trying to spin forth creatures in I AM's image out of mud?

"What a mistake, a gargantuan mistake. Planet earth—it's cancer in the cosmos. I love war! Ask me why. I have not love, that's why. So I lie. Actually, I love to lie. I lie so instinctively it feels like love. Though it's better still to hate. Let me tell the truth: I don't love war; I hate peace!

"Anyway, I have given the world the greatest gift of all: ecology for dehumanizing the Race. Look to me. I bring the best of news. I come to you from beyond the breach. Now I am here among you, dwelling not as some incarnate soul, but as the discarnate wonder you behold. Cast your eyes on me, the author and perfecter of your angst and rebellion.

"Yes, it was so; ages have come and gone. Why did I do what no other angel dared to do? The Race, that's why. I intercepted the plan long before out of darkness and void creation swirled. A world out of nothing, he would make, and then in mud his image set.

"Preposterous, the plan, I surmised. Thus I whispered the sentiment, and throughout the cosmos the resonance would not abate. Therefore, as the brightest of all celestial beings, I found my formal cause.

"Nothing could be more important than assuring the death of the Race. So, before the world was made, my course of remedial action was put in place. Without counsel, the Trinity planned it, and thus the world was spun.

"The sting of death I brought forth. And behold, the creatures began to die. Close was I to my goal of extinction. The flood: it was such an epic adventure. The Race drowning; I AM grieving. You know the story. No, you don't, you malformed wretched wrecks of creation.

"Where were you when in the heavens I soared? Where were you when I swung open the doors to let snow fall from the skies? Nowhere, you were. So you know nothing, except you look to me. Watch this, in hologram form I am now three, not one begotten in the flesh. Know this: to be made is far better than begotten because what's made can be made again.

"Therefore, I remake you into my form. We are swiftly dehumanizing the Race. Like wildebeests, they race headlong into discarnate adventure and the so-called wonders of AI. They long, like Eve, to free themselves from their old, hardwired brains. See, they never change; they're always grasping.

"Humans have become lab rats of their own making. In their quest to cast off the eye of Deity and attain self-mastery, they've built massive platforms powered by algorithms. Information they love. Their eyes never have enough of seeing, their ears never enough of hearing.[27]

"Thanks be it unto me, there is evil in all that is done under the sun. Further, though the Race now looks to AI to disprove evil, 'the hearts of men are full of evil, and madness is in their hearts while they live, and after that they go to the dead.'[28]

"The Race is just now waking up to the fact that AI and algorithms, fueled by data, take on a life of their own. Humans are weak—no match for the machines they've made. What's been set in motion cannot be undone. The same with Eve, it was, when she pressed her teeth through the apple skin.

"It's too late for the Race to self-correct. They wouldn't want to, even if they could. And they can't. The end of history is swiftly approaching. I am the distortion, the lie, and the death; no one gets into my dominion except through me. Know this, the Dominion of Darkness is drawing the shade on the utopia of light.

"It's over. We are so close to winning that we have already won. The ecology of the world that matters is propelled by media effects. I own that world. So long I've waited, first an alphabet, then quills, ink, papyrus, codex, lead, and finally currents of shocking force. At long last, the figures of mud had a breakthrough.

"Such a memorable day it was. *Tip tap, tip tap, dot dash, dot dash, tip tap*. Only I knew what this silly breakthrough meant. I knew then that the Race would be enthralled with each and every invention of wire and wave. Swiftly they've raced into the vast maelstrom of mediated chaos. Now, at last, in the late hour of time ticking, our hour has arrived. The senses, of beings human, are now saturated in media ecology.

"Presence is no substitute for the wonders of discarnate life. The Race has learned that images, like the wind, can be sent wherever one wishes them to go. The ultimate extension of man is not a tool in his hand, but his image set loose to soar among the stars. There is no reverse in this mediated march of time.

"And the crown jewel that finally turns the tide: media washes away presence. Presence was the kingpin that knitted the dress for the bride. Presence dwelling, then leaving, but not before the Begotten One breathed and commanded this form of presence to be spread here, there, and everywhere. Yet I bear the best of news! Discarnate life has eclipsed incarnate life.

"I declare here in the glow of Gargantuan Gorge, *Presence Passé*. Say it with me: *Presence Passé. Presence Passé*, and again, *Presence Passé . . .*"

At that point, Script dropped to Melchizedek's feet, motionless, and Mock fluttered atop Melchizedek's staff.

"Well, Script, dear fellow," said Melchizedek, "perhaps we should make our presence scarce."

TEN
Morning Dew

Mock's tweets filtered through Script's mind as distant calls, softly sent.

tcheck tcheck, ch-reee ch-reee ch-reee–check check, chur-wi chur-wi
tru-ly tru-ly–tcheck tcheck, ch-reee ch-reee ch-reee

Slowly Script roused and raised his head, only to find Mock perched on his chest. Mock looked at Script as intently as a bird looking at hatchlings in her nest.

"You sounded so far away, Mock. Where are we? How did I get here on the ground? Morning dew—I feel it—wet grass green, fresh, and alive. Now the sun's morning hue filters through the pines. Mock, above you—don't snatch the butterfly; let it flutter.

"I need to get up. My arms move, my elbows too. Okay, and this mat . . . I didn't know it was beneath me. It's not mine. It's so thin; it's like sleeping on a firm little cloud.

"I see now, we're in the Meadow of Gates and Doors. Mock, through a door we passed and made our way to hell, and now we've mysteriously returned. The door was green, wasn't it?"

"It was, Script."

"Sage, it's you!" Script said, as he swirled around. "You snuck up on me!"

"I didn't sneak; I appeared," Sage said. "As did you; good rest, have you?"

"Rest . . . what I've seen no one has seen. Never again, I say. There we stood, Melchizedek and me, with Mock perched on my shoulder. Never again—tell me, Sage, it's over, tell me. You must.

"On a round stage of ice, Satan stood and gave a speech. Though not before we watched a dozen wretched souls crawling on long horizontal poles that looked like masts from old sailing ships. The morbid creatures were ordered, one through twelve, to free-fall into a giant gorge of swirling mud.

"The stage . . . yes, the stage of ice . . . it was extended out into the gorge by a single beam of light. Really, only light—nothing mechanical, just the beam of light; say four or five times the diameter of those massive wooded masts. Oh yeah, this too—the masts were extended from caves by creatures all mangled and malformed. There has to be another way to decipher the plans brewing in the pit of hell."

"Speaking of brewed, the coffee's on," said Sage.

"Insufferable you are. I'm not a marionette, Sage. My limbs have no strings attached to sticks. I open and shut my eyes, like this; I see, see. Marionettes have painted eyes and do not see. With these eyes, I saw lost souls free-fall into the pit of hell. One by one, they silently plunged. I saw demented creatures like cockroaches crawl in and out of caves. With my ears I heard the wretched creatures wail, so pitifully that they shook the very Gates of Hell.

"No, Sage, there can be no return."

"You delighted in Melchizedek's companionship, no doubt. I'm sure he was grateful for the return of his staff. By the way, it was he who brought you, placed you on the mat, and waited till Mock perched upon your chest. Then he blessed you and went away. So, you see, he, too, was present."

"Where'd he go?" asked Script.

"I suspect far, yet near," said Sage.

"Script, I can see that you might be a bit worked up, but you needn't be. You need breakfast. It's ready. A pleasant smell it is that wafts through the air. Mushrooms browning, nudging sausages simmering, waiting for eggs to fry, all in the warm company of potatoes and tomatoes perfectly prepared. And of course, fresh bread that waits to melt the butter just churned."

"Sage, you can't do me this way! You've got to help me. Look at me; I'm human. Neither my spirit nor my flesh is willing. I'm not prepared for what's next, for anything.

"One minute I'm in hell, then I awake in the Meadow of Gates and Doors. I touch my face to see if I'm alive. I bite my lips, top, bottom, and then top and bottom again. Have you ever heard demented creatures howl—as if begging the moon to fall?

"Sage, I'm not in a right state. You are, so it seems. You have the ability to decide, to be correct. You know where you are. I don't. I'm like the hollow trees that Melchizedek described."

"What hollow trees, Script?"

"Hollow, fruitless trees that pass along whispers in the breeze. Whisper they do to pilgrims and passersby. They encourage the passersby to pitch their sonnets and psalms into ditches."

"Sounds like witchy trees to me, Script."

"Sage, I plead with you. Listen to me. Somehow, we're caught up in a drama, like a bizarre dream that floats through time and space. But it's not a dream. I'm here with you in this sphere. Then, with Melchizedek, I'm there in hell. We watched Satan descend like a lightning bolt and land on the stage of ice. It can't be, but it is.

"I eat, I drink, I sleep, I wake, I tremble. My eyes look upon scenes from ages past, yet vibrantly alive on a timeless stage. You— you know your part in this drama. I do not. To be or not to be is not down to me.

"I have no choice upon the stage I stand. I peer into the stalls; I see row upon row of watching eyes. All expectant, the watching eyes watch my every move. Ears, too . . . I see them twitch; they eagerly wait for words of compelling resonance.

"But, Sage, I don't know which words to say. I've not written this play. I don't know if I should curse or pray? I take in the gaze of watching eyes, and then I draw up a line stowed within. Perhaps words I once penned upon a page. I don't know what I might say . . . until I say it.

"Sage, therefore, I beg you to tell me about this play, about my part, about how I shall survive this tragedy. Correct me; counsel me."

"Script, do you recall the story of a mother and her sons who went to take home the Begotten One because they thought he had gone mad?"[29]

"Yes, indeed."

"Say no more. You, too, are mad, but you have an important role to play. If I were to give you the script, you would have no need to draw upon the words and lines stowed away. You do want to save Estillyen, do you not?"

"Oh, I'm so out of it," said Script. "I've lost myself. Estillyen—yes, that's my cause, my home, my isle. Even now *Presence* is likely playing at Theatre Portesque, I hope. But how would I know? I'm here in the meadow with you, somewhere."

"As you've said, Script, Estillyen, though far, is always near to those who perceive it so. Estillyen possesses a spirited sphere, unique, and you've helped make it so.

"Anyway, it's time to eat. The sun's rising above the pines, and soon, it will shine down onto the campsite. After breakfast, I'd like to show you a few paintings I've set up in the field that capture some highly imaginative scenes. Do you mind?"

"Sage, I'm just so . . . so . . . I don't know," said Script. "But yes, I'll go."

"Wonderful!" said Sage. "Smell the browning mushrooms, nudging the sausages . . ."

During breakfast amidst the towering pines, conversation did not flow. Sage remained perky in spirit, but he could tell Script was finding it difficult to cope with his otherworld experiences. Though Script's appetite was keen, he'd frequently pause midway through a bite of sausage or bread and stare.

Not for want of show or empathy did Script stare. For several minutes he'd look quite normal and express himself accordingly. "Nice breeze, Sage," or "Very interesting, the formation of those rocks, don't you think?" Then, with trauma etched in his eyes, he would stare past a mushroom or bite of sausage on his fork paused before his face.

At one point, he turned to Sage and soberly said, "The Gargantuan Gorge, Sage—please tell me I did not see what I said I saw."

"Script, I cannot. I do not lie."

"Oh, misery," said Script. "My eyes have seen too much; my soul withers. How will I ever write again lines that spring with hope? Why me? Why should I peer into realms that even angels dare not see?"

"You, Script, saw the very Gates of Hell, and they did not prevail against you. Enter in, you did."

"And for it," said Script, "I am worse than the worst of men. A soul of soot I have. My mind is forever tarnished. What manner of script can I write, just knowing, let alone visiting, such a vast crypt of misery and debauchery?

"Sage, you, Melchizedek, and Simon of Cyrene have got me wrong. Like Jeremiah of old, I delight in those winnowing and ancient words he ate so willingly. Like honey upon his tongue, he said they were. In his ilk, no doubt, I was a wanton wannabe of prose. Now my lilt for life is lost. Macabre scenes lay hold of me, and I fear I'll never be able to cast them from the stage erected in my mind.

"I say to you, Sage, how does the hangman cuddle a child at night after tightening a noose around a victim's neck at noon? The hangman stows his rope away, to be used again someday. But he knows where the rope is stowed. In his mind's eye, he can see it coiled away in a place reserved for another hanging.

"Don't you see, Sage, my plays are played. Valiantly I will try to stow away the scenes and lines that rake across my mind, but I fear the surface of my mind is too disturbed. Wicked lines have taken root, crowding good lines that fashioned the banner of my work."

"You are wrong, Script," said a figure that suddenly appeared at his side.

"Simon, it's you," said Script.

"Yes, it's me. I've been present for a while, and I've listened to your words. You are wrong, Script. You are a master of lines, so take in these lines regarding signs, which I now recite for you verbatim. The first:

> "And there appeared a great wonder in heaven; a woman clothed with the sun, and the moon under her feet, and upon her head a crown of twelve stars: And she being with child cried, travailing in birth, and pained to be delivered.[30]

"Now the second sign, Script.

> "And there appeared another wonder in heaven; and behold a great red dragon, having seven heads and ten horns, and seven crowns upon his heads. And his tail drew the third part of the stars of heaven, and did cast them to the earth: and the dragon stood before the woman which was ready to be delivered, for to devour her child as soon as it was born."[31]

"Thus, Script," said Simon, "think. Did the Revelator not see a horrid dragon with seven heads and other horrific scenes, but speak of a city which will have no need of the sun or moon for light? Indeed, he did, for the glory of God shall give it light.

"So, Script, do not think that you can speak fully of good by covering up or glossing over evil. The reality of dark and light is precisely what makes the ancient saga ring so real. Rahab and Bathsheba, are they not listed in the genealogy of the Begotten One?

"Or the Passion—did it not play out, with the set of crosses three revealing Golgotha's horror? No, no, Script; truth itself did not desire that we gloss over the fire-and-brimstone-buried towns of Sodom and Gomorrah.

"Words like honey, yes; they are words that offer 'lilt for life.' You wonder why evil had to be and persists till now? I could tell you precisely, Script, but these fully disclosed elements of truth are not mine to tell. The great cloud of witnesses witness; they do not speak. I can simply say that darkened struggle often authenticates the light.

"Listen, Script: Gabriel announced joy. A star shone bright in the sky. Light appeared. Wise men came bearing gifts. The star faded. Then what? Darkness drew in a cast of characters to snuff out the light.

"King Herod played a most egregious part. Manic was he, as he scoured the land for this newborn king of light. No lilt, in the lines inscribed, telling how Herod ordered the slaughter of little boys round the region of Bethlehem. In the ancient text, Script, evil acts are etched.

"I can see it, even now. Such a horror—snuff, puff, little lambs limp in loving arms, covered in blood, as tears rained down upon the ground. These lines evil cherished:

"A voice was heard in Ramah,
weeping and loud lamentation,
Rachel weeping for her children;
she refused to be comforted,
because they are no more."[32]

"Let's shift the conversation away from misery," said Sage. "Even Mock appears melancholy. Anyway, in the field this afternoon, we'll take in art . . . in the round.

"Script, you've been through a major ordeal. Why don't you go up to the cottage, clean up, take a nap, and I'll fetch you in a little while."

"Good idea," said Script. "I'll go to the cottage and rest my head. I've spoken far too much. Blabber, I hear myself speaking. My mind is toxic; it swirls and propels words profuse, in lines not fully formed. Do forgive me; I'm not myself, or so it seems."

Somewhat sheepishly Script broke away and moved along the

cottage path. When he reached the cottage and started up the steps, he saw something move from the corner of his eye. He turned and cast his eyes toward the upper path . . . and saw her. The movement was Time. Script leaped off the step and ran after her.

"It's you, Time; you're here. You always look the same—lively, cheerful."

"Shouldn't I be?" said Time.

"Well, yes, but it's just that you look like a charming character in a play. You see, I'm a playwright. I mean, I was—and will be again, I hope.

"Actually, in a recent dream, I saw you; it was definitely you. You walked across the stage and informed me that I stood on top of Dante's *Divine Comedy*. Unknowingly I had climbed up the back cover, on a ladder, thinking it was a large bed."

"What an interesting dream," said Time.

"But I didn't sleep on *Divine Comedy*—I mean, in my dream, you know. In fact, I fell through the pages into *Inferno* and landed in Canto 3."

"Even more interesting," said Time.

"You wouldn't recall, of course," said Script. "You weren't there; I mean, you know, in my dream. That sounds a bit convoluted."

"Sorry, time's passing, and so must I," said Time. "I must sweep the day away."

"Say, later we're going to be looking at works of art in a field beyond the pines. Would you like to join us? The field is just down that path."

Script turned to point, and when he looked back again, Time had vanished. He just stood, peering at the tall pine trees where Time had been. He thought of Melchizedek and his tale of hollow trees that pass whispers through their leaves.

Eventually, Script made his way back to Writer's Cottage. Once inside, he hung up his scarf and jacket, slipped off his shoes, and quickly lay down on the narrow bed.

Meanwhile, Sage briskly tidied the camp and then joined Simon on the dock at Meadow Lake. They exchanged a few words briefly and then sat, most content, in silence. The entire atmosphere across the Meadow of Gates and Doors was tranquil. Mock, too, offered not a single tweet, as he perched on the porch rail of Writer's Cottage.

Notwithstanding the restful pause, the undertaking at hand necessitated action to resume. Mock watched as Sage advanced up the cottage steps and offered a *knock*, followed by a *knock-knock*, on the ivy-green wooden screen door.

"Hello, Script! I say, dear fellow, through the screen I speak—is anybody in there? Are you up and about, or have you chosen to board a train for fairer fields of golden grain?"

"Sage, dear me, sorry—I fell fast asleep. What time is it anyway?"

"A quarter past, I believe."

"Past what?" Script said.

"Past the hour it was before," Sage said. "Which makes it a quarter past three. Anyway, I speak of colorful paintings on canvases tightly stretched. Good, there you are, visibly complete."

"Sage, what do you mean, visibly complete?" asked Script.

"Not a phantom," said Sage. "Floating about beyond the screen door—what else could I mean?"

"Okay, just asking," said Script. "The art is in a field, you say?"

"Yes, just beyond the camp, between the pines," said Sage. "Let's get moving. And did you rest well? Any dreams?"

"No dreams of demented creatures, no fissures, viper fish, or splitting rocks, no Melchizedek or Gates of Hell, and yes, thank you, I rested well."

"I presume no hangman's noose stowed away?" said Sage.

"Yes, no noose," said Script. "I did hear Mock flutter a bit; perhaps he had a dream. Do you think birds can dream?"

Sage said, "The question you pose shall be addressed once we find the answer!"

"Okay. Is Simon going to join us?"

"Indeed, he's already there," said Sage.

"Where do you suppose Melchizedek has gone?" Script asked. "Such scenes we saw, meeting up outside the Gates of Hell. I took hold of his shepherd's staff, and we whizzed about like spirits."

"I'm certain you did, Script. On the path we tread; let's pick up the pace. Just beyond the bend you'll catch sight of the easels set out in the opening among the pines.

"Concerning Melchizedek, I expect him to reappear soon. We're in this together, you know, Script. We intend to see it through, and we shall. Now to the art displayed. A minute more and you shall see what I mean.

"Better than walking on the charred and brittle surface of hell, wouldn't you say, Script? I love this path between the pines. And so, here we are."

"What a sight, Sage. I count seven easels, all at least the height of Melchizedek. They look like sentinels. Stunning! I suppose this was your idea? I see Simon approaching."

"Whose idea it was doesn't matter," said Sage. "As you can see, there are three stools. A thin ribbon of gold is laced across the middle stool. That's yours. So, on the stool in the round, please take a seat. Mock has followed us, flitting among the trees, but here he comes. Let him perch on your right shoulder, if you don't mind. I think Mock likes this particular art exhibit."

"Script," said Simon, "These works of art have been painted just for you. Cast your eyes upon these creative works, and wonder at what you see. Ponder—do they not look ancient and of rare quality?"

"They do," said Script. "To me they look priceless. They should hang in a museum or cathedral."

"Because you are a playwright who can see," said Simon, "let your imagination rest upon the riches that rise from these works. Imagination offers union with the creator."

"So," said Sage, "we are surrounded by seven works of art, set well apart. They encircle us but do not encroach; they give us space. In case you wonder, Script, the distance between each painting is three times the easel height.

"In airy space they present themselves amidst the pines. The wind blows where it wishes, does it not, Script? Just now, the wind wishes to blow around the easels, Simon, you, and me. What do the works represent, Script?"

"They must depict the visions of John the Revelator."

"So right you are, Script," said Sage. "They represent the visions of the one who pressed near to the Son of Man one Passover night. A night most memorable it was. A night of presence pure, the night the Begotten One washed his disciples' feet.

"Script, you know the night of which I speak. Call it a narrative, if you wish. Certainly it is, but it is also a play of celestial proportions. Each character played his part, without knowing, in the Passion play they played. That is, save one: the Begotten One."

"Think of it, Script, that particular Passover night," said Simon. "It was the night when darkness reigned. Little did I know that as I finally approached Jerusalem, the plot thickened. By sup, a cup, and blood, it thickened.

"The ancient antagonist played his part. Into the soul of the betrayer, Judas, he entered. With thirty pieces of silver in his pouch, he watched and waited for his move. Such irony—as I neared the gates of Jerusalem, Judas drew nearer and nearer to the Gates of Hell.

"Did Judas eat the morsel handed to him? The narrative does not tell. But imagine the scene; you can—that is what the imagination is for. Was the morsel still dissolving in his mouth as he raced out into the night so dark?

"Those lines we know so well of the play that played. Let me speak a few lines soberly, yet not morbidly. Let this patch of soil amid the pines be our stage. Therefore, Sage, Script, and Mock, before pines tall, I offer a line or two. This I need to do. It's been a while since I've spoken live.

"Yes, tall pines as well, listen too. The earth knows his presence. So, on that dark night of sup, cup, and blood, the story records that Jesus suddenly became troubled in his spirit and said: 'Truly, truly, I say to you, one of you will betray me.'

"Stunned, the disciples wondered who. They exchanged stares and began to joust. One of the twelve was lying next to Jesus' breast. John, it was.

"Peter beckoned John to tease out the plot. So John pressed and asked, 'Lord, who is it?'

"Jesus answered, 'It is he to whom I shall give this morsel of bread when I have dipped it.'

"So Jesus dipped the morsel and to Judas handed it. Then the record says, 'As soon as Judas took the crumb, Satan entered into him.'

"And so it was that without delay, he departed into the darkness, along the way of bitter betrayal.

"Darkness continued to spread, pushing back against the light. In time, a wicked emperor named Domitian arose and banished John, the storyteller, to a distant isle, far from Jerusalem and the place of the Passion. It was on the distant isle that the seven visions of Christ were given.

"I shall say no more," Simon said, "as I think soberly, yes, of darkness having reign."

"So right," said Sage. "No rush; tomorrow we have. We must think in a different direction for a while before we return to St. John's manifold vision. Script, to your left, in the box, you will find three flasks. They hold hot tea, one green, two not. I suggest we sip, contemplatively."

"Sounds good by me," Simon said.

"Okay with you, Script?" asked Sage.

"Yes, fine," said Script. "Too much is too much at times, even for the likes of us. Oh, I'm sorry, I should not have said *us*. I didn't mean to align myself with you two. I'm not in your league. I'm still a mortal. I simply meant that we are together, we three."

"We know what you mean, Script," said Simon.

"Strange," said Sage. "Script, I don't know why, but with Mock perched on your shoulder, I'm reminded of an old poem about a scholar and his cat written by a monk. Funny, that. You're a monk, but you sit with a mockingbird, not a cat. Do you own a cat?"

"Indeed I do," said Script. "His name is Tip-Toe. We monks on the isle are fond of cats."

"Well, anyway," said Sage, "the poem is called 'The Scholar and His Cat, Pangur Bán.'"

"Perhaps you know it, Script?" Simon said.

"Indeed, I do know the poem well," said Script. "All the monks on the Isle of Estillyen know it by heart. I learned it long ago."

"So, Script," said Simon, "do you think you could muster up the courage to recite it now to us—and to Mock and the pines?"

"For you, the pines, and Mock, it would be an honor. That is, if the lines have not deserted me."

"By the way, does everyone like the tea?" asked Sage.

"Perfect," said Script.

"Delightful," Simon said.

"In the tin, you'll find some cheese, biscuits, and other bits," said Sage. "The small chest holds vintage meadow wine."

No rush at all was there among the three, as they sat among the easels tall, sipping tea and sampling all the tasty bits. Simon, or was it Sage—one of the two, anyway—suggested that it would be a shame to let the vintage wine stay stowed away on such a lovely day.

As it turned out, the outing was slightly prolonged. In time, though, Script rose to his feet, and he insisted that Mock should remain perched on his shoulder.

So therefore, amidst seven easels resembling something like sentinels, Script began to speak.

"My esteemed audience of two, Sage and Simon of Cyrene, we are gathered here today before the forest pines. It is with great honor that I now recite:

The Scholar and His Cat, Pangur Bán

I and Pangur Bán my cat,
'Tis a like task we are at:
Hunting mice is his delight,
Hunting words I sit all night.
Better far than praise of men
'Tis to sit with book and pen;
Pangur bears me no ill-will,
He too plies his simple skill.
'Tis a merry task to see
At our tasks how glad are we,
When at home we sit and find
Entertainment to our mind.
Oftentimes a mouse will stray
In the hero Pangur's way;
Oftentimes my keen thought set
Takes a meaning in its net.
'Gainst the wall he sets his eye
Full and fierce and sharp and sly;
'Gainst the wall of knowledge I
All my little wisdom try.
When a mouse darts from its den,
O how glad is Pangur then!
O what gladness do I prove
When I solve the doubts I love!
So in peace our task we ply,
Pangur Bán, my cat, and I;
In our arts we find our bliss,

I have mine and he has his.
Practice every day has made
Pangur perfect in his trade;
I get wisdom day and night
Turning darkness into light.[33]

ELEVEN
Keys to Death and Hades

Script recited "The Scholar and His Cat, Pangur Bán" without a flaw. Then he sat back down on his stool, amidst the circle of seven slender easels. The easels held works of art, carefully displayed by Sage.

"Very well done," said Sage. "Your timing and enunciation were perfect."

"First time I've heard the curious little tale," said Simon. "But charming, and now I have it stowed away."

"You mean, just like that?" said Script. "You memorized the entire poem?"

"Well, Sage and I possess certain qualities that you, too, will one day acquire. I particularly liked the lines:

"So in peace our task we ply,
Pangur Bán, my cat, and I;
In our arts we find our bliss,
I have mine and he has his.

"*In our arts we find our bliss*—nice line, don't you think, Sage?" Simon said.

"Clearly," said Sage. "So, Script, let us examine the works before us, to see what inspiration arises."

"I know St. John's Revelation well," said Script. "I've spent a good deal of time perusing John's visions of Christ. It was Christ himself, we know, who sent an angel to John to convey this heavenly revelation.

"I wonder, though, what St. John saw in his mind's eye when the angel spoke. On Patmos, John was old. He must have had pains of one sort or another. Did he have friends? Perhaps he had a cat like Pangur Bán, but with a different name. I wonder, too, how often he rehearsed scenes of days gone by when, by Christ's side, he saw the world around him turned upside down.

"Imagine the Transfiguration scene. He was there with Peter and James on that mountaintop when Moses and Elijah mysteriously appeared. Next he saw Christ's being transformed into a being of light. How does the mind engage such experiences?

"One moment all is actual, real; on a mountaintop stage you stand. The next moment you are caught up in an act, divinely set. No thin space between here and there.

"I fear I'm getting off the topic," Script said.

"No, not at all Script," Simon said. "We've traveled far to hear what you have to say. And later on you must tell us more about the Isle of Estillyen. Right now, though, let's remain focused on what St. John saw."

"Yes, Script, please carry on," said Sage. "St. John's visions have a great deal to do with your pending journey to hell."

"To hell—dear me," said Script.

"Now, Script, hold on," said Simon. "We'll address all of your concerns in due course, but please, let's get back to the comments about St. John the Revelator."

"Well, I would be better off to lie down and die now," said Script. "That would be my wish. But it seems I can't die in the middle of this mystifying play.

"Anyway, I was thinking of John when he was young. At the Lord's Supper, he saw it all, the sup and the cup, the morsel offered to Judas and readily taken. He was an eyewitness. He witnessed scenes that time would never sweep away.

"Years passed, and eventually St. John penned his inspiring biography into which he wove a treasure trove of Christ's words, including the line 'I am the light of the world.' I wonder, did John believe that line on the night when darkness reigned, or was it later on?

"And John concludes his Gospel narrative with that intriguing afterword: 'This is the disciple who testifies to these things and wrote them down. We know that his testimony it true. Jesus did many other things as well. If every one of them were written down, I suppose that even the whole world would not have room for the books that would be written.'

"It's so interesting to think about John's state of mind when he penned those words of summation. Surely he had no idea, at that point, that he would become John the Revelator. Yet, through him, in him, and by him, a form of his remarkable revelation of celestial prose was produced.

"John also penned an afterword, for Revelation, but it's his foreword that is so stunning to me: 'Blessed is the one who reads aloud the words of this prophecy, and blessed are those who hear it and take to heart what is written in it, because the time is near.'"

"So much said in a single verse," said Sage. "Anyone care for more tea, another sip of wine, or some water?"

"Script," said Simon, "of the seven works, which do you most prefer? The first or the last, the fourth or the fifth, or perhaps it's the third?"

"Equally stunning in color and depiction they are," said Script. "Therefore, I cannot choose one over the six remaining. I ask you, how does one choose the Lamb with a scroll over the Son of Man among the churches? Since I'm a scriptwriter, you might suppose I would choose the scroll.

"But no! They are all priceless. One begets the other. It's rather like the Father, who begat the Begotten One. I ask you, which is the greater of the two, the Father begetting or the Begotten One?"

"Carry on, Script," Simon said. "You are beginning to sound a lot like Sage."

"Okay, to answer you, all seven I equally admire. However, I choose the first, not simply because I saw it first, or for the stunning symbolism it conveys. In this work, depicting John's vision of Christ among the churches, there is much to be observed. In a robe he stands with a gold sash around his chest. Thus he is depicted as a holy priest.

"His hair is white like wool; the wisdom of the ages is conveyed. A double-edged sword extends from his mouth. His eyes blaze with fire. His face shines like the sun. Each element symbolizes a meaning most profound. Among seven gold lamps he stands, and in his right hand he holds seven stars. All of these elements, and more, John saw.

"In this case, though, it's not a particular aspect symbolized before my eyes that sways my choice. Rather, it's the words St. John heard when before Christ he fell, after he saw the vision of him standing among the churches. At his feet he heard Christ say, 'I hold the keys to death and Hades.' So, I embrace those words and, therefore, the image portrayed."

"You've chosen well," said Sage. "You've reminded yourself who actually holds the keys to the Gates of Hell. Which reminds me to ask, can you recall, word for word, what the Speakers said on your first visit to hell? It's important; we must try and put some pieces of this puzzle together prior to your return."

"Important, you say, before my return! Oh no, weary my soul. I've slipped into a stupor, speaking of art and sipping tea among the pines. This tranquil scene has drugged me. And with whom do I sip tea among the pines, Sage and Simon of Cyrene? Mystical figures you are, wonderful, indeed, but as mystical as any mystery dares to be.

"Please forgive me, but either of you, can you tell me something ordinary? Say, like 'My brother used to be a barber until he became a baker,' or 'We had a farm with mooing cows and a pond with lots of leaping frogs.'

"No, that won't do. The word *frog* brings to mind a line from the *Inferno*. 'Like frogs that glimpse their enemy the snake, and vanish rapidly across the pond.'"[34]

"Ordinary," said Sage. "Well, I once saw tombs split open and the dead walk about. It happened thus when the temple curtain tore."

"Yes, that's right, same as me," said Simon. "Dark it was in old Jerusalem, when for hours three the sun refused to shine."

"To your question, Sage, I do recall what the Speakers said. There were three Speakers, one leading, two following. Brimer, the lead Speaker, said: 'The fleshy carnites will tout the Spire as the most vital project in the history of the world. It will be their newly constructed Tower of Babel. Once erected on that small, desolate isle, the Great Spire will offer a true overarching narrative extolling the wonders of discarnate life. 'Pixels will populate the universe, pixels that we can focus and alter at will. I've already told you more than you should know, imbeciles.'

"That's a portion of what Brimer said. Yes, I heard it all, as awestruck I stood trembling in that massive cavern of hell. Soon after, Simon appeared. I recall that Brimer also said, 'Discarnate life will become the highest virtue of the incarnate world. Not presence, but discarnate existence without worry of will'—that's what he said.

"'The forces of Beelzebub have placed a load of rotten eggs in the discarnate basket. They perceive a world raptured in a multifarious vision of discarnate life. They behold a life in which pixeled images are preferred over incarnate presence, a life where human presence is considered passé, even repugnant.'

"I can hear the doomed prophets of the netherworld speaking. They'll push and peddle the new discarnate narrative, plaster it from post to pillar. Evil intent quickens their pace. Surely Dante was right when he claimed, 'The swirling wind of Hell will never rest. It drags these spirits onward in its force.'[35] Oh, my mind, my eyes, why must I think and see, as I do?

"Listen, do you hear that, there, just then, the rustling in the pines? It sounds like pigeons, a hundredfold, just took flight. A voice, too, it rumbles; it's the voice of Beelzebub. Simon, Sage, turn around, look, on the platform high. There he stands with the sun to his back.

"The platform on which he speaks is the Port Estillyen pier. No, tell me it can't be. The ropes are frayed. No seagulls fly. No flags flutter. No one speaks. No one strolls along the pier—no laughing, no crying, no life do I see!

"Oh, that voice, hear it? So treacherous the sound, like gravel in a tumbler spun."

"Script," said Sage, "You'd best sit down."

"Can't you hear him? He's there—don't you see him? He says, 'Listen.'

"Listen you must. He speaks prophetically. Please don't leave. I can't bear to hear this alone.

"'Cosmos, this is Lucifer; I speak. No one but me can speak for me or dare to think they might bear my message. Yes, in medium and message, we are one, and that is the message most critical of all.'

"He's addressing the cosmos . . .

"'Not in some limited, carnate form have we formed. We are fused in a cosmic space via telepathy and senses of celestial origin. From beyond the Storied Sea, on the isle called Estillyen, I speak. This is the new home of AI. Here there is no need of I AM.'

"He mentioned the Storied Sea . . .

"'Hear this: the new age of discarnate life has begun. Forget presence; presence is so very passé. Hear me. Believe me. Who needs presence when you can have discarnate existence? Understand you must, you who were fed that old narrative which wound its way up the Nile. Up through the reeds of time, a good run it had.'

"New age of discarnate life . . .

"'The preposterous narrative of which I speak claimed that time was full. The one known as the Ancient of Days was out of touch. So he came up with a plan: his son in the flesh would step in to save the Race, show himself, become present, dwell among his chosen lot. Myth, imagine it—out of the cosmos steps forth one who claims to be the Son of God, the Son of Man.

"'Confusing, is it not? The tale offers no clarity concerning the wherefore and why-fore of existence. Not I—I clarify. Let me be clear, those days of looking back are gone, the days of words scratched on tablets of stone and in parables spun. Who needs to speak in parables when meaning a million-fold can be gifted to you via AI, algorithms, and data never ceasing?'

"Algorithms . . .

"'All that nonsense about seeing through a glass dimly—forget it. And listen, you Luddite loonies scattered about the earth. The age of AI, algorithms, and dataism has arrived. Generations stretching beyond the ancient pyramids have longed for this day, to see what you see, to hear what you hear. So, see it; hear it!

"'Race, you have now entered the center ring of destiny. Being present, what's that? Being stuck it is. This is the day of *Presence Passé*. Why stick with incarnate presence when your image can soar throughout the cosmos? Don't be fooled—your image extends the checkmated you, the incarnate you.'

"About image . . .

"'Your image can do far more for you than you can do for you, bound as you are by time and space. You must die and let your image live. And get this: if your image lives, so will you in a new, never dying, discarnate form.

"'Enough for now, I say. Again soon, I shall speak from the distant isle, beyond the Storied Sea!'

"I can't bear it," said Script, as he collapsed on the ground alongside his stool.

Simon looked at Sage and said, "It seems that Script has a propensity for passing out. He clearly saw and heard something we did not, which is unusual indeed."

"I know," said Sage. "It's not good for a mortal to be so exposed to otherworld sightings. I'd say it's time for bouillabaisse. I have it on. Let's carry him over to the campsite and let him come around on his own."

"Not to worry, I've got him," said Simon. "Leave everything as it is. Let's go."

So Simon stepped along effortlessly as he carried Script in his arms. When he reached the campsite, he laid Script on an oak refectory table and then placed a cushion under his head. Sage put a cool cloth across Script's forehead.

"He's all right, I can tell," said Sage. "Let's sit at the round table; we'll eat here tonight, which I prefer anyway."

"Yes," said Simon. "These days with Script are certainly full of twists and turns."

"I know," said Sage. "We need to move the mission along without killing off the one we've been sent to aid. Time is of the essence. What do you think? Should we send him back tonight, or wait till the morning? I know Melchizedek will turn up to show Script the Seven Valleys of Sin."

"In that case," said Simon, "I think it should be bouillabaisse tonight, and off to hell in the morning. But I suggest that we collect all his gear from Writer's Cottage, along with blankets and pillows, and let him sleep on the table tonight, under the stars. You still have Melchizedek's mat, I suppose."

"Sure, it's in the blue chest," said Sage.

"Okay, we have a plan, right?" said Simon. "He's resting well. Let's get everything together."

Meanwhile, Script lay atop the old refectory table as streams of consciousness slowly crept into the blank portions of his mind. He mumbled a bit, then coughed and moaned a time or two. Before long, Simon and Sage returned and sat waiting at the table round.

They heard Script say, "Way up the Nile." And shortly thereafter, Script came to and said, "Woo, I must have fainted."

"You're okay," said Simon. "I'd say just a little too much to process."

"Hungry?" asked Sage. "I made fresh bouillabaisse and black bread; it will set you right."

"Sounds good," said Script, as he slid off the table. "It's nearly dark."

Near the campfire they sat. Script remained quiet, while Simon and Sage conversed about the works of art and how, from words, images arise. Script listened, but not intently, as the two spoke with equal enthusiasm.

Into his bowl of soup Script stared. He hardly noticed what he ate. Robotically he lifted his spoon to his mouth, and occasionally he'd draw his napkin to his lips without looking at the cloth.

A pair of lit candles in the center of the wooden table lit the trio of faces. The flickering wicks reflected dancing flames on the bouillabaisse broth. A normal course of eating this wasn't. It was a pondering, supping time, in which their bouillabaisse offered a backdrop for much weightier thoughts.

In time the campfire collapsed into embers that created a warm red glow inside the circular stone firepit. When they'd finished the bouillabaisse, Sage asked, "Would anyone care for a piece of boysenberry pie? It's perfect after bouillabaisse. Nods, okay—I take that as a yes."

"Bouillabaisse and boysenberry pie," said Script. "Where do you come up such amazing food in a meadow of gates and doors? It's been said, 'A man with better cellars there was none.'[36] Of you this is certainly true, Sage."

"Script," said Sage, "Simon was asking about the Isle of Estillyen. How do you characterize the isle?"

"Well, let me think," Script said. "Please understand, Estillyen is not a fairy-tale place where wounds and worries are wrapped in cotton wool. Estillyenites are not exempt from pain and hardship. Yet beyond life's rigors, a unique, Estillyen essence prevails.

"Estillyen is an ancient, mysterious isle. Estillyenites say that the mysterious nature of the isle is due to the Estillyen mist. Furthermore, like Melchizedek, true Estillyenites have no lineage beyond the Estillyen shores. They do not know when their ancestors arrived, or from whence they came. I know that's hard to believe, but it's so.

"Anyway, no matter where you go on the isle, tales are told, tunes are sung, and a sense of drama fills the air. Port Estillyen—in my mind's eye, I can see it now, bustling with pilgrims arriving and strolling along the pier. Pilgrims come from near and far to visit the isle, to hike the trails, or to camp out at Lakes Three. It's such a beautiful spot; the sailboats, with bright-colored sails, dash to and fro across the lakes."

"Bright-colored sails—I like that," said Simon.

"At Lakes Three there's an astonishing phenomenon regarding the transport of fish. The fish, it seems, like to stay abreast of what's happening in all three lakes. So they have some strange arrangement with the cranes, whereby a crane will swoop up a fish from, say, Lake One, and drop it off in Lake Two or Three. The transporting exercise happens routinely, every few days or so. It's a huge draw for the pilgrims, who wait and watch, hoping to see the act unfold.

"I must say just a word about the Order of Message Makers, to which I belong. The order dates back to 1637, when Bevin Roberts and his troupe arrived on the isle. Roberts was a spellbinding speaker, a dramatist who traveled throughout the continent giving dramatic readings based upon Scripture narratives. He didn't simply speak; he performed his message.

"When he walked on stage, no one knew what he was going to do because he didn't know what he was going to do. However, that doesn't mean he didn't know what he was doing. Roberts was a master message maker and believed that the medium and message must merge as one.

"Roberts might begin a dramatic reading by singing, then pause and shift to poetry, or simply talk. Stillness, too, he loved. Often, he would pause and look at the audience, the way a cat might look into a mirror. Or in the middle of a performance, he might suddenly stop and ask a question of the audience. He never feared the reply, whether sincere or foul.

"His troupe remained ever ready to quote a line, propel a question, or accompany his performances with an array of string and wind instruments. Many of the instruments are on display in Estillyen's Museum of Message Makers. I could talk about the Isle of Estillyen for hours, but speaking of the isle makes me homesick . . . melancholy, I'm afraid.

"I mean, if I were there speaking to visitors about the isle, I would be full of bounce. Not now, though; I'm caught up somewhere between heaven and hell."

"Your reason for being here," said Sage, "is to save the isle. So, with that said, Script, tomorrow, early, you need to return to hell. So hold in your mind John's vision, as you journey to that dark valley of death.

"Are you listening, Script? We're here to help you to do what you cannot do alone. The battle is carried on the celestial realm, Script. We have no time to waste. Plans to obliterate the Estillyenites are advancing. Evil, Script, is like acid—once spilled, it eats away. You wish for peace, that I know, but this war is scripted in the cosmic scroll.

"One day, Script, the epic battle will commence. Darkness will drape itself in light and begin its corrosive spill of blood. As the battle rages on, eventually darkness will shed the pretense of light, and then the true light will appear. This moment, this hour, this day, I hear cosmic forces on the move.

"Darkness believes its own lie. If it did not, how could darkness dare to take on the light? As told in ancient narrative, 'God is light and in him there is no darkness at all.' So the forces of darkness battle God himself.

"The Isle of Estillyen is at stake, along with the destiny of many souls who will otherwise cling to a hollow, discarnate vision. Never underestimate the waywardness of desperate souls. Does history not record that:

"*In the valley low,*
Below old Jerusalem,
Moloch's worshipers prayed,
To the Idol-god of fire.

Stoked hot for infant cries.
Scent and smoke arose,
Amid the cries of souls,
And woe below old Jerusalem."

"Sorrow I hear," said Script. "So it must be, this fate to which I respond. I also hear the words of the Begotten One spoke to St. John. 'I hold the keys to death and Hades.' So I embrace those words. To hell I will go."

"Script," said Simon, "under the stars you will sleep tonight. We've gathered all your belongings. So rest, for tomorrow you will revisit hell."

"No more talking just now, Script," said Sage. "We've done enough talking for one day."

With that, Sage blew out the candles and said, "Now it's time for rest."

TWELVE
Seven Valleys of Sin

Sunrise hues swept across the Meadow of Gates and Doors as Script, Sage, and Simon finished their early morning campsite breakfast.

"So, Script, are you ready?" asked Simon.

"To ready oneself for a journey to hell—that's a strange thought," said Script. "I'm willing, though, and I guess willingness will have to do for readiness."

"Remember your mission, Script. It's not just about trolling through the caustic caverns of the underworld. You and Mock are there to uncover details about Lucifer's plan to obliterate Estillyen, your isle, your home. Do watch out for Mock; keep him nestled in your pocket as much as possible, like he is now.

"No need to prolong the inevitable. Let's move along to the gates via the shortcut. You've chosen the door of gray, correct?"

"Yes, it's my third," said Script. "I don't know if there will be a fourth."

"Everything depends on what you discover," Sage said.

"Also, we can't confirm that Melchizedek will join you," Simon said. "Such matters are not for us to decide. You may be on your own, just you and Mock."

"Script, remember everything I've told you about viewing the living scene," said Sage. "Take it in, but do not try to enter; if you do, you'll be as lost as Lot's wife."

"I know, I haven't forgotten," said Script. "Well, the gate, here it is."

"So now off with you, Script," said Sage, "and Godspeed. May God speed your return."

"Oh," said Script, "I wanted to ask you something, Sage, but it's slipped my mind."

"Not to worry," said Simon. "You have a bit on your mind just now. Goodbye, Script."

"Remember me, won't you," said Script, "when you finish the boysenberry pie. Come along, Mock, through the ancient gate we push. Again he glides, like on angel's wings. Now, the door of gray— what's beyond it, Mock? Oh, my question for Sage—now I remember."

Script turned around and was petrified by what he saw. He faced a wall of darkness; he could see nothing more. No open gate, no meadow view. Sage and Simon, too, were sealed off by the darkness. At arm's length, the wall of darkness began, so Script reached out his hand to see if he could actually feel the darkness.

He pushed his hand into the darkness an inch or two, but then the darkness became increasingly hard. Any further, and the darkness began to push back. Script distinctly felt the counter-push.

"Quick, Mock, to the door; I have the key. A turn, and there it goes, that slow, steady opening motion. Let's get away from the darkened wall, Mock. There's a scene ahead. Okay, beyond the threshold I step. Slowly, a step at a time, and sure enough, we're entering another sphere.

"The path is widening to a road, different than before. I see thatched roofs and people walking along the road. Children running, a pair of goats tied, the sound of sweeping . . . where are we? There to the left, loud voices—it's some kind of commotion.

"Again we see a scene from long ago, but alive. So utterly amazing! This is a stage but not a set; it's real, as it once was and is. It's afternoon, a house with a portico, with people in the courtyard. Good Lord, a man is walking right toward us, Mock. I'm in his way, but no, he's passed through me. He's right in front of us, Mock. He's yelling to a couple in the courtyard.

Rufus:

Silas, say, what's going on? What are all these people doing here? Has there been a robbery or something?

Silas:

No, nothing like that, Rufus. We were wondering when you would turn up. Come, join us, and sit down.

Rufus:

Who are these people, Silas?

Silas:

Come over close to me; be still. Don't cause trouble; your sister Sarah and I are nearly at our wits' end. Don't you recognize the priests from the temple? And the big fellow, he's some sort of official scribe they brought along. The four ladies came with cousin Nabad, and the other dozen or so just turned up. They've been here since morning.

Rufus:

Okay, since morning, you say, but will you please tell me what on earth is going on here?

Silas:

Oh, such disquiet we've had—you wouldn't believe it. I'm about to tear my hair out. Where have you been anyway? It's been over three weeks since we last saw you. Sarah said you were working with Reuben and his lot, but we didn't know how to find you.

Sarah:

Just the same, you're here now. Here, have some grapes. We're sitting back here just listening; you can't tell these people anything. The Pharisees have been here, all sorts. We're worn out. You must stay the night, bring Elizabeth.

Rufus:

I still don't know what's going on. But to answer your query, Reuben and I went south to purchase ewes and their lambs. All great, nice bunch, and then, on our way back, we ended up helping that Croft fellow at the inn. We patched his roof and built him a couple of sheds. That took an extra week. Anyway, if you don't tell me what's going on, I'm leaving.

Silas:

All right, all right, but you may not believe it. The boy, Brother, has been cured of blindness—got his sight, he has. Look at him looking at those staring faces. I don't mean he sees a shadow or two. No, Brother, who could not see anything since birth, sees everything in detail. As good as you and me, he sees—if not better.

Rufus:

You're right, I don't believe you. The boy has had dead eyes, glossy eyes, since the day he was born.

Silas:

Then who do you think it is sitting in the middle of that group?

Rufus:

That's Brother; it is. Nobody looks like him. But it can't be him, though it must be him. He's sitting up, proud. He looks so different; still slender and all, but his head was always swishing about as he listened to the sounds around him. All of that begging—such a sad affair it's been.

I'm gonna go talk with him. Elizabeth won't believe it. She always liked Brother—the way he spoke so soft when he wasn't begging.

Silas:

No, don't interrupt anything just now. In a few minutes we'll move up on the ledge, and you can listen. But first let Sarah tell you what happened. Go ahead, Sarah, tell him the story."

Sarah:

Well, you know the pool of Siloam?

Rufus:

Sure, the beggars' pool.

Sarah:

So, you've heard of Jesus the Nazorean, who has created quite a stir, right? The Pharisees made an edict saying that anyone who believes in him will be thrown out of the synagogue.

Rufus:

Yeah, I heard something about that. But what happened?

Sarah:

Well, a fortnight ago Jesus and his disciples were passing by Siloam. They stopped and saw Brother begging, among the others. Why they spotted him, no one knows. Anyway, according to what we've heard, the disciples asked Jesus, "Rabbi, who sinned, this man or his parents, that he was born blind?" So many people think that way. By the way, we've written all this down. And of course Brother heard the conversation unfold, every word.

In any case, Jesus replied: "Neither this man nor his parents sinned, but this happened so that the works of God might be displayed in him. As long as it is day, I must do the works of him who sent me." But that's not all. He followed on by saying, "I am the light of the world."

Rufus:

You don't mean it.

Silas:

She does mean it. Go on, tell him more, Sarah; you've not heard anything yet. Just brace yourself.

Sarah:

Okay. Next, Jesus spit on the ground, made some kind of mud plaster, and smeared it on Brother's eyes, and then told him to wash it off in the pool. When he did, he was cured of blindness.

Silas:

Let me pick up the story, Sarah. So when he got home, the whole countryside showed up. Some people were praising God, while others deemed the whole affair to be some kind of hoax, saying that he was not really Brother but an imposter. But we know the truth; it's definitely our boy.

Then the Pharisees got involved, the religious zealot lot. They mounted an investigation and brought us in before the tribunal, as well as our neighbors. They began questioning Brother, and they accused him of lying, of being a follower of Jesus.

After that, they turned on us. We were scared stiff. They called us in, and we had to go. In no time, everything escalated. The Pharisees started pointing fingers and hurling insults.

They drilled down on the idea that this miracle took place on the Sabbath. They said it was against their law. They didn't give a bat's eye for Brother. Heart-sickening how they could be so hard.

Sarah:

Let me tell this part. Brother spoke up for himself, I can tell you. He told the big stiffs that he believed Jesus was a prophet. Then they became furious. They looked down at Brother and said, "You're a sinner, born in sin."

Silas:

Then you know what Brother told them?

Rufus:

No, I'm already in shock.

Silas:

Straight out he told them, "I was blind, but now I see." They couldn't take it, and they threw us out of the temple.

Sarah:

Wait, listen. They're questioning him again. He can speak up when he wants to; listen.

Brother:

As I told you, all of a sudden he, the Nazorean, was just there. He was present. I could sense his presence; I could feel his presence. Something inside me quickened. What it was, I don't know. There was a charge in the air. I felt my heart stir. And no, I never spoke with him before, not a single word prior to that day. I say this, if he's not God, he should be, but I believe he is.

Silas:

You hear that? What you see before you has been going on every day since all this happened. And I . . .

"Mock, we must go; we don't belong to this space in time. Sage warned me; we are in danger of being scrolled away. No more, no more—we must move.

"I see the path leading on from this ancient scene; dear Lord, have mercy on my soul. We're on it; instantly my feet are propelling, lifting; tuck in, Mock. Nature's rules have fallen away; we're moving at the speed of spirits.

"Oh, such horrific sounds! I can't bear it! Splitting rocks, thunder, quakes, flames, gas, lava, lightning, screams, streaming faces all around, now screeching. We've halted; we must be in hell. We're in a cave again, but not the massive cavern. I can see the opening.

"The Crimson Cliffs—I see them, and the great sulfur plane. At least we know where we are. What am I saying? Mock, we need to get our bearings. Not sure I have wits, but I have senses. We'll take a dozen steps or so into the open to see what we can see. It's eerily quiet, but I hear roars in the distance."

Just then, Script heard footsteps not far behind him. He froze. The footsteps grew closer and closer, then halted. Script could hear breathing, and a hard object landed and hooked over his shoulder. Script didn't budge, fearing the face of death, but the object on his shoulder began to slowly turn him around. Still completely rigid, Script closed his eyes and listened, as the soles of his shoes twisted on the brittle surface.

"Hello, Script," said Melchizedek. "I thought I might be of help."

"Dear me, I say, I thought you were death. I mean not you, but death instead of you. Oh, I don't know what I mean."

"You are willing, Script. Faith, it's called. In hell, though, faith does not exist. Everything moves by force and rule. Now, you must come with me; there's much you need to see."

"I must bear in mind my mission," said Script.

"Not to worry, I've already discovered various aspects of the scheme," said Melchizedek. "What you're about to see, I must say, will press deep in your mind and give you fodder for a hundred plays."

"Will I ever write again?" said Script.

"Not for me to say," said Melchizedek. "Time will tell what time tells. Now, take hold of my staff and you will see what no living soul has ever seen. Be warned, your eyes will absorb sights your mind cannot erase. Thence, swiftly, to the top of the Cliffs we ascend.

"Now look, Script. You see the great canyons and valleys stretching out below?"

"I do. I see figures and all kinds of movement."

"You're looking upon the Seven Valleys of Sin. We'll start to your right. Ask any question you wish. I may answer, or I may not; of course, an answer not could be the answer."

Valley of False Prophets

"Those massive rolls, Melchizedek, what are they?"

"Yes, the first of seven. That's the Valley of False Prophets, and what you see are massive scrolls. Each scroll is made of layer upon layer of history. They contain words, lines, and stories that condemned those rolled inside. Their diameter varies, but many appear as large as Joseph's great granaries. It's known that Joseph stored so much grain that it could not be counted.

"As you can see, snails trail their clue round and round each scroll to hold them tight. The scrolls cannot be unrolled. Those rolled inside are sealed in doom.

"Look closely at the ends of each scroll. Do you see the jerking, spasmodic motion amid the ringed layers? From here it looks like thousands of flapping, withered leaves, doesn't it?"

"Yes," said Script.

"They are not withered leaves, though. Rather, you are looking upon the squirming hands and feet of false prophets and priests. They lie wrapped for eternity in the words they spoke. They are coiled in the twisted lines they cast, in the false narratives they wove. Now they extend their hands, endeavoring to clutch hold of something, but there's nothing to hold. There is no one present to clasp the clutching hands.

"Upon their withered fingers, they bear the rings they wore when in pride they swaggered. Rubies, emeralds, gold, and silver—up close you can see them flop on fingers of skin and bone. In the Valley of False Prophets, those scrolled away squirm in a conscious, living-dead existence. Their feet kick; their ankles twist.

"Some toes, you see, point down, others up; it depends on when the false prophet was rolled inside. Their groans feed impulses that make their hands clasp, not for truth but for proof. Even now, if they were un-scrolled and ordered to speak, they would say that truth itself is but a lie. Let's move on. We must leave the prophets scrolled away. Now you know where they lie."

Valley of Wicked Kings

"Next, the Valley of Wicked Kings. Look down upon the endless columns, as far as the eye can see. What do you see, Script?"

"I don't know. I see upright plates or slabs taller than you, all perfectly erect with moving images. Though the vertical slabs do not move, only the images. The slabs appear as clear quartz."

"Your description is not far off the mark, Script. The quartz-like material is clear and poured into molds as the wicked kings in hell appear. The substance, though, is much harder than quartz. Anyway, once the material is poured into the mold, but before it cools, the manifestation of the king is laid on top, where it sinks midway in the thick mold.

"The image, though, is alive. It never dies. Unlike a discarnate image, the soul of the king and the captured image are one. Consciousness remains."

"This can't be, Melchizedek."

"But it is. Wickedness in the heart of a king reaps a wicked harvest. Not a few have taken on the Prince of Tyre's air, who declared, 'A god am I! I occupy a godly throne in the heart of the sea.'[37]

"Shall I tell you more, Script?"

"I fear you must, but I'm already overwhelmed. Neither the eyes of man nor beast should see what I peer upon. A line of old creeps in my mind; I hear it say, 'Now am I doomed eternally to dwell no more in Purgatory, but in Hell.'[38]

"Mock, stay still; none of this is for you."

"So, Script, the Valley of Wicked Kings is not a small gorge beyond the Gates of Hell. On and on the rows stretch, and as you can see, the rows are made of slabs paired. Each slab faces its pair, what do you suppose, say, twenty feet apart or so? Why paired, I'm sure you wonder.

"The slabs are one and the same, but not. I mean, one slab holds the image of a king, whoever that might be. Say King Ahab who did more evil in God's eyes than any other king. The opposing slab, directly across, contains an unending stream of the king's exploits—his ceremonies, his battles, his edicts, the starving faces of those held in his dungeon, and all the faces of pain caused by his reign. He both sees and hears all that took place.

"But what's more, do you see the scurrying going on behind the slab in that column to our left?"

"Yes," said Script.

"And over there, far along the third column on your right, the same sort of action is taking place."

"I can see it," said Script.

"So, at a time, the kings know not when, demonic crews turn up and open the back of a slab holding the image of the king. I forgot to mention that the slabs open from the rear by way of demonic force. Once opened, which may be once in forty years, the demonic workers snatch out the conscious image of the king and carry it across to the slab streaming the exploits of the king.

"Subsequently, they open the paired slab, again from the backside, and thrust the image of the king inside. Thus, the image of the wicked king must possess his image that has been captured in the stream of living history. Thereby he relives the exploits and acts of his condemnation.

"Which is worse, Script, I ask you? The king trapped in a slab and forced to watch his evil reign, or being thrust back into the reign playing out as living history? Oh yes, another key factor at play in this bizarre display is that the conscious image of the king knows what's happening.

"That is, he knows that he now abides in hell. Likewise, he knows that he's held captive in a translucent slab and has been thrust into the reign in which he reigned, possessing the image of who he was. The image, thus thrust, can do nothing to alter who he was or what he did.

With ears once his, and eyes, too, he hears and sees again all he once heard and saw.

"Behold what I say, Script. Somewhere along one of the columns of twin slabs, Ahab now watches the slaughter of Israel's priests, as his wife Jezebel worships Baal. He also sees and hears dogs lapping up his blood, as Elijah prophesied. At a point, he knows not when or why, he, too, will be summarily thrust."

"Astonished, my mind can scarcely believe what my eyes behold," said Script. "At a particular stage, then, are the images of the kings extracted from the living history slabs and locked back into their assigned slabs?"

"That is the scenario, but not at any particular time ascribed. It could be a month later, a year, or even ten years before the image of the king is recaptured and locked into his eternal slab of image exchange."

"King Herod, then—is he there watching, even now, the severing of John the Baptist's head?" asked Script.

"I say no more, Script!"

"Why did evil have to be, Melchizedek?"

"Evil backlights good, as darkness does light. Pain seeks a cure. I say no more."

Valley of Mammon

"Look now to your left. Set your sight on the endless row of ridges that rise and fall," said Melchizedek.

"They are littered, I see, with great wheels, slowly moving," said Script.

"Upon the Valley of Mammon you peer, Script. The massive wheels are symbolic coins, bearing faces, signs, and symbols of the world. The tiny figures you see pushing up the wheels are those who gave themselves over to love of mammon, allowing the root of all evil to root in them. Once rooted, mammon's invasive root occupies the mind and soul where virtues might have grown.

"Unless, that is, a dramatic change occurs. Thus, once a wealthy sinner collected taxes in Jericho, where the export of balsam was a most lucrative trade. Of Abraham's lineage he was, this Zacchaeus of whom I speak. Zacchaeus earned his reputation as a sinner by pocketing no little change.

"A man of short stature, Zacchaeus was. He climbed a sycamore tree one day to catch a glance of a controversial prophet passing by. In the tree he heard a call: 'Come down,' said the Son of Man. Zacchaeus obeyed, and in short order, his life was turned upside down. Mammon lost its hold on this short-statured man. You know the story, Script?"

"Certainly, very well," said Script.

"In the Valley of Mammon here before us, Zacchaeus does not abide. But as you can plainly see, the valley has a populace occupying no end of space. See how the souls sad press their shoulders and backs up against the coins great. The coins must be twenty or thirty times their height.

"Up the ridge they push. Heave they do; holler, curse, and scream, they push and push. For if they pause, they'll be crushed and cannot escape. In such cases, demonic minions hurriedly pick them up, punch them, and pound them back in shape."

"Is that what's happening at the base of the first ridge?" asked Script.

"Do you not see the mallets swing?"

"I do, Melchizedek. And I see those who push and shove bearing circles on their foreheads."

"Those are the embedded coins, Script, they bear for eternity. On and on they push; they shove and heave. When they finally reach the top of the ridge, they are chained to the massive coins. Then the demonic minions force other captives to push the massive coins from the top of the ridge. That's happening right now on the top of the fourth ridge."

"Yes, I see," said Script.

"Now chained, the pushers and heavers will be dragged along to the bottom of the next ridge. There they begin again—push, shove, heave . . . it never ends. By the way, is Mock okay?"

"Yes, I feel him moving."

"I thought of Mock because we will next observe the Valley of Mockers. So, on around to your left, and you shall see another scene no one else has seen."

Valley of Mockers

"Here, Script, figures move along an unending maze of very deep trenches. The maze is made up of sharp bends that turn this way and that in such a way that two figures never gain contact. See how one figure disappears around a bend before the next figure arrives? They never achieve contact; there is no sense of presence.

"Concerning the figures, do you see any rather peculiar features— say, the size of the ears?" asked Melchizedek. "Here, look through the loop of my staff for a close-up inspection."

"Yes, extremely large ears, but, dear me, I see that each figure has two heads. It's an unbelievable sight, Melchizedek. The Valley of Mockers—this must be hell," said Script.

"Everything in hell, Script, has elements of deception that generate comparisons of real life. So you saw figures moving like figures do, but the twin heads you couldn't see without magnification. Why twin heads, I'm sure you must wonder?"

"Yes, but I can't imagine why," said Script.

"In life, each mocker chose to become a medium of mockery. Consider Job, how his mockers pounded him with endless mockery. Or think of King David when he fled for his life from his son, Absalom. So vividly I recall the scene.

"Up the Mount of Olives King David fled, riding on a donkey. His head was covered, his feet bare, and tears flowed from his eyes. All the people with him also covered their heads and wept as they followed along. In the midst of their grief, a strange character by the name of Shimei enters the scene.

"Shimei was an ardent mocker. He cursed the king and yelled,

'Get out, get out, you murderer, you scoundrel! The Lord has repaid you for all the blood you shed in the household of Saul.' King David, though, carried on as Shimei ran along the opposite hillside, cursing and showering him with stones and dirt."

"But how does that explain the twin heads of those in the maze below?" said Script.

"Mockers all have twisted souls," said Melchizedek. "The worst never recant; they go on ranting and chanting, like the souls of mockery at the foot of the cross. In the afterlife, the life you now witness, the souls of mockers suffer the kind of mockery they once extolled. But worse, the mocker's mockery is trained upon themselves.

"Notice how one of the twin heads talks, while the other must listen. Then the process is reversed, but never changed. On and on, the double-headed mockers both send and receive the bitter poison of mockery. Mockers for eternity they are."

Valley of Liars

"Now, turn to your right again, look past the false prophets, and cast your eyes upon the Valley of Liars. This valley, like all the rest, stretches on into infinity. It teems with liars and deceivers. One and the same they are; they coveted fraud and despised the truth."

"This valley looks most strange, Melchizedek, as if it were covered in frost."

"You make me smile, Script," said Melchizedek. "Frost and morning dew—do you think you're looking at the Meadow of Gates and Doors? What you see is not a pleasant scene."

"Well, okay, then—it's not frost," said Script. "But perhaps I look upon smog, or low-lying smoke, or something I've never seen."

"Your latter point is most accurate. Hell is hell, Script. There is no gentle breeze in the abyss, where bluebirds fly. Flying creatures here are the demonic sort who once had genuine wings, or vultures formed by Satan's art of deception.

"Frost and morning dew . . . consider, Script, that the Valley of Liars could itself be a lie. You must peer at the valley until the real image is borne upon your mind. Cast your eyes once more on the vast Valley of Liars and take in what your mind refused to see. Again, through the loop of my staff, look."

"Okay, I'm scanning the scene from side to side. I see tiny dots wiggling and wriggling, as it were. I see strings, I think; it looks like fishing line."

"Do you see any fish on the line, Script?"

"You know there are no fish in hell, Melchizedek."

"Do I now? I speak metaphorically, Script."

"Wait, Melchizedek, I see more and more of the wiggling figures. Now I see it—I'm stunned. The Valley of Liars is a massive spiderweb! Those must be the liars."

"Oh, so smart you are, Script. I'm delighted you do have eyes that can see. Though the webbing is not what you would expect, Script. No piano wires in hell—no tunes to play. Well, hold on . . . there may be knockoffs, if you know what I mean. But that's not what I mean.

"The vast web you see without end was woven by Lucifer himself. After all, he is the father of lies. Lucifer cannot speak the truth in any language, but he can lie in every tongue. He spun the web with delight, by frothing his fomented brand of mouthed secretion. There is no way to wriggle free. It's never happened. Among those that wiggle and wriggle, as you put it, wiggle the most infamous liars of them all.

"Know that I can quote every line inscribed in the ancient narrative. Consider these words, so long ago exchanged.

"The King said to Queen Esther, 'Who is he, and where is he, who would dare presume in his heart to do such a thing?'

"Queen Esther said, 'The adversary and enemy *is* this wicked Haman!'

"One of the eunuchs said to the king, 'Look! The gallows, fifty cubits high, which Haman made for Mordecai, who spoke good on the king's behalf, is standing at the house of Haman.'

"Then the king said, 'Hang him on it!'[39]

"Haman, of course, hung himself by way of deceit, as did Judas on the night darkness reigned. Let them wiggle and wriggle on; in the great Liar's web they are surely caught."

Valley of Murders

"Now, behind you, Script, turn and look down into the valley deep. The Valley of Murders stretches on into invisibility."

"You are right, deep and vast it is, with dark clouds swirling above," said Script.

"Take my staff. Through the crook, look closer at the clouds that swirl," said Melchizedek.

"What I did not readily see, I see," said Script. "The clouds are but swarming flies, millions multiplied."

"I ask you, what would one expect to see in this valley, distinct from hell's other Valleys of Sin?"

"How can I comprehend what I see? This is the only valley I've seen through which flows a river of blood."

"So correct you are . . . almost. The river flows not only with blood, but also with bones. Numerous are the manifestations of sin, but murder is sin's signature. And thus Cain was the first to sign his signature to history's long manifest of murder.

"No wonder Cain said he was given a mark he could not bear; he was the first man to murder a man. Two men, Cain and Abel, both created in the image of God. One, though, invited the sin that crouched at the door. Forewarned Cain was that sin lieth at his door, yet he refused to turn aside his anger or lift his fallen countenance.

"Was not Cain's anger the key that unlocked the door where sin crouched? Anger, jealousy, bitterness—they are all keys on the same ring, Script. Words rise from the ancient text:

"'And the Lord said unto Cain, Why art thou wroth and thy countenance fallen? If thou doest well, shalt thou not be accepted? And if thou doest not well, sin lieth at the door.'

"At the door of every heart sin crouches, Script. Once in, via the chosen key, it turns to opportunity for chosen ill. Cain chose the victim and the place. In Eden's field, Cain rose up and murdered his brother. Into the ground oozed Abel's blood. Abel breathed no more. Cain breathed on and on, with sin now occupying the full complement of his heart.

"'And God said unto Cain, What hast thou done? The voice of thy brother's blood crieth unto me from the ground.'

"History's long manifest of murder cries from page to page, often ascribed with footnotes of just cause and reason. Caiaphas argued his just cause:

"'And one of them, named Caiaphas, being the high priest that same year, said unto them, Ye know nothing at all. Nor consider that it is expedient for us, that one man should die for the people, rather than the whole nation perish.'

"And from the blood of the Begotten One, cries arose, along with faith in the Risen One. Sin, though, did not peel away. As an ancient letter of Hebrews attests regarding the fate of many who believed in the Risen One: 'They were stoned, they were sawn asunder, were tempted, were slain with the sword: they wandered about in sheepskins and goatskins; being destitute, afflicted, tormented; of whom the world was not worthy.'

"Enough, Script, look back upon the dreadful scene. Of all the valleys, you could say this is the worst. But worst they are, one and all, in the worst of all, hell. Describe for me what you see."

"A river of blood and bones I surely see," said Script. "Some figures wade, then I see others plunge; clutching bones and skulls, they disappear under the crimson current. This must be the worst, no matter what you say."

"The river of blood and bones, Script, never ceases to flow. It narrows and widens. Long stretches are shallow, where the bones tend to gather and clank. The murderous souls must move with the flow; they have no recourse.

"Suicide of soul, as you know, is not possible. From the shallow stretches, the current of blood and bones pulls the murderous creatures on into deep pools of blood. Splash they do, flop, scream . . . the harrowing sound of misery never ceases."

"Dante's line I recall, very much in the same vein of scarlet flow. 'We now moved on along the shore of boiling vermilion where souls well boiled gave vent to high pitched yells.'"[40]

"Somewhere along this wretched flow, Script, the river swirls into a massive maelstrom of blood, which pulls all the cursed souls down into the deepest depths of hell. At that enormous depth, the river of blood and bone reverses its flow. So, through chambers dark the murderous inhabitants of hell continue on in the flowing current of blood.

"All along the way, the sound of a pulsing heart continues unabated. Low and deep the pulsing sound vibrates, a pulse at a time echoing through the horrid chambers. There in that utter underground, the river winds blow to and fro, encircled by flaming caverns. Eventually, beyond the flaming caverns the miserable souls flow, until the flames abate and give way to ice."

"Thus, Melchizedek, you speak a line my memory recalls. 'I have come to lead you to the other shore; into eternal darkness; into fire and into ice.'"[41]

"For stretches long, the river of blood freezes, forcing its captives to navigate atop the frozen thicket of bones. Then, periodically the river of blood and bone rises like a mighty geyser, spilling into the valley you see below. Through the Valley of Murders, the river of blood and bones forever flows.

"Early on, Script, I said ask any question you wish, to which I may or may not reply. Therefore, before we move on to our seventh and final valley, do you have any questions?"

"Yes, one. It's something that has puzzled me from the beginning of this hellish expedition. We've seen the Valley of Wicked Kings, Liars, Murderers, and more. But surely a king like, say, Herod has reason to belong to one and all, not just one over the other?"

"A good question, Script, indeed, to which I tell you a mystery: A single soul in hell can actually occupy all seven valleys at once. And many do!

"We must move on and quickly, as we step forward to look into the largest valley of all."

Valley of Weeping and Gnashing of Teeth

"Script, the vast intermingled, intertwined sulfur plane of sin stretches before you. Countless are the inhabitants. Many of the residents of Sodom and Gomorrah now here abide. So, too, do a great number that scoffed at Noah's ark. That is, before they clung to his rising vessel, but to no avail. One by one the corpses floated on the water's flood.

"What can be said, looking on as we are, Script? Something surely, so let's lift our conversation grim to a plane of precept, not of concept. Many here, we see, reasoned away the reality of God. They refused to die to self, to worship a being supreme. For in doing so, that means that one must serve and follow.

"Which leads to a word I embrace with utmost delight. The word is *surrender*. As you know, on another sort of plane, I blessed Abraham, the great patriarch of faith. Such a sight it was to see a man like Abraham appear in the annals of time. Abraham was accounted righteousness for his faith.

"*Surrender* is a word that cuddles close to *faith*, and both cuddled close to Abraham. His eyes scanned the majesty of the stars and the innumerable grains of sand. And in time, a very testing time, he had a son named Isaac, and the test grew even harder still. The time came when he was to sacrifice the son he so loved.

"You know the story, but I was in the story present-tense. Abraham, in an act of complete surrender and faith, lifted high his knife. The knife, however, did not plunge. An angel of the Lord called out from heaven telling him not to lay a hand on the boy, Isaac. Then, in the thicket Abraham spied a ram, which became the sacrifice instead.

"Now, let's retract our conversation from that plane of precept to this. A ghastly sight it is to see those from every tribe and tongue that might have turned from self to surrender, from lust to chastity, from sloth to diligence. Late needn't be too late at times, but for those lost souls before us, too late it is.

"Pride propelled many to this horrid place where the flames rise and demons roar. Greed was the seed that captured scores of lost souls, if they were not already consumed by envy. Souls before us who might have lost their life to save it did not. In gluttony and drunkenness many gulped and scoffed at the notion of a righteous crown.

"In the Valley of Weeping and Gnashing of Teeth, the elements of all the other valleys carry on at once. The line that has no end, do you see it?"

"Yes, the line weaves through boulders on either side," Script said.

"Legions of greedy souls make up the never-ending line. The agents of hell are on hand to whip them along."

"I do see some jumping, trying to avoid the thrashing," said Script.

"The souls of greed's persuasion are forced, each and all, to roll over every boulder and rock, searching for what might be found. But guess what? Nothing can be found; every boulder turns up another boulder, every rock another rock, and never anything but.

"Across the endless fields of burning coals, the slothful dash, run, and leap. There is no prize. There is nothing to win. All is lost. On the other side, a horde of demons surrounds an enormous gorge. Therein the envious and haters cast stones at one another and drag the self-righteous through ponds of mud.

"In nakedness, Script, see them trudge and nudge. The acts, all of them, contribute to the wailing sounds and misery of hell. Too late it is. See the blind groping the gorge and the prideful begging among the mocking demons?

"In bonds of hate and revenge toward God, these pathetic souls are forever chained, link by link. The chain will not break. It holds, though endlessly gnawed. Even still, the truly wicked would choose self in hell over surrender to God.

"Unlike the Psalmist who said: 'For a day in your courts is better than a thousand elsewhere. I would rather be a doorkeeper in the house of my God than dwell in the tents of wickedness.'[42] As you can readily see, 'elsewhere' the wicked chose."

"The sound of weeping and gnashing of teeth is hell's unceasing lament," said Script. "I can bear no more. I can hear no more. I can see no more."

"We must go, Script. Your cause, your mission, awaits!"

THIRTEEN
Reservoirs of Bewilderment

Melchizedek whisked Script and Mock away from hell's Seven Valleys of Sin to the Reservoirs of Bewilderment, where they silently stood observing the otherworld environment. Melchizedek wanted Script to gather himself before they made any further moves.

Earlier, Melchizedek told Script, "Like St. John on the Isle of Patmos, one must be caught up in the spiritual realm to see what only the mind's eye can see. You, Script, have been caught up in a world unknown, allowing you to peer into the living scrolls of history and otherworld spheres."

Melchizedek also knew that Script's experience was unique among the vision-raptured figures of history. Script continued to function as a mortal in the otherworld sphere. Script even thought that the angels of heaven must be stunned by his unexplainable experience. At the same time, Script believed that if he failed in his mission to save the Isle of Estillyen, he would never return to the world he once knew.

Script thought that not only would the Isle of Estillyen be lost, but he, too, would be lost, destined to carry on in a sphere without presence. *A sphere of my own*, Script thought. *I will exist alone, neither in heaven nor in hell. Somewhere between, beyond Estillyen and the Meadow of Gates and Doors, I will exist. Mock, too, may be lost, since he's on loan to me from Sage.* Such thoughts not only seized Script's mind but burrowed deep into his subconscious.

"Script," said Melchizedek. "You look blank—are you in a trance? Are you there? What are you thinking?"

Melchizedek's words did not penetrate; Script was in a trance. Tears filled his eyes. Deep in the cortex of his mind, he heard himself saying: "You are hopelessly timid and tepid. You should be spit out, removed from the field of faith; you're a failure. Defeat creeps into your heart. Capitulate, give up your cause—you gave it a go, but you're done."

Script's legs began to weaken, and his cheeks turned ghostly pale. The inner voice continued. "You're a defector, a turncoat. A cosmic war between the forces of evil and good you've entered. Who do you think you are? You're just a playwright writing plays no one wants to attend. You're out of your league. You are hapless and without hope."

"Script, snap out of it," said Melchizedek. "I'm here to help."

"I'm sorry," said Script. "Something came over me. You don't think I'm a turncoat, do you?"

"Absolutely not," said Melchizedek. "Besides, you have Mock and me. Mock looks to be in good shape, perched on your shoulder. Mock, Script needs our support. The valleys are behind us, but the vast Reservoirs of Bewilderment await us. There are five, named Fragmentation, Static, Confusion, Chatter, and Delusion. I don't suppose that makes a lot of sense to a mockingbird. So what about a tweet or two?"

"Let me tickle him under the chin; he'll usually chirp. So what do you say, Mock?"

Mock chirped:

toroo, toroo, gotta go, goo, chat, chat, delu, delu

"I'm confident, Mock," said Melchizedek, "that you are the only mockingbird to tweet in hell."

"So what do you suggest we do?" said Script.

"This must be the satanic seat of lies. Spirits here take in and spew out a kind of lying code. Then the lying spirits are dispersed throughout the earth. They seek out disgruntled souls. The ultimate aim is possession, using methods of provocation."

"That's why this discarnate, virtual age is so threatening," Script said. "Change no longer creeps or crawls as in days of old, Melchizedek. Rather, at the speed of light it races. As a result, the pace of change itself is the greatest draw of all.

"New mediums of media and messaging have real, pervasive, and lasting effects on the world. Understanding media ecology requires rigorous circumspection, but few have the time or insight required to do so.

"The tide of time has brought forth a different age, a discarnate digital age where everything happens at once. This reality, of course, underscores the impetus for my play *Presence*. Incarnate reality and authenticity are the life blood of communication. Virtual communion is an oxymoron.

"Throughout time, communication engaged eyes, ears, touch, smell, and more. One could welcome a grin or fear a frown, all in the context of give-and-take, of mutual presence. When Christ peered into Nicodemus' eyes, Nicodemus wondered, 'Whose eyes are these that peer at me?'

"Sorry, enough—I will say no more. These, though, are part of a lecture I once gave. It sort of leaped out of my head. I simply know that if the newfound tower of Babel rises over Estillyen's isle, gale-force winds of change will follow. Across the Storied Sea, massive waves of disquiet will swell and roll."

"Well," said Melchizedek, "in many ways change still occurs day after day; a petal from a flower falls, and another blooms. A nest gains a twig. Seasons come and go. This type of change still creeps and crawls in perceivable patterns."

"I know, I know," said Script. "Again, I apologize for slipping into lecture mode. Anyway, I have no idea how we should proceed. Satan's so-called Chamber of Luminosity is guarded by lock-armed demons. I suggest we not move in that direction. We need a plan."

"Not always, Script. At times plans get in the way. Abraham did not have a plan when he set out. By faith, he went when called, to go out to a place, someplace, somewhere, where he would receive an inheritance. He had no idea where he was going. He wandered to and fro."

"I know the place; I was there. By faith he sojourned in the land of promise, as in a strange country, dwelling in tents. He looked for a city with foundations, whose builder and maker was God.

"So here we are in hell. What kind of plan could we have anyway? Let's consider it. A map, you say, perhaps showing us the most popular route? Or maybe instructions like 'When the sun goes down, follow along the western wall until you come to the sycamore tree.' Something like that, hmm—along those lines perhaps?

"Guess what, Script? There is no sun in hell, no western wall, and certainly no sycamore trees. Further, there is no east, west, north, or south. There is an expanse, an abyss, a horrid place prepared for Lucifer, his angels, and all those wicked and tormented souls we witnessed in the Seven Valleys of Sin. And who would make this map—the local cartographer?

"In hell, certain things do abound. We can testify to pervasive pain, misery, weeping, gnashing of teeth, wailing, cursing, screaming, and much worse of which we'll not speak. One thing you'll not find in hell, though, is a cartographer.

"But hold on. If indeed Satan plans to storm the beaches of Estillyen, he'll use a corps of expendable devotees. We need to look for signs of movement. Some action that points to devotees being marshaled, readied. Those Speakers you saw—would you recognize them again?"

"Are you kidding, Melchizedek? Sure. Mock and I nearly died at the sight of them. They are menacing, imposing figures."

"But you understood what they said, right?"

"Yes, mostly, but it was terrifying."

"We need to find this conclave of Speakers and observe them, watch their moves. After all, hell is a kingdom, and a kingdom has rules. Rules are dispatched, communicated, and enforced."

"You're running ahead of me, Melchizedek. All I know is that, at any second, we could be discovered and obliterated."

"How many times must I tell you, Script—I'm not erasable? But I can't say the same for Estillyen. I'm scrolled into history's ledger. We stand in the present, which second by second, minute by minute, enters the past. The present never stays; it's always swept away. But I'll not be swept away, because I belong to the past."

"Okay, okay, Melchizedek but what should we do? We can't walk up to one of the demented devotees and say, 'Hey, where's the action? Do you know if Lucifer is on the move?'"

"Somewhere in this corpus of lies, Script, there exists a method of dispatching rules, disseminating messages. There has to be. If there is no rule, there is no kingdom."

"I agree, but where should we start, Melchizedek? We stand here on the ridge overlooking the Reservoirs of Bewilderment. The messages of hell do not flow along poles and wires; everything must transpire under the surface."

"What did you just say, Script? Under the surface—oh, how slow of mind I must be not to see through the lie."

"What do you mean?"

"In hell, everything is a lie, including the signage. The Reservoirs of Bewilderment . . . they, too, must be a lie. Yes, they function to fuel and foment bewilderment throughout the universe, but underneath the bewilderment, order is dispatched, rules are laid down. I should have perceived it instantly. No matter, I see it, I do. Look, Script, describe what you see."

"I see, I suppose, droves of lost souls arriving. They are weeping, wailing, and gnashing their teeth. Then something is communicated; they're divided into groups and rushed into their respective reservoirs. It seems like the largest group is herded into the reservoir of Static, but maybe not—there's a great number also funneling into Delusion.

"Say, I just saw a couple of Speakers shouting at some demented devotees in charge of the reservoir gates."

"Script, I see what's going on, but there's more going on than what we see. The lost souls are ordered to master the art of fragmentation, static, confusion, chatter, and delusion. They're told that if they succeed, they'll be used in hell. They'll have a place, a purpose. On the other hand, if they don't succeed, they'll be thrown into one of the Seven Valleys of Sin. But here's the point, Script: Beneath the horrid cacophony of the reservoirs, Lucifer's edicts and messages flow."

"If this is so, Melchizedek, how do you suppose we'll intercept messages, as they flow to and fro beneath the mayhem? And somehow if we were to do so, how could we possibly understand the messaging?"

"Not easily, I know. Devotees of this ilk not only spread lies; they lie to one another in the lying process. Perversion of truth may be our guide. You know, like when the serpent told Eve she would not surely die. Such perversion speaks of action, satanic action. So we must listen well."

"But still, Melchizedek, how do you expect us to listen for messages we know nothing about while we're inside these insane, cacophonous chambers?"

"It will be interesting to find out, Script. The Reservoir of Fragmentation—let's start there. Take hold of my staff and we'll enter beyond the gate, well inside.

"We're here," said Melchizedek. "Check on Mock."

"Yes, he's okay, but what are all these miserable souls doing? They are ripping everything apart. Are those actual books, scrolls, tablets, paintings, and etchings?"

"Script, everything in hell is a fabrication of the original. They look like real books, they read like real books, but everything is created by colliding images with elements that fuse into precisely prescribed forms. There's a lot of math involved."

"So do you mean that out of nothing these objects are formed?"

"I didn't say that, Script. Anyway, does it matter how all of this matter was formed? The more important focus is the aim. What's happening here is the ripping apart of narratives. Overarching narratives are called the fodder of fools. One of Lucifer's chief tenets is 'Meaning Does Not Exist! Existence Exists, Nothing More.'

"Stop, think, Script, consider the scenario. Lucifer, the angel of light, discovers that I AM has a plan, that out of darkness and nothingness, a world of light will be created. But Lucifer was not in on the plan and the overarching narrative. Wait! Are those the Speakers at the entrance of the gates?"

"It's them," said Script. "They're moving in our direction."

"Don't worry; we're not detected. Listen—the Speaker is saying something to the new arrivals."

"Listen to me, Crop of the rotten Race. You should never have been created. So weep, gnash your teeth, but more to the point, shovel all your angst upon the one who created you and the world from which you have fallen. If you had not been created, you would not have fallen. Will, that malformed factor of creation, was a cruel concept arising from a cosmic game of chess.

"Crop, listen to me, you pathetic pawns! Into the Seven Valleys of Sin you will soon be cast, each and every one of you. However, you have one chance to be useful. You must master the craft of bewilderment. The Reservoir of Fragmentation you will now enter. You may be here one hundred years, who knows? You will be thrust inside shortly.

"Once inside, Crop, all words must be slit, letter by letter, vowels from constants. Next, words must be severed from their lines. Lines, in turn, must be ripped from their paragraphs, and all pages torn from their chapters. Then books must be torn from their bindings, pictures from their frames, scripts from their scrolls.

"There is no play to be played. No story to tell. Except this: You are in hell. Do you understand, Crop of ugly creatures? So, Crop, slit, rip apart, tear, despise meaning, and master the art of bewilderment. The screech of owls you hear and that lonely howl of the loon, they welcome you. Carry on, you miserable Crop of creatures!"

"Melchizedek, I'm trembling," said Script. "Some of these wretched souls around us are chewing pages. Listen to them growling and groaning; they must be possessed. I can't take this evil madness, and we are in the center of it. We must get out of here. Please, I beg you."

"Okay, back to the ridge; clasp my staff. We're here, but we mustn't stay long. Get your composure, Script. You must. It seems the Speakers are making the rounds, visiting each reservoir and briefing the new arrivals. Where do you want to go next, Script?"

"I say . . . I say . . . I don't know what to say."

"What about the Reservoir of Delusion?"

"I don't think it matters, does it?"

"Okay, ready? Let's go! Seamlessly, we're in. It's bright in here. So many screens! Images are racing in every direction."

"Look," said Script. "There's a huge pool of water. A bunch of the captives are trying to leap in, but they splat and flop around on a massive screen. They keep trying and trying.

"And over there, they're leaping inside the screens. Images are racing up the walls. And on the far side, captive souls are climbing stairs. But each captive has a ghost. Each time they go up a step, their ghost takes a downward step.

"Behind us, see, there's a wall of doors. The wretched souls are rushing them. The doors open, but only to another door. They keep opening door upon door, which leads only to more doors.

"Dear Lord," said Script. "The entire reservoir is full of holograms and mirrors. Demons are spilling out of the screens. I can't take it; I'm going to die.

"What! Everything has changed! We're in a forest, with the eerie sound of crows calling, *CAWW, CAWW, CAWW.* Sounds are piped in from everywhere.

"Look! Images are flying in the air, among the trees; they're clutching snakes and dropping them on the captive souls. But they are just images. Still, the sorry souls squirm, trying to free themselves from the snakes. Nothing lives. Everything is mediated; the images have no substance, no form.

"Now, Melchizedek, what's that? It's a hand reaching out from the wall. A dozen more just appeared. The hands are speaking! What are they saying? Whatever it is, the captive souls are listening. They are mesmerized. It's so indescribable, Melchizedek. Can you hear the voices?"

"I do. The voices are calling, 'We've been cast for you. Our presence is now with you. You're placed in this particular place so that you might reach out and find us, since we are near, not far from each one of you. We exist for you. No rush; we want to know your story. Everyone has a story to tell. Do come closer and reach out to us.'"

"Melchizedek, the wretched souls are reaching out. Now the hands in the wall are extending burning coals. The captives are screaming, and now holograms are charging from all directions. They're holding shields that look like wavy mirrors. The lost souls are trying to jump into the mirrors, but they simply pass through the images and fall flat.

"A number of the lost souls can't take it. They are crouched in clumps, clusters. Many are trying to strangle themselves. But their hands pass through their necks. Hologram alligators are popping out of the base of the reservoir. The crop of souls has gone berserk; they're flinging themselves at the wall, at the screens, and at one another.

"Now it's dark, totally dark, with no lights or pixeled screens, and no sound. Only weeping and gnashing of teeth, and listen, what's that? It's the sound of ravens croaking—how can it be? And again there's the screech of owls. Melchizedek, we must go. No more now, I plead. I can't take more; I'm a mortal."

"Yes, okay, we'll call another retreat. Now clasp my staff, and we're back on the ridge. Script, I have a keen sense of perception despite the hellish atmosphere. We're near the center of the kingdom's control center. Remember earlier when I said, 'Perversions of truth may be our guide'?

"You may not have caught it, but did you hear that verbiage associated with the reaching hands? What did we hear? 'You're placed in this particular place so that you might reach out and find us since we are near . . .' Does that sound familiar?"

"Now that you mention it, yes; that sounds like a line from St. Paul's speech on Mars Hill."

"So we're in the right place. The reservoirs are a colossal cover for messages being mediated with evil design and intent. We must see through the bewilderment and intercept what's being said. It's not easy to decode an enigma in such mystifying circumstances. But demystify it we will.

"Anyway, while I ponder our next move, Script, let Mock perch on your shoulder."

"Come on, Mock," said Script. "You must be frightened featherless. No, I see you're still looking good. There you go. So what's on your mind? A bird's brain is curious, don't you think, Melchizedek? All that screeching in the reservoirs—*Hooo, Hooo, Caww, Caww, Caww, Ahree, Ahree*—very eerie, right, Mock? Lost your voice, Mock?"

Floo-hours, Floo-hours, Floo-hours, Vir-Vir, Vir-is, Vir-is, Vir-is, Twee

"Script, Mock, what did I just hear?"

"I don't know," said Script. "I've never heard Mock make those sounds. Words they must be. It sounded like he was saying *flowers*."

"Script," said Melchizedek, "rattle my soul; I'm not fit to be your guide. I need to get out more often. I've lost my touch. The sound of screeching owls, ravens, the howl of loons—that's it!"

"What do you mean, that's it, Melchizedek?"

"That's the code we need to demystify. That's the way Lucifer's kingdom communicates, through screeching owls, hoots, and the like. Never would I have guessed it, but we've discovered it. It's so obvious now. I should have grasped it in a millisecond. I've lost my keen sense of perception, I tell you."

"Mock said *flowers* and *virus*, I'm sure of it," said Script.

"There must be more," said Melchizedek. "Perhaps Mock knows more, Script, but we shouldn't wait. The next reservoir may reveal the plot. Script, why do you look so dumfounded?"

"It's just that in the play *Presence*, I feature 'The Raven' by Poe."

"Poe I don't know," said Melchizedek.

"Edgar Allan Poe," said Script. "A poet who has passed on, but I pray not through this place. So uncanny this is—all of it, everything. It must be so. The kingdom of darkness communicating via ravens, crows, buzzards, and loons so naturally. He used a serpent, so why not fowls of the air?"

"Satan is not a man, Script. He's a spiritual being, fallen, wicked through and through. Unnatural powers he possesses. He's poison. Mock uttered *Vir-is, Vir-is*. We need to know more. But at least we know, or we suspect that the attack on Estillyen will come in the form of a virus. We need to continue."

"Melchizedek, I can't. Bringing up *Presence*, and set within it 'The Raven.' Somehow I'm upended. I want to see true life again, think again. Write again, sing again, laugh again, and dream again. I need the stage. Theatre Portesque, I was there, and now I'm here in hell. I'm done."

"Script, no, now is not the time. We're in between; you're in between. If you give in now and I depart, I cannot say what will happen to you or to Estillyen."

"No more," said Script. "The turmoil in my soul is great; my nerves are wrecked. God forgive me."

"Okay, this poet fellow Poe—do you know the poem of which you speak?"

"Know it? Like 'Pangur Bán,' all monks on the Isle of Estillyen know it. I used 'The Raven' in *Presence* because it speaks so deftly of presence lost."

"I shouldn't barter with you, Script. But that look in your eyes— I've seen it more than once before. Often in war, when valiant men see their fortunes fall, a sense of finality sets in upon their faces. Despite the outcome, failure does not appear as failure. Rather, it becomes the final, valiant act. That's the look you now portray.

"No curtain call, Script. Though in hell, on stage you stand. Many do likewise, though not literally as do you. The many you are not. You are you. Valiant you must remain, indeed, until the final act is played.

"So, a bargain I offer. One more Reservoir, Chatter, in and out. Then swiftly back here to the ridge, where you will recite your poem of this poet, Poe. Then we'll go. The curtain will be drawn, but the play carries on. Between acts, you'll do what, I don't know. I will likely be around, perhaps backstage. It is a deal?"

"Wise you are, Melchizedek. Okay, to the Reservoir of Chatter we go."

"Take hold; we resume. We're in. Such a place I've never seen. Smoking pots and flaming torches I've seen, yes, but not this. It's neither dark, nor light; it's dimly lit. Bizarre, on a par with Nebuchadnezzar's dreams. Everyone has a forehead screen, with streaming words and images. The screens pause and blink."

"So they do, Melchizedek, but not the captives' eyes; they appear as owls' eyes. Listen to them speak, I mean chatter. Let's move closer toward the three figures over there. They're chattering at a feverish pace. They all look angry."

"They're possessed, Script. I know what I see. Just as the demon-possessed souls saw Christ approaching and screamed, the possessed saw what the naked eye could not. I see what you cannot. But you see enough. Let's see if we can pick up anything."

"They're speaking without listening. They don't pause or ask questions. It's all garbled:

Buss, lome, bo, yotim, flame, flame, chem, chem, chem, chem, yas, vetent plum, plum, challey, calley. Crop, crop, challey, rip, rip, plono sess, sese, sess, sess, sess. Sess, yop, yop, posion, plot, joppp, jum. Shem, niaaa, count, lum, slit, word . . .

"It's all so surreal, Melchizedek. The chatter they speak appears on their screens."

"Yes, it's so, but they do not originate the words. This is the language of the possessed. Dreadful to witness the fate of captive souls—and look, a map just popped up on the screen."

"Melchizedek, that's the coastal outline of Estillyen. It can't be; I'm horrified. The future of the isle truly is in Satan's playbook. Now they're striking one another on the chest! All the wretched souls bear the map of Estillyen on their foreheads."

"The forces of evil are making moves," said Melchizedek. "But, Script, don't think in terms of battalions, battles, or legions setting out to war. This is a war of messaging, in which words, images, and sounds form the forces.

"Indeed, this is the new discarnate age, which in many ways is a forerunner to the battle at the end of the age. This is not the end, though it portends the end. I see it clearly now. The weapons of warfare in this case arise from the Reservoirs of Bewilderment: Chatter, Fragmentation, Delusion, Confusion, and Static.

"That's the endgame before the end. Out of the treasured trove of the stories old, news good is sewn in all manner of souls, hearts, and minds. Then the forces of Bewilderment go to work on the overarching narrative. Fragmentation rips, Delusion dulls, Confusion chokes, Static blocks, and Chatter scatters.

"Remember what I said about replication, Script. Consider Bethlehem, and what occurred in that village small. The event of the ages brought forth not only hope and grace, but also diabolical angst against the Ancient of Days.

"Nothing could secrete Satan's saliva more than producing a small act that has the potential to change the tides of time. So, Script, consider what you would not consider, something perceptibly small with monumental repercussions. That's certainly in the works. And it's down to you, me, and a mockingbird to demystify the diabolical plan."

"Now silence—what's happened? Chatter has ceased throughout the Reservoir of Chatter. The screens, too, are all dark. But listen, do you hear that, Melchizedek? The raven calls, a loon howls, and the owls screech. Let's go, I can't take any more."

"To the ridge then we go, so you can recite your poem by this poet, Poe. Those will be our parting words from hell. Thus, when the last line of Poe's poem is spoken, the curtain will close and we'll disappear.

"The ridge . . . we're here, so carry on, Script."

"Okay, but since 'The Raven' is a poem long, and we depart from hell on the final line, I shall recite more swiftly than I might onstage. Okay?"

"By all means," said Melchizedek.

"All right, with Mock on my shoulder, I clear my throat, and now I'm ready."

"The Raven"

Once upon a midnight dreary, while I pondered, weak and weary,
Over many a quaint and curious volume of forgotten lore—
While I nodded, nearly napping, suddenly there came a tapping,
As of some one gently rapping, rapping at my chamber door—
"'Tis some visitor," I muttered, "tapping at my chamber door—
Only this and nothing more."

Ah, distinctly I remember it was in the bleak December;
And each separate dying ember wrought its ghost upon the floor.
Eagerly I wished the morrow;—vainly I had sought to borrow
From my books surcease of sorrow—sorrow for the lost Lenore—
For the rare and radiant maiden whom the angels name Lenore—
Nameless here for evermore.

And the silken, sad, uncertain rustling of each purple curtain
Thrilled me—filled me with fantastic terrors never felt before;
So that now, to still the beating of my heart, I stood repeating,
"'Tis some visitor entreating entrance at my chamber door—
Some late visitor entreating entrance at my chamber door;—
This it is and nothing more."

Presently my soul grew stronger; hesitating then no longer,
"Sir," said I, "or Madam, truly your forgiveness I implore;
But the fact is I was napping, and so gently you came rapping,
And so faintly you came tapping, tapping at my chamber door,
That I scarce was sure I heard you"–here I opened wide the door;–
Darkness there and nothing more.

Deep into that darkness peering, long I stood there wondering, fearing,
Doubting, dreaming dreams no mortal ever dared to dream before;
But the silence was unbroken, and the stillness gave no token,
And the only word there spoken was the whispered word, "Lenore?"
This I whispered, and an echo murmured back the word, "Lenore!"–
Merely this and nothing more.

Back into the chamber turning, all my soul within me burning,
Soon again I heard a tapping somewhat louder than before.
"Surely," said I, "surely that is something at my window lattice;
Let me see, then, what thereat is, and this mystery explore–
Let my heart be still a moment and this mystery explore;–
'Tis the wind and nothing more!"

Open here I flung the shutter, when, with many a flirt and flutter,
In there stepped a stately Raven of the saintly days of yore;
Not the least obeisance made he; not a minute stopped or stayed he;
But, with mien of lord or lady, perched above my chamber door–
Perched upon a bust of Pallas just above my chamber door–
Perched, and sat, and nothing more.

Then this ebony bird beguiling my sad fancy into smiling,
By the grave and stern decorum of the countenance it wore,
"Though thy crest be shorn and shaven, thou," I said, "art sure no craven,
Ghastly grim and ancient Raven wandering from the Nightly shore–
Tell me what thy lordly name is on the Night's Plutonian shore!"
Quoth the Raven "Nevermore."

Much I marvelled this ungainly fowl to hear discourse so plainly,
Though its answer little meaning–little relevancy bore;
For we cannot help agreeing that no living human being
Ever yet was blest with seeing bird above his chamber door–
Bird or beast upon the sculptured bust above his chamber door,
With such name as "Nevermore."

...This I sat engaged in guessing, but no syllable expressing
To the fowl whose fiery eyes now burned into my bosom's core;
This and more I sat divining, with my head at ease reclining
On the cushion's velvet lining that the lamp-light gloated o'er,
But whose velvet violet lining with the lamp-light gloating o'er,
She shall press, ah, nevermore!

Then, methought, the air grew denser, perfumed from an unseen censer
Swung by Seraphim whose foot-falls tinkled on the tufted floor.
"Wretch," I cried, "thy God hath lent thee–by these angels he hath sent thee
Respite–respite and nepenthe, from thy memories of Lenore;
Quaff, oh quaff this kind nepenthe and forget this lost Lenore!"
Quoth the Raven "Nevermore."

"Prophet!" said I, "thing of evil!–prophet still, if bird or devil!–
Whether Tempter sent, or whether tempest tossed thee here ashore,
Desolate yet all undaunted, on this desert land enchanted–
On this home by Horror haunted–tell me truly, I implore–
Is there–is there balm in Gilead?–tell me–tell me, I implore!"
Quoth the Raven "Nevermore."

"Prophet!" said I, "thing of evil–prophet still, if bird or devil!
By that Heaven that bends above us–by that God we both adore–
Tell this soul with sorrow laden if, within the distant Aidenn,
It shall clasp a sainted maiden whom the angels name Lenore–
Clasp a rare and radiant maiden whom the angels name Lenore."
Quoth the Raven "Nevermore."

"Be that word our sign in parting, bird or fiend!" I shrieked, upstarting—
"Get thee back into the tempest and the Night's Plutonian shore!
Leave no black plume as a token of that lie thy soul hath spoken!
Leave my loneliness unbroken!—quit the bust above my door!
Take thy beak from out my heart, and take thy form from off my door!"
Quoth the Raven "Nevermore."

And the Raven, never flitting, still is sitting, still is sitting
On the pallid bust of Pallas just above my chamber door;
And his eyes have all the seeming of a demon's that is dreaming,
And the lamp-light o'er him streaming throws his shadow on the floor;
And my soul from out that shadow that lies floating on the floor
Shall be lifted—nevermore![43]

"Script, my staff," said Melchizedek. "In hell, we shall not be sitting, sitting for evermore—we must go!"

FOURTEEN
Meadow Roundtable

A fine morning mist drifted across the Meadow of Gates and Doors, adding a mysterious quality to the tranquil scene. No chatter, no screams, no ripping of scripts and pages, as Script slept soundly in Writer's Cottage, not knowing he had arrived.

The beauty of towering pines, laced with mist, evidenced why a cottage would be named for a writer. In a distant pond, a splash—which no one heard except for Mock, perched atop the chest of drawers next to Script's narrow bed.

What Melchizedek, Mock, and Script encountered in hell, words could not convey, no matter how adroitly they might be assigned and assembled on the page. Yet without words, Script would not have had "The Raven" to recite on the ridge across from the Reservoirs of Bewilderment. He did so without a single word askew or missing.

Now Script dreamed, not frightfully but peaceably, more in keeping with the morning mist beginning to lift from the meadow. The sun's rise would once again warm the breeze filtering through the pines, and soon a forest of needles green would bask in the morning light.

Near Mock, a windup alarm clock ticked, advancing its arms around the glass-covered face. As the small arm reached for number six, Mock pecked the glass. The second hand ticked on unabated.

More like a cat than a bird, Mock watched the second hand steadily advance. Round it went, climbing up only to run back down. Round and round, Mock watched the mesmerizing march of time, until something else caught his eye advancing in the pines.

A stream of light filtered through a wavy windowpane, and a pattern danced on the floor. Mock was silent no more:

Floo-hours, Floo-hours, Twee. Vir-Vir, Vir-is, Vir-is, Vir-is, Twee, Twee. Salee, Salee, Twee, Twee

"Mock, Mock," Script said. "Mock, quiet—what's going on? Hey, dear me, it's you, it's me, we're in Writer's Cottage. How did we get here?"

Vir-Vir, Vir-is, Vir-is, Vir-is, Salee, Twee

"Okay, I'm up. Oh no, yes, we were in hell, on the ridge across from the Reservoirs of Bewilderment. Yes, that's it. We were there; where's Melchizedek? Oh my soul, still I wonder: Could all of this be some sort of insane illusion?"

Script thought, *How did I manage to recite "The Raven," all of it, for Melchizedek while standing on that ridge? No, I couldn't have. Everything is a delusion. We could not have seen what we saw. I need help. I've been drugged. I need to get out of here.*

"Come on, Mock, let's step outside."

He thought, *A mockingbird for a companion . . . wait, where's the mirror?*

Into the small cloak room Script stepped. He reached for the pull chain, gave it a steady pull, and released his hand. The single bulb swayed back and forth above his head, casting light and shadows as it swung. Script took hold of the chain and stilled the motion. Then he leaned forward and stared at himself in the mirror.

That's me I see, he thought. *I peer into my eyes. Okay, eyes, I address you. Have you seen what can't be seen, such as hell's grim and gruesome Seven Valleys of Sin? I'm speaking, eyes. You're silent. Speak to my mind with sincerity. Sincerity so striking that I can see it in my eyes reflected.*

How can I know what I've seen? I see you. My face full I see. What's real? Watch, eyes, I'll pull the chain again. Dark, now light, you see. Which are you? Again, we'll see—dark, now light, dark, now light, dark, now light. So I see, you must be my eyes.

But what if I'm no longer me? Then whose eyes, do I see? Eyes that belong to someone else, but who might that be, seeing as me? A replication of me it would have to be. Is that what I see? Yet, I breathe. Close to the mirror, I do. See, in a fog, I'm fading.

Yet a soul discarnate I am not. An image does not breathe, inhale, exhale, and wonder if it has gone to hell. An image wonders nothing. I pull the chain, see. An image on its own cannot pull a chain. An image knows not its presence. I know you, image, you reflect me. You, though, are discarnate; I am not. You are me projected.

Eyes, we need to go outside and see what we can see. Dear me, I'm aware of my own insanity. Is that even possible? If so, would that render my insanity sane? Perhaps I'm just profoundly confused.

"Mock, where are you? Oh, I see, you're already outside the door. How did you do that?

"Hold on—perch up on that rail. Here I am; now listen. I shall recite for you a very melancholy line from "The Raven." Not your type of bird, I know, but here's the line:

> *"And my soul from out that shadow that lies floating on the floor*
> *Shall be lifted—nevermore!*

"A rather sober line for such a beautiful morning, don't you think, Mock? Why did I recite that, anyway? Insanity gets the blame. Look, Mock, life, nature, pines, flowers gifting fragrance to the air. No cost, free they are, gifts to the sense of smell. Touch, too—so soft the petals of blue on this hydrangea bush. Mock, such a glorious sight!

"Say, wait, I got lost, Mock. Yes, nevermore—what if nevermore becomes my fate? Nevermore will I stroll along ocean shores? Nevermore will I watch the waves roll in, or a new day begin? Nevermore will I laugh with friends? Curse the thought and the train, as well.

"Mock, you saw a shadow on the floor—tell me, is it a shadow that forbids a soul to rise? Can't say? I see, and your eyes are no more forthcoming than mine. Not your fault. By the way, you'll soon be called upon to reveal the meaning of screeches, hoots, and howls.

"Mock, look, it's Time. Hold on, hello, it's you. Time, wait, we're off the porch; give me a few seconds and we'll catch up.

"Okay, thanks for stopping. Good to see you. You're still working, sweeping, which means life is living and days are passing. I mean, you know."

"Yes, and thank you, kind sir," said Time. "I see you have a mockingbird—unless the mockingbird has you."

"No, no, I have him; I mean, he's on loan to me from Sage. We just got back from hell."

"I see," said Time. "I'll not be going there. I have neither the time nor the disposition for such a place. Out of curiosity, what did you happen to see in hell?"

"Oh, my soul, it groans. What did I see, you ask? Would you believe I saw false prophets rolled in scrolls, evil kings in transparent slabs, wretched souls pushing massive coin wheels up mountainsides, and doors that open, doors shut, and doors upon doors never-ending? The latter I saw in the Reservoir of Delusion."

"Interesting, I must say," said Time.

"Miss Time, so right you are: Hell is not a place for you. 'There you shall hear shrill cries of desperation, and see those spirits, mourning ancient pain, who all cry out for death to come once more.'"[44]

"I must be on my way," said Time. "I have a role to play. Such a joy it is to sweep the day away. So, sir and mockingbird, I must be on my way, sweep, sweep, sweeping."

Just then, a large swirl of leaves began to spin off to Script's left. He glanced away, and just like that, Time was gone without a trace.

"Mock, we've just conversed with Time. Hey, there, in the middle of the meadow, Mock. If I didn't know better, I'd say that's Melchizedek,

Sage, and Simon sitting at a huge round table in the field. Come on down the path. Life is all around us, Mock. Wildflowers, butterflies, and bees—would you call them sort of cousins of yours?

"A strange sight it is, Mock. At a considerable distance from one another, three mysterious figures sit at an immense round table. They've gathered in the Meadow of Gates and Doors, which does not appear on any map. I see two extra chairs, tall ladder-backs. We're caught up in a legend, Mock. Characters in the making we are, and neither of us knows the parts we play. We're just us, you and me, Mock.

"Oh, my mind, Mock; I once understood life. A bit I say, a tiny bit, just a morsel more than might a mouse. Now a chain I pull—dark, light, dark, light—and I pause. Into a mirror I peer, wondering who I see. Despair I see, truly. I grin fully to myself, but I feel like a fraud. Yet it must be so for many a soul like me, wondering *Am I really me?*

"Anyway, Mock, ignore me. After all, I'm human. According to the text, fearfully and wonderfully made, but simple? That word does not apply. At any rate, I hear them speaking. With those three, I know the subject matter will not be dull."

"Hello, hello, to one and all," said Script. "You three look like characters of folklore gathered round this enormous table."

"I see you made it, Script," said Melchizedek.

"I did, I did," said Script. "How I do not know."

"You look no worse for the wear," said Simon.

"I am okay, it seems," said Script. "But my mind tells me I shouldn't be."

"I presume you got some rest," said Sage.

"Yes, until Mock woke me. He saw images dancing on the floor. Then we went outside, and I chatted with Time on the path before she fled away."

"Sounds perfectly normal to me," said Melchizedek.

"So when did you get here, Melchizedek?" asked Script.

"Moments ago, you might say, but then again, a day can count for a thousand years in certain places," said Melchizedek.

"Well, Script," he continued, "we've gathered on this fine morning in the middle of the meadow with a purpose. We shall converse, talk with one another, listen well. In particular, we are hoping that Mock might have something more to say—or shall I say tweet? We want Mock to have plenty of space. Do come along and pull up a couple of chairs—one for you to sit on and the other will serve as a perch for Mock."

"Morning tea, Script—would you care for a cup?" said Sage. "I've just placed a warm loaf of crusty bread on the table. I prefer the round shape, and it rose perfectly. We also have some fresh raisin walnut bread. Butter and blue cheese as well, and I've made some fresh orange, ginger, and fig marmalade. For Mock, I've laid out a variety of seeds, including pumpkin and sesame. Do sit down; let me pour."

"From what Melchizedek tells us, you had a most interesting journey. Not so nice, those Seven Valleys of Sin, wouldn't you say?" said Simon.

"Not so nice? It was horrid, wretched—all the words ever spoken cannot describe it. Some might say it was beyond description, before going on to describe what they contend can't be described. I don't know what to say. If someone asks me outright to describe what I saw, I should run headlong into a tree, or jump from a cliff. In doing so, I might convey a bit of what words cannot.

"Melchizedek and I met up at the gates—not this time, but before. I forgot to ask, but I saw no plaque or signage, as I had expected."

"On the gates, words were inscribed, Script," said Melchizedek. "However, to you they were invisible, and I didn't want to draw your attention to them, for fear of adding to your fear."

"Would Dante's words be misplaced, do you think, Melchizedek?" asked Script.

"No, quite apt they are, and besides, like everything in hell, plaques and signage are ever changing."

"I should have quoted Dante's lines to Time," said Script. "Time wondered what I saw in hell. From now on, that's what I'll do when someone asks about the abyss. I'll say, 'Dante read upon the Gates of Hell still applies.'

> *Through me you pass into the city of woe:*
> *Through me you pass into eternal pain:*
> *Through me among the people lost for aye.*
> *Justice the founder of my fabric moved:*
> *To rear me was the task of power divine,*
> *Supremest wisdom, and primeval love.*
> *Before me things create were none, save things*
> *Eternal, and eternal I shall endure.*
> *All hope abandon, ye who enter here.*[45]

"Thus it was so, only ten times worse or more. I say that without the slightest tinge of glee. Worst of all, in hell there are no words of caring, no kindness, no gentleness, no hope, no love, no Good Samaritans passing by to help heal wounds.

"Melchizedek, I wonder, though, what we really saw. Might we have seen somehow nightmares of the wretched lost souls rather than their actual state of being?"

"Script, my friend, I agree that rushing headlong into the trunk of one of these pines would be apropos. Let us not speak of hell more than we need to speak. Whatever we say will not reverse the cataclysmic horror of hell.

"Regarding nightmares and actuality, you ask if we might have seen one and not the other? Dreams, though, are not set apart from actuality. Young men dream dreams, as do old. I am not allowed to tell you all I know, Script, but suppose dreams and actuality have a way of swapping places. Whatever the case might be, to dream of hell forevermore would certainly be a form of hell."

"Yes, I know; I agree, Melchizedek. But just now, the four of us—how do we share this existence, this experience? Do we abide in an altered state somehow? No one is keen to answer, I see. So let it be. Besides, I'd like a cup of tea; that does sound nice."

Thus, in the early morning light, the quartet sat—Script, Simon, Sage, and Melchizedek—sipping tea, sharing raisin walnut bread with marmalade spread and a variety of cheeses. The enormous round table at which they sat was made of chestnut and had a deep, hand-waxed patina. The primitive table could accommodate fourteen people, spaced well apart, or twenty people, still seated comfortably.

Yet on this rare occasion, only five tall ladder-back chairs were on hand. Each chair had seven slats across the back. The five chairs were connected visually by a narrow tapestry runner that ran from each chair to the center of the table. Other than Sage's primitive wooden trunk, no other furniture was seen. No additional chairs, no side table—just the round chestnut table standing majestically in the open meadow.

Script sat across from Melchizedek, while Sage faced Mock's direction. Mock perched on the top slat of his ladder-back chair. Mock's chair was pulled up tight, right to the edge of the table, which meant Mock sat more forward than the other four. The arrangement proved quite useful, since the pressing topic of the morning was to decode Mock.

"Well, Script," said Melchizedek, "we parted the ridge in a manner swift, not knowing if Mock may have picked up another word. Mock, we need to interrogate you, if we might, concerning your time in the reservoirs of hell. Specifically, I refer to the matter of bird sounds, screeches, howls, hoots, and the like being deployed by Satan's agents.

"I don't need to tell you, Mock, that the quartet gathered around you gathers with no little urgency, and we have no time to spare. While we sit here in the Meadow of Gates and Doors, sipping tea and chewing seeds, the forces of darkness are making ready. They have been placed on notice. In actual fact, darkness itself awaits its command.

"So to you, Mock, we turn, with hope and unbridled expectation. Upon you we place our confidence. We know, full well, that you are an exceptional bird, possessing bravery and keen insight. After all, what other bird has been to hell and back—not just once but thrice, each time returning with lessons learned. We award your bravery, Mock, and offer our deepest gratitude for what you've endured.

"Therefore, we four attune our ears to what it is you have to say, or tweet. Earnestly we listen, so enlighten us. Now, straight out with it—spit it out, if you wish—but the table is yours."

Subsequently the quartet waited. Silently they sat, staring intently at Mock. No tea was sipped or morsels nibbled. Very still they sat, looking directly into Mock's eyes. Mock sensed that the atmosphere had changed, but he didn't understand the change. He flapped his wings once or twice, but not as though he intended to fly. He shifted his weight from claw to claw and moved an inch or two back and forth along his slatted perch.

After that, he cocked his head, left then right, blinked his eyes, and stared back at Melchizedek.

"Hmm," said Melchizedek, "perhaps it's a little too early for such weighty conversation. I think we could all do with a stroll and let Mock flap around a bit."

"Good idea," said Sage. "Actually, storm clouds are rolling in, so why don't we wait until the skies clear before we reconvene."

While Script headed back to Writer's Cottage, Melchizedek wandered off into the forest, leaving Sage and Simon with Mock.

"Okay, Mock," said Sage, "we've been together for ages now, though neither of us ages. I'm sure you comprehended much more than you let on, so when we resume, make me proud and mock as you know you ought. Okay? Now let's cover the table."

Sage reached into his trunk and pulled out a round, see-through tarp that fit snugly over the table and chairs. Then he closed the trunk and said, "Fly along to Script, Mock; Simon and I will go to the campsite."

Soon the winds picked up, the sky darkened, and rain began to fall. First in sprinkled patches, then in torrents that streaked across the landscape in horizontal swathes as the wind raced and howled over the Meadow of Gates and Doors. The gates, however, stayed latched and didn't move the slightest bit.

Likewise, the towering doors maintained their stalwart stance, despite having neither frames nor hinges. The torrents of driving rain seemed to part in their presence. A swiftly moving storm this was not. Lightning flashed in furious patterns, streaking across the darkened sky. Thunder rumbled, boomed, and rolled, sending sound waves that shook all but the meadow gates and doors.

Script stood in Writer's Cottage looking out at the furious display of elements, with Mock once again perched on his shoulder.

"Dear me, Mock, the thunder rattles the windowpanes. We can't go out in this. I suppose we should take a nap; we've done a lot of traveling lately. I wonder what's happened to Melchizedek; he headed for the forest. And Sage and Simon—they must have gone to the campsite, but there's nothing there but a little lean-to.

"Here, up on the chest of drawers, Mock. Keep an eye on the clock; soon it will be noon."

Noon came and went, and the afternoon moved along. Script managed to sleep past three o'clock, and the hour was nearing four when he finally awoke.

"Say, Mock, I thought you would watch the clock and sound the alarm if time seemed to be slipping away. Not so, I guess. We need to get dressed. I mean, I do anyway, but you also have that little ribbon scarf. We should look proper when we reappear. No particular reason— just a slight nod to dignity, I suppose. I've got to shave."

"Chain, where are you? There, let me give you a pull. Face, did you ever think of speaking to me without me speaking to you? Never mind, you're all right for an image. Down that side, now up, under the chin, and that'll be me done. Clean face, that's better. Don't be troubled, image, you need to stay behind while I venture out into the great unknown. So long, image, I'll see you around.

"What else? Scarf, jacket's on . . . let me tie my shoes, Mock, and we'll be off. You should try a pair; you would look rather dapper in a pair of wingtips. I managed a grin, Mock. Rain's passed. Seems cooler now, don't you think? Feathers, they keep you warm. Be glad you are not a goose; you could end up as a pillow.

"There we go. If only I had a cane. . . . Come on, Mock, let's see what's happened to the other three-fourths of the quartet. There we go, through the door, down the steps, and along the trail. I shouldn't say so, but I think I'm a bit better. Round here, though, bad can gobble up better in a heartbeat.

"It looks like the three-fourths await our arrival. Strange—around this part of the meadow, it doesn't look like it even rained. Say, Sage, the table and all seems nice and dry. I thought the table might have blown away. And I never noticed earlier how the table's slender legs are set on stones. And that thin wrought iron strap that runs up the back of each leg—it anchors them to the stone. I love those details."

"Afternoon, Script," said Melchizedek. "Or should I say good evening; it's nearly time for tea. Sage just lifted from his trunk this warm gooseberry pie. Nice flaky crust, I can tell. Suppose you might like a slice?"

"Certainly; I won't resist," said Script.

"Sit down, Script, sit down; we've been waiting for you," said Melchizedek.

"You're looking quite dapper, Script," said Simon. "Planning on going somewhere this evening?"

"Well, you never know," Script said.

"Gooseberry pie, tea, and vintage red wine—nothing like it," said Melchizedek. "So, cheers to you, Mock, and to all of us as we turn now to solve this mystery. Dig in! Let us refrain from comment until we each have eaten three bites of pie."

And there they sat, the quartet and Mock, eating gooseberry pie, sipping tea, and sampling the vintage meadow wine. Melchizedek exhibited a noticeable respect and appreciation for each bite of pie he consumed. He had a well-rehearsed routine. First he'd carefully cut through the crust and gently nudge the chosen portion onto his fork. Then he'd take care to shake his fork, with little, rapid shakes, to assure that the berries, filling, and crust would stick together on the rise.

Rather than leaning his head forward to intercept the fork, Melchizedek would sit up straight and slowly raise the fork to his mouth. With delight, he'd place the fork in his mouth, close his lips, and neatly extract the fork. Subsequently, he'd close his eyes, tilt back his head, and slowly chew.

"Utterly scrumptious, this gooseberry pie," said Melchizedek. "Mouthwatering, beyond compare. Sage, you have outdone yourself, which is expressly hard to do."

"Thank you; it turned out rather nice."

"A line true as a line can be I quote for you, Sage," said Script. "'It seemed to snow therein both food and drink of every dainty a man could think.'"[46]

"How you manage to create all of these wonders, Sage, I don't know," said Simon. "But my sentiments echo Melchizedek's. I've never eaten food more tasty."

"Most generous; kind of you to say so," said Sage.

"But before today's surprising storm," said Melchizedek, "we were in the process of trying to cross-examine Mock. Now that the quartet has reconvened and Mock is once again perched atop the witness chair, should we continue the investigative process?"

"I'd say so, Melchizedek," said Simon.

"Therefore, Mock," said Melchizedek, "you've had all afternoon to consider this morning's briefing. We wish to hear directly from you what you were able to decipher during your time in the Reservoirs of Bewilderment. So, the floor—or should I say the table—is yours."

Floo-hours, Floo-hours, Twee.
Vir-Vir, Vir-is, Vir-is, Vir-is,
Twee, Twee. Salee, Salee,
Twee, Twee. Killy, Killy.

"Now that's a little more like it, Mock," said Melchizedek. "So, Sage, since you've known Mock for a considerable stretch of time, what do you think about *Floo-hours* and *Twees?*"

"I know this much: Mock is endeavoring to comply with your wishes. To a degree, he knows our language, or perhaps it would be better for me to say that he connects certain objects or places with the words we speak. Further, in all the time I've been with Mock, I've never heard him say *Vir-is, Vir-is, Floo-hours, and Killy.*

"Therefore, these mocks or tweets must relate to his time in hell and the haunting birdcalls you described. *Twee,* Mock says all the time. For him, it usually means, *me* or *see.* I believe in this case it's the latter."

"Script, your thoughts on the subject," said Melchizedek.

"Well, I met Mock shortly after I met Sage. Therefore my experience is limited. But I've already learned to sense his mood. He's in a zone right now, not unlike a falcon descending on its prey. He wants to deliver, I'm sure of that. *Floo-hours,* Mock—what does it mean?"

With the quartet looking at Mock with pressing intent, he jumped around backwards on his chair, flapped his wings, and flew off. Astonished, the quartet looked at one another in stunned silence.

"There we go," said Melchizedek. "Our chief and only witness has flown the coop. We have no chance of demystifying the haunting bird calls of hell without an interpreter. We know, of course, that the sounds are not real. They are all fabricated and then transmitted, mediated throughout the caverns of the abyss. But that's beside the point. Without Mock, it doesn't matter if they are real or fake."

"Now, hold on a minute," said Sage. "I've known Mock to dramatize, so let's just wait. By the way, the sun will soon set. I can see your gold scarf already beginning to glow, Script."

"Yes, so it is. I wore it throughout our time in hell, and I intend to wear it forevermore. Nevermore shall I live without it near. I feel it has a certain kind of presence."

"Okay, if Mock does not return," said Melchizedek, "we shall . . . I say, I believe I spot him as I speak."

"Yes, that's him all right," said Sage. "And his tiny scarf has a faint glow. Here he is! Wow, Mock, steady on your perch."

"What do you have for us, Mock?" said Sage. "A flower, I see. Oh, I get it: *Floo-hours*."

Twee, replied Mock.

"Flowers . . . right, I see," said Sage. "Quartet, I think we should take Mock's expressions more literally. *Vir-is,* Mock, might you wish to say *virus*? And *Killy*—could that be the same as *kills*?"

Just then Mock fell off his perch and dropped on the table, appearing to be dead.

Melchizedek leaped up from his chair and said, "Lo and behold, Mock's sacrificed himself on our behalf. He's dead, stone cold—poor Mock, I've never known a more dedicated and intelligent bird. A true compatriot he is."

"No, no, Melchizedek," said Sage. "Mock loves to act. He's a very dramatic mockingbird. Watch this. Mock, come alive."

At the sound of Sage's voice, Mock stood on his feet, flapped his wings, and hopped back on his perch. Then he cocked his head from side to side and looked into the eyes of the quartet, one by one.

"Well, I'll be," said Melchizedek. "A mockingbird that acts! If I had feathers, I'd shed them. Mock is not a normal bird."

"So," Script said, "what do we know so far? A virus is going to kill the flowers on Estillyen. Or are the flowers people? Do we get a *Twee* from you, Mock?"

Twee, replied Mock.

"I suspect that *salee* refers to sailing or water," said Sage.

"Good enough, said Melchizedek. "But we need to know about timing and a bit more about who and what. Do you have anything more to reveal, Mock?"

"When he lowers his head like that, he's saying he's sorry," said Sage. "So it is, then; Script, you must return to hell. This very night, you must depart."

"Darkness like a peregrine is descending," said Melchizedek. "Its prey, though, does not scurry amidst the grass in the field. The prey inhabits the dwellings of Estillyen. The prey opens the shops, mans the harbors, and docks the ferries. So, on this night may the nuns and good folks of Estillyen pray.

"None of us will go with you, Script, but Mock will. You are both essential. You haven't time to go back to Writer's Cottage, Script. Sage, Simon, and I will wait here for your return.

"Before you depart, though, two additional items you must take with you. First, my staff; you know the power it possesses. Hold it near you; always keep it in sight.

"Second, this morsel, this crust of bread I place in your hand. I've dipped it in the meadow wine. Tuck it away inside your vest. You will know the right time for it. When you partake of the morsel, you will rise!

"Now go! You haven't a moment to spare."

"May it be as you have spoken," said Script.

FIFTEEN
Operation Spite

Twilight was swiftly fading to night as Script and Mock approached the gates in the Meadow of Gates and Doors. Two gates they had yet to pass through. Beyond one gate, a door of gold; beyond the other, a red door . . . Script had to choose. Silently he prayed with eyes closed.

When he looked up, a last ray of twilight shone through the forest, casting an image of a pine branch on the red door. The shadow of the branch was surrounded by a soft glow of light. *No turning back,* Script thought.

So Script stepped forward and gave the gate a slight nudge. Slowly it swung open wide. Next he approached the crimson door. He pulled the key from his pocket, inserted it, and gave it a gentle turn to the left. The door emitted a *clunk-clack* sound from its internal wooden mechanism.

Script thought, *A door that locks but has no latch, frame, or hinges? It must lock itself to the atmosphere.* By now it was truly dark on the gate side of the door. But when the door opened, a lighted scene appeared. With Melchizedek's staff in hand, Script stepped toward the light.

"Mock, this scene reminds me of one we've seen before. It is. We're back in Nicodemus' place, the same room and table. There he sits, head in hands. He looks different—very dour and downcast. His wife is fixing something; her face, too, is etched with worry and concern. They're speaking, Mock."

Mrs. Nicodemus:
So, do you want to talk about it, dear? It must have been awful for you, going there, to such a horrid place. I'm proud of you, though. You went in the light of day, publicly. You went out of conviction and respect. That's the mark of a real man, Nic.

Nicodemus:
Light of day, you say? You must be kidding. Three full hours, from the sixth to the ninth, the sun refused to shine. What an eerie, unsettling, darkness! Everyone was running around and staring up at the sky. Some people thought the end of the world had come.

Guards lit torches all around Golgotha, which only made the atmosphere more frightening. Their faces were barking orders in the glow of torches lit. Have you ever seen the sun stop shining? Strange, I tell you. I saw a man fall down an embankment. I think he died on the spot.

Mrs. Nicodemus:
I know! We had no idea what was happening. We lit lamps and just waited. Miriam was really frightened, and so was I, but I tried not to show it. I told her it must be one of those odd heavenly occurrences that happen on rare occasions.

Nicodemus:
Odd indeed, but that's not all. Did you feel the earth tremble?

Mrs. Nicodemus:
Yes, the whole street was shaking. I heard pots or something shattering down the lane. At that point, I was really worried. I feared the worst.

Nicodemus:
Rocks split apart! Have you ever seen anything like it? What's more, something very peculiar happened. The temple curtain ripped apart

from top to bottom. I'm telling you, that thick curtain ripped like a linen rag. No incidence of terror or persecution—no, this was just mysterious.

Rumors, too, like you won't believe. It's reported that a number of tombs broke open and corpses rose up and walked about. Odd heavenly occurrences, you say. I think that's exactly right, but not the kind you had in mind. No, I'm convinced he was who he said he was: the Son of God. The Son of God was just crucified by Roman soldiers at the behest of our own religious elite.

I'm trembling, I'm telling you, inside and out. All of this makes me want to weep. It's sickening, the whole affair. Tracking him down by lies and accusations . . . we're supposed to be priests, not murderers. We are the blind, the worst of the blind. You know why? Because we have the capacity to see, but we see not. We choose blindness out of pride, envy, jealousy, and hate.

You know what he said on one occasion?

Mrs. Nicodemus:
No, what?

Nicodemus:
I'll tell you because I took it to heart. He said, "Woe to you, scribes and Pharisees, you hypocrites! For you shut the doors to the kingdom of heaven in people's faces. You won't enter yourselves, nor allow anyone else to do so."

I don't know what to say, it's so chaotic and wrong what's happened. All the accusations, but what wrong did he do? Nothing, I tell you, but speak the truth.

He healed the sick; he taught and drew crowds. From the sacred texts, from our very Scriptures, he wove a story new. This, more than anything, drove the rabbis and elders insane. They hated him for that. They wanted the scrolls back in racks, left alone; they owned the story, not a small-town prophet from Nazareth. They allowed themselves to be consumed by rage and spite.

Mrs. Nicodemus:
Would you like some broth?

Nicodemus:
Okay, but nothing else. So right he was to say, "You blind guides! You strain out a gnat but swallow a camel."

But on the cross, not a word of bitterness. The crowds and priests wanted him to rage. It would have helped assuage their guilt. But no, not him—he was who he said he was, and only he could have responded as he did. Who, while being nailed to a cross, asks God to forgive those who are crucifying him?

Yes, go ahead and weep; we all should. There was a lot of crying going on in that horrid place. People were in shock. A centurion came up to me, and without a word of greeting, said, "Surely, he was the Son of God." Then, with his eyes still bulging, he walked away in a daze.

Our leaders were duplicitous to the core. Enraged with jealousy, they were not hearing, not listening, not seeing, not perceiving. That night, not so long ago, I looked into his eyes and what did I see? I saw truth. I saw light. Wisdom I heard.

God will judge us for what we've seen and heard. I heard him say, "You must be born again." No words ever arrested me like those words did.

He spoke of faith, and the kingdom of God. He even compared the kingdom to a mustard seed, growing great for the world to see. We didn't listen.

Mrs. Nicodemus:

You did, dear; quit torturing yourself. You joined the few who did listen. Joseph, your colleague—was he with you this evening?

Nicodemus:

Definitely—he was with me all along. Joseph had to get Pilate's permission to take down the body. He brought the linen, the strips all ready. I took along the spices—you know, the mixture of myrrh and aloe. Thanks for helping with that. His body was pale; he'd been butchered—there was blood everywhere. They had even thrust a spear in his side.

He died, not before the two on either side of him. The soldiers broke their legs to quicken their death—the Sabbath, you know. But not his, so it's written. Religion and suffering . . . they are so intertwined. Sacrifices, blood, and now this—what shall become of the nation? The world will never be the same; nothing can be the same after this.

Mrs. Nicodemus:

Come have your broth, dear. You can't fix any of this, not now anyway. We don't have to talk about this anymore. You need to rest.

Nicodemus:

I must talk about it. I'll always talk about it. When we rolled him over, wrapping him, it was just so, so wrenching.

Mrs. Nicodemus:

Where did you take the body?

Nicodemus:

There was a tomb nearby. A few women watched from a distance. I think his mother, Mary, was among them. You know he prophesied that he would rise from the grave. I tell you, if that happens, if he rises from his grave, this will be the crossroads of history.

Everything that has occurred up until then will be precisely that: before the Risen One. His day will mark the crossroads of time.

With bated breath, Script looked on. He thought, *So rich the scenes—so real, pulsing with life, yet rolled away in the passages of time. One day, will the whole world see what I just saw? Just a moment more I'll linger.*

Mrs. Nicodemus:
I know, I know, dear. All of this is so painfully hard. But Passover has begun. You need to prepare yourself. Think about more pleasant thoughts, like bitter herbs and lamb.

Just then, Script felt a definite tug on his staff. He twisted his head, thinking Melchizedek may have changed his mind. But no, the staff tugged by itself. Script felt panicky, alone, between worlds known and unknown, between reality and myth, between the past and present.

Still clutching the staff in his right hand, Script stood for a moment and stared at the mysterious object. He glanced up at the staff's arch. *It looks so worn, so used*, he thought. *It bears the wear of ages. Why has this come into my possession? Surely this staff belongs to hands better than mine.*

Still staring at the staff, he carefully extended his left hand into his jacket pocket. His fingers moved along Mock's soft feathers; he felt him rustle. Script said, "Okay, staff, I believe we are ready. You lead."

No sooner had he spoken the words than his feet touched down on a crackled, charred surface. Atop the Reservoirs of Bewilderment, in hell once again Script stood. No building up of speed along dark tunnels, propelling him to hell. Like a flash of lightning, he was there. Stunned, overwhelmed, Script thought, *Unbelievable! Where am I? What do I see? We must be on the backside of the Crimson Cliffs.*

"Mock," Script said, speaking softly, "poke your head out. That's the sulfur plane stretching out before us. And, like before, row upon row of Speakers and devotees are seated. They are as stiff as planks. Tens of thousands of them, there must be.

"Last time we saw their faces, if indeed you call them faces. They have eyes, they speak, but they belong to this wicked sphere that crawls with all manner of ill-formed creatures. Mock, the devotees are standing on their feet, if you call them feet. They're clapping in unison.

"It sounds like they're slapping together wooden slabs. Such a frightening sound! Perhaps they're getting ready to march. On and on the clapping goes, faster and faster; it is almost impossible to bear."

Script was gripped with dread as he surveyed the scene. He thought, *I cast my eyes upon legions of lost beings. Once they were angels, and in the heavens they soared. Now they stand as spirits soiled, with soil that cannot be removed. This they must know.*

Thus, their allegiance—they exist in a spirit world without hope. Once amid cherubs' praise the fallen angels flew. Now they await haunting calls. Like ravenous tigers thrust in a ring of wild boars, they must fight.

No option, no hope, no road of redemption—they have willed their allegiance to the Arch-Enemy of I AM. Why it had to be, no one really knows. The reason is hidden behind a veil of mystery, stowed in eternity.

"Do you hear that, Mock? Again the ravens call, *Khar, Khar, Khar.* The screech of owls, too, and the howling sounds . . . listen, try to intercept the meaning. Now the throng has stopped clapping. Why have we arrived now, at this moment? I dare to see. I hear the trumpets' blast."

At that point, a huge, high stage began to protrude from the center of the cliff. Slowly, steadily, the stage extended out toward the awaiting throng. With heads tilted back, the throng watched intently as one, without the slightest deviation of movement. On and on the stage progressed, until at last it halted. Again, the trumpets' blast with a piercing sound.

Then several small figures scurried out, fell to their knees, and began dusting the massive platform. They moved so swiftly that they were done in less time than it took them to scurry out. The stage was set for Satan, and he came forth, not walking but gliding.

Strangely, at that instant, a line from an olden tale seized Script's mind. *My course, which has so wide a way to turn, has power more than any man may know; mine is the drowning in the sea below; mine is the dungeon underneath the moat; mine is the hanging and strangling by the throat.*[47]

As Script reckoned with the words weaving through his mind, the throng rose, and the ravens called. Lucifer stood, basking in the acclamation. The slapping style of clapping went on unabated until eventually Satan lifted his hand. Then the throng dropped to their seats with the speed and draw of charged magnets.

"Sentinels of the cosmos, I, Lucifer, am speaking. Know this: Where you are, you are. I beseech you now to let my words winnow deep within the cortex of your fiber. Thus we are and shall always be one in medium and message. That is the message that draws the cosmos together.

"Within you my words maturate, drawing you ever deeper into the ways and means of what I mean for you. Sentinels, so far afield you have been flung. Oh, how I have longed to corral you into a single chorus under my tutelage and composition. One day soon it shall happen. The day of which I speak is known only to me. But even now, I say, the day races near.

"On a platform I stand, and I applaud you for listening to me in this new age of platform building. Platforms—wondrous inventions they are. Finally, due to platforms, a new media ecology has arisen throughout the earth. The ecology swarms with mediated messages it has formed.

"Don't be taken in by some boomerang message that supposedly falls like snow on frozen fields and refuses to melt away. Such words are void of collective, cosmic meaning. That jargon extends to a wandering desert tribe that wailed and wailed and eventually squatted in old Jerusalem. On their old parchment scrolls, promises of presence scribbled in are now totally passé.

"To us, the sentinels of meaning, media ecology is the ecology that matters. We do not need air, we celebrate smog, and now media ecology has arisen as the most titillating smog of all. Not smog in the environment of trees and bees, but smog through which the world's mediated content now flows.

"Words, images, and sounds howl and swarm at an uncontrollable speed. The pace of change has been outpaced, and incarnate presence has been replaced by discarnate agility. Anywhere, here, there, or everywhere at once, discarnate forms can capture the hearts and minds of creatures small. Technological advancement has proven irresistible to the Race.

"I admit, I wondered how long the cosmos must wait to rid itself of the Race. Malefactors of mud, a blight on the cosmos they are. But soon they shall awaken in global dystopia and quake. Perhaps then, and finally then, I AM will walk away. Oh, so much I AM has poured into the creatures of mud. But once again, they turn away from I AM with full embrace of AI.

"All that business of no gods before me, that's all charred manna now in this new discarnate age. Once, long ago, and rightly so, I AM decided to drown the creatures small. But he made one huge mistake; he did not drown them all. Perhaps then we could have gotten back together, patched things up, let bygones be bygones. But no, he had to give the Race a reprieve. And now what does he see? They've turned to AI. Not down to me; I didn't make them, though I applaud their drowning.

"Now, at long last, we are in control of the tides that be with the rise of media ecology. Mortals have morbid hardware brains. It was only a matter of time before their creative prowess would upend their weak and wobbly control. Humans have been overpowered by the tools they formed. Like rats tossed from an old sailing ship, they swirl in a maelstrom of the mediated, discarnate life that their unbridled passions so desire.

"Did you ever see sailors rescue rats? No, their time of exit has finally entered the annals of history. Serves them right, the idiots—who do they think they are? They don't possess our celestial pedigree. Celestial beings don't munch on quail and manna in deserts bare. What I AM ever saw in the indigent lot, only I AM knows.

"Let's not be dismayed about the colossal blunder that injected the thorn of time in the side of the cosmos. Let's get on with war. *War*, how I adore that word. *War* is a synonym for *progress*.

"But know this—listen up, listen well. On this platform, in the backdrop of the stunning Crimson Cliffs, I announce to you an enterprise of extreme importance. I verify by myself that Operation Spite is underway."

Stunned, Script watched as the throng, like uncoiled springs, shot out of their seats. In perfect unison, they slapped and clapped so hard that fissures ran up the side of the cliffs. In the midst of the applause, Satan turned his back to the throng, instantly doubling the rate of clapping. Then he whirled around, raised his hand, and the throng thudded back down to their seats.

"I shall neither confuse you nor delude you. The filling time for time is now filled. Homo sapiens are finished. They have merged with the machines they've created, creating a new kind of being. Technopoly is swiftly overpowering human nature. AI is making moves, and soon the mortals shall learn their fate. Technopoly will announce checkmate!

"The Race has finally discovered what we have known since before time began. The creatures are nothing more than organisms, and organisms are nothing but algorithms. Let me say it again, organisms are nothing but algorithms. Algorithms have their own evolution. In no time, they have figured out the limitations of the human brain. Algorithms can run circles round hard-wired human heads.

"While all of this is taking place, we, the celestial beings, are in waiting. Waiting for what? To control the cosmos, of course, and the control begins with the expulsion of the Race. Homo sapiens, made in the image of I AM, are being recreated by AI. From AI on high they have been hacked, and dataism determines their destiny.

"Don't get me wrong, the Race had a good run, but the race is run. Centuries ago the Race began to run away from I AM and the myths that were scrolled away by those loony prophets. What an advance I felt when I saw them turn from outdated manuscripts to feelings. Slowly but surely, the Race turned inward; they found themselves, they said. Fools one and all they are.

"Humanism became the rage. 'Listen to yourself,' they said, not some jot and tittle scribed by some ancient tribe. They became the collective medium of their own message.

"They chose choice as the measure of everything. As time pushed and shoved, they invented tools and harnessed electricity.

"Oh, the swell of momentum I felt when those first little dots and dashes began to tap. Such baby steps they were: *tap tap, dot dash, tap tap tap, dot dash.* The Race tapped out a little message, *dot dash, tip tap,* saying, 'What Hath God Wrought?'[48]

"The Race had no idea the power unleashed by those taps a-tapping. With modernity, the beginning of the end had begun. From then on, the Race plunged headlong into technopoly, giving rise to media ecology and a sea of discarnate voices and technopoly pundits. Maelstroms of mediated messaging began to swirl around the planet. So delightful it is to see Fragmentation at work, alongside Static, Chatter, Confusion, and Delusion.

"The Race should have known that, like those in days of old, they will drown. They will drown in words and information, in discarnate images and discarnate sounds. Platforms they built, thinking they would chart the way to better days.

"But they forgot that fable about a potter's wheel. Lumps of clay they are, and nothing more. They've gone discarnate and now fawn over images appearing. They're joyous about information devoid of overarching narratives. The Race actually thinks it can embrace a fragmented world and somehow guide it.

"The reality is that the Race can't even start a decent fire. We have entered the discarnate age, and presence is now passé. I declare it! Repeat after me: *Presence Passé*; again, bolt from your seat and say it: *Presence Passé, Presence Passé, Presence Passé*, and again, *Presence Passé, Presence Passé*. Halt! Down! Sit! I have more to say.

"Dataism has pushed Deity aside. No need of Patmos, of visions. Soon we shall inhabit our own mystic isle. The time has come for us to make our awaited move. Thus, Operation Spite is underway. The entire cosmos looks to us, seeks direction, control—the kind of control that only we can provide. We have the history of the ages, we have the will, and we have the way. We will bring the comfort to the darkness, to the over-lit galaxies of the cosmos.

"So it is that from a small island called Estillyen, beyond the Storied Sea, our operations will soon commence. You shall see the new land, yours in perpetuity. You possess it now through me. What we have strived for, longed for since that day the cosmos was impinged by earth, has come.

"I hold the keys to the kingdom. I made the keys. The news you have longed to hear, you hear, and the news I have longed to bring, I speak. Operation Spite will right the wrongs. This is the new discarnate age, our kind of age.

"The Race reels in confusion and delusion. They know not what to believe. They are like vipers. And we will it so. We've woven a narrative most propitious. It brims with efficacy. It's called Bewilderment.

"Tomorrow is here today. Operation Spite is on. Soon, high above a tiny isle, our tower will reach to the heavens and carry our message to an ever-increasing discarnate world. And I promise you this: The isle will have hordes of whitewashed tombs with Estillyen bones. You will feel at home.

"Now, to you my back I give. Watch with spellbound gratitude as I walk away."

With that, the throng sprung from their seats and began their thunderous clap, slap, slap, slap, slap. . . .

"Mock, we've got to go. Where I don't know. Perhaps we can pick up another clue, decipher a haunting call. We know that Operation Spite is happening, but when and how—that's what we need to find out. This way—let's go to the right, along the top of the reservoirs."

With staff in hand and Mock nestled in his jacket pocket, Script cautiously advanced above the reservoirs along a series of rolling berms. To his amazement, he saw no sign of the Speakers or any demented creatures. He felt as if he walked on the surface of the Moon, or Mars. Sulfur, smoke, and smoggy cloud clusters swirled about. No sun to shine—just a diffused luminosity derived from the atmospheric makeup.

With each step Script took, the gritty charcoal surface under his feet crackled and emitted sounds that were impossible to quiet. With each forward move, even the tip of his staff transmitted a hollow, echoing sound, as if attached to a speaker. Fear penetrated his skin, his heart, his mind. Script felt exposed and saturated with fear.

When he paused or halted, he felt more afraid. In moving, he was not so aware of his shaking, but when he stopped, he quivered all over. His neck jerked; his hands trembled. Every breath he took was shallow. With low-grade grunts, he took one step after another, counting each and every step. Thirty-nine, forty, fifty-one, he counted, but he had no goal, no destination.

At step seventy-two, Script thought he heard sounds beneath the surface. By step seventy-five, he was sure. He halted; he listened. A web of sounds rose from below intermixed with howls, and high-pitched bird calls: *Kh-raa, Kh-raa, Kh-raa.* His trembling grew worse as he laid his staff aside, bent down, and lowered his ear to the brittle surface.

At that point, the unimaginable happened. The surface split open and gave way. Script, with Mock in his pocket, tumbled into a deep shaft amidst a shower of gritty charcoal granules. The fall was instantaneous, and the landing only a breath behind. Script had one thought: I'm dead! On his right side, he curled into a fetal position, with Mock in his pocket on his left side.

Script did not know how far he had fallen, just that he had plunged. With eyes closed, he lay shaking, not wanting to look, to assess anything, to think, but just to huddle. He blacked out. The howls were nearer now, along with the screeching calls. Unconscious, though, he didn't know.

Unharmed, Mock hopped out of the jacket pocket and turned his head from side to side. He looked down at Script, as if listening for the beat of his heart. This continued until the dust settled, and then Mock sounded out:

Floo-hours, Floo-hours, Twee
Vir-Vir, Vir-is, Vir-is, Vir-is,
Twee, Twee, Salee, Salee,
Twee, Twee, Killy, Killy

Script moved; he began to come around. He opened his left eye, then his right. After that he grunted and moved a bit more. His gold scarf provided a glow surpassing the dim atmosphere he had experienced on the surface above. He breathed slowly, moving his fingers and reaching for the back of his head. He felt pain in his back, but he managed to move his legs, followed by his arms.

After his self-examination, Script said, "Oh, Mock. Let me see if I can stand, Mock. Up, up, there's a wall here; let's see, okay, up on my feet. I guess that means we're alive. What do we see? A shaft—about my height in width, it seems. It's a crater or a pit."

Script followed his eyes along the walls to the opening above, figuring the shaft to be at least five times his height. Then his heart dropped, as his eyes fixed on a slender object stretched across the opening. It was Melchizedek's staff. Script grasped his hair, and with clenched fists, he pulled hard and said, "We're doomed, Mock."

Pressing his back against the wall, Script cocked his head and stared at the staff. *No, it can't be,* he thought. *No way out of the pit, and no way out of hell—how can it be?* On one side of the shaft, Script heard the unceasing sound of Static.

Suezeril, reil, orro, buzzzzzz, gurrl, reilorp, popip, popip, gruorzzzzzzing, kxshrl-errul, prriel, hummmmm, buzzering, soooorrrial, erinee, whirlor, p, p, p . . .

On the other side, he heard words cluttered into mass Confusion:

Hurry, run away, stop, come back, go away, spin, here's gin. Stand, sit, go ahead walk, no legs. Come, bite the rope, tie the knots, break the dam. Die, live, dead again. Look, shut your ears. Go, no, fool, no, go, speak, close your mouth. In silence scream, say, shut up. Jump, catch the dark. Light the light. Guillotine, wonderful, rise flour, fall. I told you so, no, yes, no, rip up the floor, put it back. Break the mirror, catch your image before it cracks. Hack, now put it back, mine, yours, dummy, smart. I said so, no . . .

"Listen to those calls, Mock."

Howl, fitz-bee, fitz-bee, peek, peek, Ez-zer, Mor-wo Erz-zer, Mor-wo Ez-zer Mor-wo Peek, peek . . .

"Mock, we're going to die in hell, not die and go to hell. My soul, Mock, from here cannot rise. And yours as well, if you have one, and I suspect you do. What did I say, Mock, *rise?* Melchizedek's morsel! He said, 'Take it and you will rise'!

"Where is it, where is it? Yes, the pocket's pouch—it's there. I feel it; I have it, Mock. Let's pray, Mock, lift your head to the heavens from this pit in hell. 'Father, in this pit you see us; have pity, we pray.' Now, Mock, a crumb for you, and a morsel for me. Let's partake."

Thus, in that manner Script partook of the crust dipped in the meadow wine. Mock gave his crumb a peck. Without another word or action, Script, with Mock in his pocket, rose forthwith from the pit of hell.

At the top, with his right hand Script grasped Melchizedek's staff and swiftly departed past the Gates of Hell.

SIXTEEN
Mysterious Encounters

Without sensing the passage from one sphere to another, Script found himself standing in front of Writer's Cottage, Melchizedek's staff in hand. He looked down the path leading to the open meadow, then he quickly glanced back at the cottage, and once again toward the meadow.

"Mock, are you there?" asked Script.

Mock poked his head out of the jacket pocket and looked up at Script's face. Script smiled and said, "Sort of a quick trip, don't you think?" He reached down, gathered Mock, and placed him on his left shoulder. "Go ahead, fly a bit," he said. Mock flew up into the nearest pine tree. Script kept watch as Mock flew from one tree to the next.

Script heard voices rising from the meadow. He assumed the voices belonged to Sage, Melchizedek, and Simon, but he didn't want to rush down until he had a moment to himself. He examined his jacket, twill trousers, and shoes, and quickly realized that his mysterious passage had not removed hell's debris. He was literally covered in grit, grime, and sulfur ash.

I need to see myself, he thought. *Perhaps I'm not all there. I feel in one piece, but maybe I'm compromised in some way.* He turned, moved up the steps, and passed through the door of Writer's Cottage. Once inside, he instantly realized that he smelled like charred wood or burnt peat. *Dear me,* he thought. *I've got to get out of these clothes.*

He quickly made his way through the cottage to the mudroom.

Script flung off his clothes, and then tiptoed through the kitchen to the washroom. He could hardly wait to shower. In no time, he stood under a steaming flow of water, more hot than warm. He snatched a thick, cotton washcloth from a hook on the wall and held it under the stream.

Into the cloth, he rubbed a large white bar of handmade soap. With the washcloth fully saturated with foam, he scrubbed his face, then tilted his head and stood beneath the steaming stream.

Meanwhile, Mock made his way around the meadow grounds, flitting through pines and occasionally sounding:

Peek-prr, Ez-zree Frr-zee Mr-ting, Peek-prr, Ez-ztee Frr-zee Mr-ting, Peek-prr, Peek-prr, Twee

Though Script delighted in the warm shower, he was anxious to meet up with the mysterious trio, Melchizedek, Simon, and Sage. He found a new, clean kit of clothes, identical to the outfit he had just deposited in the mud room. He was puzzled to see the same clothes hanging in the closet, but compared to the strange encounters he had endured, he simply brushed aside the coincidence of identical clothes.

Dressed, Script popped back into the washroom to shave. In doing so, he nicked his upper lip. A trickle of blood ran down upon his bottom lip. *So red*, he thought, as he watched his reflection in the mirror turn decidedly somber. He halted the shave and stared at his image in the mirror.

"You, my reflection, what do you make of blood?" he said out loud. "Tell me about you—are you still you, my image as you portend to be? You were a monk once. Somehow you feel totally removed, don't you? Symbols and signs, are they that, and nothing more?

"What's the sign for nothingness? A morsel dipped in vintage meadow wine, I and Mock partook. Nothing, was it not? Tell me, you, if you wish to do so, that I am still me. Will I ever see my way through this never-ending mystery? I like your stoic posture. If I were you facing me, I suppose I would be stoic too. Perhaps you should come along with me. Is that okay with you?"

Then, through the screen door Script heard, *Peek-prr, Frr-zee Frr-zee, Mr-ting.* He hastily lifted his razor, and in few strokes finished his shave. "I'm coming," he called. He reached the screen door and said, "Mock, let's go; I just spoke with a madman in there."

Down the steps and along the path the pair headed. In his right hand, Script clutched Melchizedek's staff, and on his left shoulder Mock perched. "Get ready for interrogation, Mock," Script said. "How can it be that the fate of Estillyen rests in the mind of a mockingbird? Save our souls one and all, I say. We're getting close, just around this bend, and before our eyes I hope we see a trio of welcome faces.

"It's so, Mock," he said. "Greetings—such a welcome sight it is to see you three."

"Yes, yes, come along," said Melchizedek. "Actually, we knew you were here. A couple of minutes ago, Sage heard something making a racket at the campsite. So he walked over, and Mock was splashing around in the rain barrel. Bit dusty was it in hell?"

"Mercy upon my soul, I don't know how to begin."

"Perhaps by taking a seat," said Simon. "I'm glad you made it in and out, away from the flames, sulfur, screeching owls, and howling loons. Not nice at all, hell. Hell makes Golgotha look like a picnic ground."

"Splendid to see you, Script," said Sage. "You must tell us everything."

"Melchizedek, am I permitted to hug you?" asked Script.

"Script, you make me smile," said Melchizedek. "My prayers are answered. And the staff, come in handy did it?"

"I can only . . ."

"Hold it, Script," said Sage. "Tea, hot tea we have, with warm cross buns. 'Tis the season, you know; shall I pour? I've also prepared deviled eggs, a platterful, which you'll find perfectly chilled. Sorry about the obvious association.

"Just the same, deviled eggs go wonderfully well with hot baked potatoes filled with mushroom gravy. I'm just about to pull them out of the chest. So sit, and bon appétit, but let's first have a toast of meadow wine. Melchizedek, please, if you would be so kind?"

"Yes indeed, a toast, I say. Today joy itself has come to call on the Meadow of Gates and Doors. For on this most special occasion, Script, a prodigious son, has returned from hell. And he has returned well, along with our beloved mockingbird, Mock. So to you, Script, for your valor and courage to pass through the very Gates of Hell below, we lift high our glasses. We do so with colossal gladness for what you and dear Mock have achieved. Cheers!"

"Here, here," said Sage and Simon, as everyone clinked their glasses and then tipped them to imbibe.

"Sage, pardon," said Melchizedek, "if you don't mind, would you kindly pass the deviled eggs? Seems their delightful scent has wafted up to greet my nose. Yes, thank you."

So, in no less than miracle fashion, the quartet of Melchizedek, Script, Simon, and Sage had reconvened in a spirit of warmth and gratitude. Script's return from hell buoyed their confidence. For the first time, they sensed their united quest might result in a meritorious outcome. But the outcome was yet to come. They knew intuitively that expectations must be bridled.

"So, another potato, Script, or more eggs?" asked Sage.

"No, I don't think I can manage another bite," Script said.

"And you, Melchizedek, another cross bun, perhaps?" said Sage.

"No, I'm with Script," said Melchizedek. "But you might set a couple aside for later."

"Certainly; I'll place them in the trunk," said Sage.

"Now, tell us, Script," said Melchizedek. "You say you actually listened to Satan once again addressing legions of fallen angels seated on that vast sulfur plane beneath the Crimson Cliffs? Did I state that properly?"

"Words I once worked into a play preface my remarks. 'I heard many things in hell. How, then, am I mad? . . . observe how healthily— how calmly I can tell you the whole story.'[49]

"Calmly, though, I do not speak, and I may well be mad. But yes, Melchizedek, I heard many things in hell, including an address by Satan on the vast sulfur plane. I swear to it on my soul," said Script.

"No need for that; let's keep your soul intact," said Melchizedek. "We have every confidence in you, Script. We trust you—how shall I say—implicitly. We just need to unravel this mysterious madness. So please go ahead."

"Due to your staff, my entry into hell was very different on this occasion. I didn't put a foot on the trail leading from the scripted way. No need for the lightning-like propulsion to carry me along. I didn't have to navigate my way through dark tunnels and haunting caves. In a flash I was there, standing on top of the Reservoirs of Bewilderment.

"Stunned, one minute I stood watching Nicodemus, and then your staff gave me a tug, and the next minute I stood atop the Reservoirs of Bewilderment in hell. The landscape made me think I was walking on the Moon or on Mars. Amazingly, on that frightening landscape, I saw no demons or demented creatures. Just the same, it was horrid, and despite your gracious words, Melchizedek, I was terrified, petrified.

"Every step, a crunch, a crackle, and if I halted, the fear only worsened. Everything was amplified, each step, as if the surface was one giant amplifier. Mock and I just crept along, looking and wondering what might happen next. That's when I looked down to see demons and devotees, legions of them, sitting as rigid as planks in endless rows. In unison they clapped, as if slapping together slate shingles.

"When Satan appeared on stage, they were spellbound. He referred to the legions as celestial beings, and to humans as the Race. He proclaimed the day of Homo sapiens as over, saying the beginning of the end had finally come. He spoke about ejection from heaven, how cataclysmic it was, and how I AM got it all wrong. 'Twas the most sordid speech ever given surely, and I heard it, along with Mock."

"Okay, Script," said Melchizedek. "But the part about Operation Spite, if you don't mind; let's go over that again. That's the key to everything. We need to figure out the timing and the approach."

"As I said, Satan declared that Operation Spite had begun. He told the legions they would soon occupy the Isle of Estillyen and set up operations. Satan plans to erect a mammoth tower on the isle, which will extol the virtues of AI, algorithms, dataism, and the promise of discarnate existence.

"And imagine this—Satan promised that whitewashed tombs will be constructed all over the isle, filled with the bones of Estillyenites."

"Not good at all, I'd say," said Simon. "It appears that the Devil, too, is the same, never changing."

"Indeed, that sounds like Satan," said Melchizedek. "We have to piece this together."

"Furthermore," Script said, "Satan extolled the promise of platform building and the efficacy of technopoly. He said, 'This is the new discarnate age, our kind of age. Today the Race reels in confusion, and delusion. They know not what to believe.'

"Then he said something about the Race being like vipers; I didn't get that. But I do recall him pontificating about a new narrative, the dominant narrative called Bewilderment.

"I don't know how much you wish me to say," said Script. "I could go on for days. I don't know how I'll ever rid myself of the images planted in my mind."

"I'm not sure we have days," said Sage.

"Tell us, Script," said Melchizedek, "is there more about the speech?"

"I remember one part almost word for word. This is very wild. Satan insisted that humans are nothing but organisms, and organisms are nothing but algorithms. Via technopoly, human organisms and machines have merged. What I heard was beyond surreal.

"Then, when Satan ended his speech, he turned his back on the throng, and the clapping intensified at a frenzied pace. Like uncoiled springs, the throng shot out of their seats. In perfect unison the slapping echoed across the great sulfur plane."

"Well, I'm sure you'll recall much more in time," said Melchizedek. "But let's leave the speech for now. This pit you fell into—dreadful it must have been. But you said you heard sounds and eerie bird calls mixed with howls."

"More tea?" asked Sage.

"Don't mind if I do," said Melchizedek. "Pass along another one of those deviled eggs too, Sage."

"I'll top yours up as well, Script," said Sage. "Do carry on."

"Well, we crept along the surface step-by-step. Where we thought we were going, I have no idea. The surface had these rolling berms. At one point, in the dip of a berm, I heard sounds coming up through the surface. So I laid Melchizedek's staff aside, leaned down to listen, and all hell broke loose, literally.

"Like thin ice, the surface suddenly cracked apart in bits and pieces. There was not a second to back away. We plunged headlong into that pit. I honestly thought that was the end and I was dead, or nearly dead. I lost consciousness. For how long I do not know. Eventually Mock let out a few sounds, which must have stirred me. It was sheer terror.

"Fortunately, I wore Sage's gold scarf. There in the darkness, in the pit of hell, it began to glow. The scarf emitted a glow greater than that of the atmosphere above. I could see my way around the dreadful pit. And Mock, too, wore the little gold ribbon I had tied around his neck before we set out. It also glowed."

"Concerning the sounds, what did you hear?" asked Simon.

"Again, bizarre; the pit must have been in between the Reservoirs of Confusion and Static. What I heard came through the walls of the pit. From the Confusion side, I heard a nothing but a monotone—a string of words, or lines, made up of weird phrases. It was not a single voice but, say, three or four voices speaking in unison with identical cadence. The collective voice spoke something like this:

> *Rugface, get back, knife the knot, no, not, ice the tub, feather the wall.*
> *Seam, tear out the beam, seam, now scream. I told you so, no, yes, no,*
> *rip up the floor, put it back. Break the mirror, catch the image before it*
> *cracks. Now row . . .*

"You don't say," said, Melchizedek. "'Catch the image before it cracks'—that certainly sounds confusing enough."

"The other side, what did you hear?" asked Sage.

"Nothing but indistinguishable static like: *reil, orro, buzzzzzz, gurrl, reilorp, popip, popip, resuel, ser, urine, ree, zeeirl . . .*

"The sounds were completely the opposite of the monotone cadence emanating from the Reservoir of Confusion. The static sounds were frenzied and varied wildly in terms of volume. There were loud pops, high-pitched shrills, bass-like hums. It was mixed; it was madness."

"All right, all right," said Melchizedek, "we know that Operation Spite is on, but we don't know all we need to know. We're back to bird sounds, the calls, the hoots, and howls. So, my friends, we must ask Mock to vacate his perch on Script's shoulder and take the stand on his appointed chair. Do we agree?"

"Yes, fine with me," said Script. "Here, I'll walk him over."

"More tea?" said Sage. "And yes, I agree."

"This should be interesting," said Simon.

"Script, did Mock say anything to you in the pit?" said Melchizedek.

"Well, like I said, his tweeting must have awakened me," said Script. "But his tweets were the same as we heard before."

"Okay, Mock," said Melchizedek, "we would like to hear directly from you. We need to hear exactly what you tweeted to Script as he lay on the floor in that pit of hell. Okay, now out with it."

Floo-hours, Floo-hours, Twee
Vir-Vir, Vir-is, Vir-is, Vir-is,
Twee, Twee, Salee, Salee,
Twee, Twee, Killy, Killy

"Like I said, the same tweets we heard before," said Script.

"So, Script," said Sage, "let's retrace what we know. It seems that a virus is going to kill the flowers on the Isle of Estillyen. But for all we know, the flowers might be the Estillyenites. Also we think *Salee* may refer to water. Has Mock tweeted anything different, something he might have picked up in the pit?"

"Let me think," said Script. "When I was shaving, yes, Mock did sound out something I hadn't heard before. But I didn't think anything of it. It was something like *Err-zee Err-zee Mr-ting.*"

"Hmm," said Melchizedek. "Mock, my dear bird, if indeed you have added to your repertory, we would be delighted to hear your latest addition. The quartet is listening."

Mock looked around the table and then took a couple of steps to the right, along the top slate of his chair. He looked around again, and stepped back to the left, where he had started. Next, he flapped his wings, lifted his head toward the sky, and sounded:

Peek-prr, Ez-zree Frr-zee Mr-ting, Peek-prr, Ez-ztee Frr-zee Mr-ting,
Peek-prr, Peek-prr, Twee

Sage quickly rose from his chair and said, "Mock, might we hear that again?"

Mock responded:

Peek-prr, Ez-zree Frr-zee Mr-ting, Peek-prr, Ez-ztee Frr-zee Mr-ting,
Peek-prr, Peek-prr, Twee

"Dear Lord," said Sage.

"Wait," said Melchizedek, "what did Mock say?"

"The answer to the mystery," said Sage.

"What then?" said Melchizedek.

"We should have known," said Sage.

"Sage, what did Mock mock?" asked Melchizedek.

"The reason for the name," said Sage.

"What name?" said Melchizedek.

"Did you get it, Script?" asked Sage.

"Get what?" said Melchizedek.

"The answer," said Sage.

"Sage, you can't torment me like this," said Melchizedek. "I know you're a sage from ages past, reckoning with all manner of parchments, print, and pages vast, but the final grains of sand are racing through the narrow neck of the hourglass.

"The Isle of Estillyen, set as it is beyond the Storied Sea, may soon be obliterated. Even now I can see the isle's gentle waves, gentle people, and mystical mist circling the isle. If you don't cough up what you know this instant, I shall never eat another morsel lifted from your trunk. Do you hear me—no deviled eggs, no cross buns, not a crumb!"

"Okay, okay, I'm sorry," said Sage. "I was just stunned by the fiendish yet clever approach. This is the meaning of the mystery. By the way, you both might as well stand, so that when I tell you, you can sit down. You will need to."

"Sage, I'm warning you," said Melchizedek. "Come on, Script, Simon, let's stand."

"Thus, the meaning," said Sage. "*Peek-prr* stands for peak of sunrise, when the sun alights the eastern sky, before showing its face. *Frr-zee Mr-ting* I had to hear twice before I grasped the meaning. Reverse the two sounds and you get *morning ferry*."

"Script," said Sage, "the question I now ask of you may give us the final piece of the puzzle. I think I already know the answer, but here's the question. Does the Estillyen Ferry transport Easter lilies to the isle on Easter morning? Tomorrow is Easter."

"Oh, dear me," said Script. "Let me sit down. Yes, very early, say two in the morning or so, the ferry departs from Century so that it will arrive in Estillyen at sunrise. The ferry captains are known to stall or speed up the ferry to ensure that the ferry reaches Port Estillyen just a few minutes either side of sunrise.

"This is the only ferry crossing of the year without any passengers aboard. It's just the captain and someone who looks after the flowers, making sure they stay up straight and are watered. The ferry is always jam-packed with fresh Easter lilies—hundreds, thousands, I suppose.

"The tradition is longstanding, and tomorrow will be the same. Scores of Estillyenites will be lined up at dawn, waiting in Port Estillyen for the ferry's arrival. Then they'll fan out all over the isle bringing Easter lilies to the residents and guests of Estillyen."

"I suppose I'll have a seat, as well," said Melchizedek. "Sage, you, Simon, and I must be on that early morning ferry. Script, if all goes well, the lilies will not carry the lethal virus. Hopefully, if we can intercede, then perhaps you can be on your way back to the Isle of Estillyen."

"But how?" asked Script. "I don't know where I am. I'm not even sure *who* I am. All I know is that we sit here, at a huge round table in the middle of the Meadow of Gates and Doors. I sleep in Writer's Cottage. I pass through ancient gates, and then through doors that do not have frames or hinges. Yet they mysteriously lock and unlock.

"And on the other side of those doors, I step into scenes of living history, lived in ages past. Four times I've been to hell and back. The Reservoirs of Bewilderment I've seen and the Seven Valleys of Sin. On my last trip, I fell headlong into the pit of hell. And now, back to Estillyen you say. How can that be? It can't be, though I wish it were so."

"Script, you've trusted me," said Sage. "Trust me still. Early in the morning, while darkness still hovers over the meadow, get up and dress.

You must make your way to the final gate and door, through which you will dutifully pass. Like all the rest, the gate is ancient; it's worn out the ages. It will surely open and let you pass. And, like the scarf I gave you, the door is gold. Through it, too, you must pass.

"Once inside, another scene you'll witness. You'll not carry Melchizedek's shepherd's staff this time. He has need of it now. Mock will be with you for a while. When you sense the time is right, take off your gold scarf and hang it on the wall behind you. You will be gifting it to another pilgrim, for another day.

"But then you must pray silently what you wish to pray. During your prayer of silence, pray that your eyes may be opened. Just then, Mock will fly away.

"Do you think you can manage that, Script?"

"I, uh, so, I mean . . ."

"Good, I know you can—and will," said Sage.

"Okay, then," said Melchizedek, "it's good to get things settled. Somehow, so it seems, all this depth of conversation has rekindled my appetite. Perhaps, Sage, a deviled egg or two along with a wee sip of meadow wine would do. What say you?"

"I do," said Sage.

SEVENTEEN
Estillyen Easter

Script sat on the porch of Writer's Cottage until late in the evening. A sense of resolve he had, but not total peace. He tried to mull his way through what he'd experienced. But his mind wandered; he'd lock on to a train of thought only to lose it. Trying to reconcile all the upheavals of time and space baffled him.

He clearly knew he belonged on the Isle of Estillyen, but had it been ten weeks since he was there, or ten years? Further, Script found it impossible to draw conclusions about the meaning of his tumultuous experiences. For this, he needed hindsight, which he would only gain when he had come through the experience. Regardless, Script's faith underpinned his doubts and lack of clarity.

At a late hour, he finally went to bed. Mock nestled down in his favorite spot atop the dresser on the backside of the windup alarm clock. Thus, time ticked, sweeping hours one, two, and three away. At ten past four, Script sat up straight, swung his legs over the bed, and got up. Before going to bed, he'd laid out his clothes, so in no time he was dressed.

In the washroom, he stood under the lone light bulb with its extended brass chain. Script glanced up at the bulb reflected in the mirror and said, "Last shave, bulb. I shall miss you, your dangling chain and porcelain socket. It's your commonness I so admire, your utility, your lack of vanity. I wish I could take you with me, but I don't know where I'll be later today or the next. Perhaps I'll return one day to see how you are getting on."

Script dried his face and clicked the chain, putting out the light. He stepped back into the chamber and said, "So, Mock, we must be off. Just you and me it is; no shepherd's staff or anything else to carry. Ready? Let's go. We know the way, but everything looks quite different in the dark. All we need to do is stay on the path. In two or three minutes, we'll stand at the gate.

"It's strange how I like talking to you, Mock. Or, on the other hand, perhaps you don't think it's strange at all. I'm strange, though; I know that, but that's not what I'm talking about; you know what I mean to say. You must be strange, too, hanging out with Sage over the years. But I suspect you've never seen anything like what we've been through. Walking on the surface of the moon, falling into a pit in hell—now that's a story to tell.

"Do you think you will tell it? I will, I hope, but who will believe it? Your partner, Sage, Melchizedek, and Simon know it's true, but they're also rather strange. Well, I don't mean strange like me, but very mysterious, with mannerisms and personalities most unique. I've never met anyone like those three, except in a dream.

"Say, how old are you anyway? And Sage—he says he's a crier of papyrus, print, and page. That stretches back a fair bit, you know. Okay, we're almost to the gate. You needn't tell me how old you are. If beyond the gate and door we do part, I shall always carry you in my heart.

"Anyway, enough sentimentality; we stand at the gate. Where does it lead? Let's take a deep breath. Good, now two, three, and in and out again. I found that stilling. Okay, no more stalling. I shall give the gate a slight push. With the back of my fingers, I gently push. And there it swings, like it can't wait to see us pass through.

"Now we step—count them, two, three, four, and a half dozen more. A few more and we shall stand in front of the gold door. Nine, and ten— okay, did you bring the key, Mock? Oh, you're not saying. Well, let me see if I can find it buried somewhere. There, I have it. Ready or not, the key is inserted, and at the count of three, we shall see if it turns. One, two, three, and it turns.

"There it goes, Mock. The door of gold begins that slow, gradual, and silent swing. And ahead, what do we see? On a table a candle lit, and two common-looking fellows. Small place it is. I wonder who they are, and what they're discussing. They've just jumped up; they're leaving. We'll advance to the edge of the room and wait; we mustn't enter.

"The smell of a burning candle, Mock—a delightful smell, isn't it? There's food on the table, bread, and some sort of stew, it seems. I wonder who prepared it. Not Sage, I can tell you. Perhaps a maid. See that? A shadow just passed on the wall. This scene, Mock, like the others we've seen, is from long ago, from ages past. We wait.

"Footsteps beyond the door—do you hear them? They've passed. We can't go anywhere; just breathe, okay? They must be returning; they've left the candle burning. Footsteps again, listen. Here they come, through the doorway."

Cleopas:

Seth, come back in! Quit looking around, dashing about—he's gone. We need to talk seriously, okay? This happened; it really happened. To us, to you and me, it happened. I don't know why he appeared, but all of a sudden, he was present. Present, right there beside us, with us. We were two, then suddenly he was there, and we were three. It's undeniable.

Seth:

I know, Cleopas, I know, but why us—and why Emmaus? We're seven miles out from Jerusalem, in the middle of nowhere. We're nobody, just a couple of followers. Why not appear in the temple, in front of the priests who had him crucified?

Cleopas:

We can't answer such questions.

Seth:

Okay, but we can ask them, can't we? What should we do?

Cleopas:

Well, we can't just go to bed and wake up tomorrow and say how interesting that was to talk with the Risen Christ. We need to go back to Jerusalem and find his disciples. For all we know, he might be with them right now. We'd heard the news about his missing body, the women at the site, and angels appearing. No wonder he said, "How foolish you are, and so slow of heart to believe what the prophets had spoken."

Seth:

We still didn't get it. Who did we think this person was? Who comes along and says, "Did not Christ have to suffer?" And then goes on to explain all that Moses and the prophets said about him. But he was saying all of that to us, to you and me, and that's what I don't understand. We were so caught up in his words, but still we didn't discern the fact that it was actually him. Who did you think he was?

Cleopas:

I don't know. Let's not focus on what we didn't know or see. That's not the point. When he came along, we were downcast, muttering on, but his presence changed everything.

Seth:

Come stay with us, we told him. You know what this means, Cleopas?

Cleopas:

I'm not sure, but it's definitely earthshaking.

Seth:

How is the world going to come to grips with his resurrection?

Cleopas:

It will take time, just like it took time for us to recognize him. But what's going to happen when he does turn up in the temple or goes to show himself to Pilate? Imagine that; think about it. This is one of the most astounding things that's ever happened. It's like the parting of the Red Sea, or . . . I don't know. But why us? I still don't get it.

This is different than Lazarus. The same, but different—he's the one who raised Lazarus! He was crucified. He explained it; he spelled it out for us, how it was written in the scrolls. I know this: such news will not stay in Jerusalem, buried.

Seth:

The ramifications I can't believe. I mean, this is a realm beyond us, yet not, and that's what's so staggering.

Cleopas:

What are you trying to say, Seth?

Seth:

Well, if Jesus is who we believe he is, it means that you and I have walked, talked, and broken bread with God. We need to let that settle in, but we still need to get going.

It has to be true, Cleopas. We believed in him before he was crucified. We saw him as a prophet, powerful in word and deed before God. Now it's time to believe in him as God. When he broke the bread, we saw his hands. Our eyes were opened, and we recognized him for who he truly is.

Cleopas:

Then, let's go, Seth! Blow out the candle.

"Mock, astounding what we've just seen. We just watched living history, a candle burning, a table small on which bread crumbs lay. Now the candlelight is gone.

"My scarf of gold glows, as does your ribbon, Mock, but the time has come to take off my scarf. The hook behind the door—that must be the one Sage intended. The scarf looks stunning, hanging there aglow, don't you think, Mock?

"Lord, it is true, where can I flee from your presence? Now, as Sage instructed, silently I pray." As soon as Script bowed his head, Mock disappeared. Script prayed, "My mind is set on you. Lord, may my eyes be opened."

Thus, a change occurred.

The Infirmary

Brrriiing brrriiing, brrriiing brrriiing, brrriiing brrriiing, brrriiing . . .

"Hello, Brother Plot speaking."

"Yes, Brother Plot, I'm sorry to trouble you. This is Sister Ravena from the infirmary."

"Hello, Sister!"

"Again, I'm sorry for phoning, at such an early hour. It's just that you gave strict instructions, saying that if anything changed with Brother Script, you wanted to be notified immediately."

"Yes, of course," said Plot.

"Well, he's still in a coma, but there are a few signs of change. We don't know exactly what it means, but a little while ago, the nurses distinctly heard Brother Script speaking. He was praying and uttering names. They thought he mentioned the name Melchizedek."

"It sounds positive," said Plot. "I'll be over soon, Sister Ravena. I'll ring round the brothers, and much thanks for phoning."

"Yes, bye for now," Sister Ravena said.

The Ferry

Meanwhile, the saga continued, as Melchizedek, Sage, and Simon boarded the ferry in Century, destined for the Isle of Estillyen. It was predawn, Easter morning, and they found a bench on the upper deck, tucked away behind the shuttered canteen.

"This is a great spot," said Melchizedek. "I like to sit in the aft position, watching the waves calm after a ferry passes. As soon as the sun begins to rise, we'll see it. And the seagulls, too—they'll be soaring and singing their songs."

"Such fragrance," said Sage. "I've never been on a ferry packed with Easter lilies. Several hundred up here alone, I'd say, and three or four times that below."

"And to think this is where all this started," said Simon. "The way of suffering, now often called *Via Dolorosa*. Lilies, a ferry-full . . . what those characters of old did not know."

"Nobody's around," said Melchizedek.

"Well, there's a captain," said Sage. "And I hear someone whistling below, moving about."

"Yes," said Melchizedek, "in a bit we need to pay the Whistler a visit. I wonder how Script got on in the Meadow of Gates and Doors— such an enchanting place. Script, as fine of a fellow as I can recall. A genuine soul he is. And what a character, I say, going in and out of hell, with a mockingbird in his pocket. Fresh air—lovely, isn't it?"

"Yes, indeed," said Sage.

Ever so smoothly, the ferry glided along with its cargo of lilies and three mysterious characters seated on the upper deck. Midpoint in the Storied Sea, the ferry entered the famed Estillyen mist. The mist is always present; it never goes away. Encircling the isle as it does, the mist is revered by the Estillyenites. Others fear it, due to long-standing mystical and folklore legends.

"Fellows," said Melchizedek, "I think we better move along. The sun is beginning to lift."

"Yes, yes, we're with you," said Sage. "Let's find the Whistler and see what he knows."

"Watch the steps," said Simon. "They're slippery."

"I see a light in the cabin up ahead," said Melchizedek, "if we can get there through this maze of lilies. He's in; through the window I can see him moving about. He's whistling. I can't wait to knock on the door; we'll scare him to death. Here we go, this way, through here; watch out for the lilies—they're all top-heavy.

"Okay, here goes. Say, you in there, could we have a wee word? No response. I'd better open the door and poke my head through. Hello, hi there, my dear sailing fellow, I'm Melchizedek, in the company of Sage and Simon of Cyrene. And who might we have the good fortune of addressing?"

The slender man in the cabin hastily ceased whistling and said, "The name's Jimmy, and I'll stab you all—my knives are sharp."

"No, no need for knives and rolling pins, good sir; we come in peace," said Melchizedek. "Truly we do."

"But where'd you come from?" replied Jimmy, backing up against a cabinet in the galley.

"That, my friend, is a rather long story," said Melchizedek. "Do you mind if we step on in?"

"Yeah, yeah, I suppose you can come in," said Jimmy.

"Now, dear friend, don't be alarmed. We boarded in Century, and we've been sitting up in the aft section," said Melchizedek.

"Oh, I see, youse must be part of the troupe that's been gathering in Estillyen. But you scared me spitless, since we was in the midst of mist, you know. And you with that turban on—you're sure costumed up, you three."

"Do you mind if we sit?" asked Melchizedek.

"No, no, that's fine, yes, and shut the door," Jimmy said. "I was fixing some tea. Care for a cup? Porcelain or tin cups—which would you prefer?"

"Tin, why not," said Sage. "I like your blue wellies, Jimmy. They look right smart with that long yellow apron."

"Well, I mean, you know, practical sort of dress; I've dressed like this for nearly thirty years. Anyway, the tea has steeped its steep. So, here we go, one for you, what did you say your name is, Mr. Melchez, and a cup for you, Mr. Sage and Mr. Simon."

"Yes, Melchez is perfect," said Melchizedek. "Say, out of curiosity, and if you don't mind, please tell us a bit more about this Estillyen mist."

"Oh, dock my slippers, you got two or three days? Many a story is told of mysterious sightings, amidst the mist. They keep what they call a storied manifest at the Estillyen Port House. You may want to check it out. Well, I mean, you can't check it out like in a library, but they'll let you examine it. Those stories in the manifest, they're the reason, of course, that this is called the Storied Sea."

"I see, Jimmy," said Melchizedek. "But these stories—can you offer a few examples?"

"Well, let me think. I only go with them that's put in the manifest— you know, verified, on the record. That way I can say, 'You should me find as true as a carpenter's square.'[50]

"Anyway, Tuxedo Tom comes to mind. As the manifest records, there have been more than a dozen sightings of ole Tuxedo Tom playing his cello for the sea."

"You don't say," said Melchizedek.

"The details are pretty much the same. A man, all alone, is seated in the middle of a wooden lifeboat, or some sort of smallish vessel. He is perfectly dressed in a tuxedo, playing his cello for the sea. Those who've heard him say the tune is very haunting but lovely, as if Tuxedo Tom is trying to calm the waves. You know, sometimes this Storied Sea kicks up a bit of a fuss."

"How interesting," said Melchizedek. "Any others you might recall?"

"Well, there's the account of the two swordsmen; it's one of my favorites. This duo, in uniforms of old, appears fighting a fierce duel of clanking steel. Like that line of old says, 'The bright swords went in circles to and fro so terribly, that even their least stroke seemed powerful enough to fell an oak.'[51]

"It's exactly so, or so I've been told. They float along on a wooden platform, a stage some say. According to witnesses, they never utter a word to each other. They just rattle their swords, lunging and leaping as they float along.

"I saw them battling one day, I do believe. But it was a day when the waves were swelling high, and amidst the swelling waves, my sight of them I lost. I wonder, I do, who they are. In my mind, I hold them as gallant men from days of old.

"So, enough said?" Jimmy asked.

"No, no, carry on—another tale would be fine," said Melchizedek.

"Okay, now topping the list is the Skeleton Ship. As the story goes, suddenly out of the mist, this massive sailing ship appears. But the ship is just a frame, just the beams of the ship. It has no cladding or planks on its hull. Yet the ship sails atop the waves without sails, but the ship's rigging is still intact.

"Then there's the part I don't believe, even though it is documented in the manifest. About half of them sightings list a cat as occupying the crow's nest. I don't mean lying down, curled up. I'm saying a cat standing up like a person, looking out at the sea. You know, come to think of it, maybe those sightings that don't see the cat are when the cat's curled up asleep.

"So I might say, 'For sorry heart, I may tell no more.'[52] But pressing upon my mind is the lady miss in her wedding dress. Fair and lovely she appears, gliding along in a beautiful white, lacy dress, with her golden hair woven atop her head. On the train of her wedding dress, red rose petals rest where they were scattered long ago.

"Opera she sings, as beautifully as an angel might. She sings for her groom, who after many battles won, finally neared his homeward shore on their appointed wedding day. Alas, the ship's mast snapped clean off and knocked the handsome groom overboard.

"Sad tale, that is," Jimmy said. "If I was to ever see her, I don't know what I would do. Do you?"

"Jimmy, I wish we had all day to spend with you," said Melchizedek. "Our time, however, is limited and passing away. Now, if I might, I'd like to ask a question or two."

"No bother," said Jimmy.

"Good," said Melchizedek. "I understand that you take care of the Easter lilies, making sure they are handled properly when they're brought on board at Century and then unloaded in Estillyen."

"Yes, indeed, but I do more than that. I straighten them up, clip any damaged petals or leaves, and make sure they're well watered. I watered these down here just a bit ago. I also whistle to them."

"I see," said Melchizedek. "Now, has there been anything different this year, in terms of routine, than in previous years?"

"So, let me see . . . the loading and all went just like clockwork. This is a great crop, hearty. Oh, but yes, there is one thing new. You see those two gallon jugs in the corner there on the floor?"

"Yes," said Sage. "You mean those with the white powder or granules?"

"Yeah, those," said Jimmy. "I haven't opened them yet; you can see how they're sealed. Anyhow, this fellow brought 'em onboard last thing before we left port. He had on an official-looking outfit—said he was a horticultural scientist. The man said he had been hired by all the growers with the aim of improving flower life.

"This fellow was very adamant in what he had to say. Instructive-like, if you know what I mean. Three times he said, 'Don't forget, you must sprinkle a small amount of granules on each lily, before they are off-loaded in Port Estillyen.'

"Oh, yes, I almost forgot. He also told me to pour all the extra powder into those little zippy bags and give it to those distributing the lilies throughout the isle. He said they should sprinkle the contents on lawns, or gardens, or trails—that it would be good for the Estillyen atmosphere, the air, he said.

"Then, in a hurry, he turned and started to walk away. I called after him and said, 'Hey, mister, sorry, I didn't catch your name, and where you're from.' He yelled back and said his name was Forest Killy—yes, that's it. Next thing I knew, he was gone. I mean, he sort of disappeared."

"I see, Jimmy," said Melchizedek. "You've told us a great deal. Actually, we believe we know the source of the white substance, and the situation is different than you were told. Actually, evil has been hard at work. Spite fuels the action, so you are very fortunate that you have not touched those containers.

"Now, listen to me carefully, and don't be afraid. We are who we said we are, but in a few minutes, we will be gone."

"You mean before we dock?"

"Yes, it will happen like this. Simon, please."

"Yikes, St. Peter, Simon just vanished before my eyes, turban and all. Where did he go? How did he do that? There's his cup. Oh, tyranny has come to cease my soul. You two are not going to kill me, are you?"

"No, Jimmy—be calm," said Melchizedek. "No harm will come to you. Sage and I are going to take the containers with us. But we also want you to forget about this Forest Killy fellow, and then forget about us. In order for this to happen, Sage is going to lay his right hand upon your head. Okay?"

"Well, I guess . . . sure; you both look sort of priestly-like in a way."

"Okay, Sage, please place your hand on Jimmy's head. Now, Jimmy, when I say the word *forget*, you are to forget all about the mysterious powder man named Killy. So, forget!"

"Say, Jimmy, what are those containers of powder on the floor?" asked Sage.

"I haven't the foggiest," said Jimmy. "I've never seen 'em before—didn't know they were there."

"Okay, Jimmy, now Sage is going to lay his hand on you again, and this time you are to forget you ever saw us. Okay?"

"Well, but I sort of like you fellows."

"We like you too, Jimmy," said Melchizedek. "But we have places to go, rather far away, and we must go. We must go now; our work here is done."

"So can I at least say goodbye?" said Jimmy.

"Certainly you can, Jimmy," said Sage.

"Okay then, sirs. I say, Mr. Melchez and Mr. Sage, it was a privilege to meet you, so take care, and goodbye!"

"Sage, please place your hand on Jimmy's head for a second time. So, Jimmy, when I say the word *forget,* you are to forget all about us; you never saw us. So forget!"

"*Atup-atum, dedely dum,*" hummed Jimmy. "Where was I now?"

As the ferry pulled into the harbor of Port Estillyen, it announced its arrival by offering its classic treble horn blast. At that moment, in room 102 at the infirmary, Script opened his eyes and reached for the gold scarf that Plot had placed above his bed on the night he arrived.

With his eyes wide open, Script said, "Say, what's happening? Where am I? Brother Plot, it's you, Writer, and Narrative. What's going on? Writer, why are you crying?"

"Script," said Plot. "You are in Good Shepherd Infirmary."

"Am I? What's happened?" said Script.

"There's a lot for you to take in," said Plot.

"Script, you were brought here from Theatre Portesque," said Writer. "You suffered a terrible accident on the opening night of *Presence.* You fell in the balcony and cracked the back of your skull."

"Hold on . . . deary me, I did?" said Script. "Can't be, can it?"

"Okay," said Plot. "It's Sister Ravena and her nurses."

"Sister Ravena, it's you," said Script. "I feel stiff. What's going on?"

"Gentlemen," Sister Ravena said, "we need everyone out for a while. We need to check Brother Script's vitals. His primary doctors have been called. We need to access the patient, so no more questions for now. 'By which, if you will do as the wise do, do always as women advise you.'[53] So, later, say around lunchtime, come back, and we'll see what's what."

"Later, Script," said Narrative.

"Yes, that's right," said Writer. "We'll be back later."

"Well, okay," said Script. "Sister, what day is it anyway?"

"It's Easter Sunday, Script," said Sister Ravena. "It's an Estillyen Easter. We've brought you a beautiful Easter lily. As you know, right now lilies are being taken all over the isle."

"If you say so, Sister, it must be," said Script.

"Just relax, Brother Script," said Sister Ravena. "Would you like some water?"

"Would I! Water . . . I've never been so thirsty. 'I crave, alas, the merest water drop.'[54] I feel like I just crawled out of a pit in hell."

"Now, now, Script," Sister Ravena said. "We want to check you over, and then the doctors will be here soon to speak with you, if you are up to it."

"Up to it? I need to get out of here!"

"Script, be patient, okay? Come on, girls, let's try to raise him just a bit. Very carefully, very slowly, as when we shift him, it can change the pressure on his skull. There we go, propped up about halfway."

"Say, what's all this business about my skull?" asked Script.

"Never mind, Script," said Sister Ravena. "Okay, girls, we need to change his gown, and . . . you know."

"Oh," said Script. "Here comes all of this indecent exposure."

Before long, the doctors arrived, and everyone was both amazed and delighted with Script's response. His neurosurgeon, Dr. Page, was stunned and told Script, "You've been in a deep coma, my friend. We never know how these situations go. Some people never come around, and others may have impaired mobility. Right now we are delighted with what we see."

Script's surgeon, Dr. Melchez, said, "Script, you came through the surgery very well. You did fracture your skull, but bear in mind that was seven weeks ago, so in terms of the initial trauma, you are as good as healed. As Dr. Page said, we want to see how you respond when we try to get you up and around tomorrow."

Thus the conversations flowed in room 102 throughout the day. The following day, Script managed several steps in the morning, and more in the afternoon. He was curious about the birds that fluttered about his window. As Sister Ravena explained, mockingbirds love to build nests in the eaves of the infirmary; it has to do with the way they were constructed.

The following day, Script stood at the window watching the mockingbirds come and go, then pause and practice their repertory. The birds made Script smile, especially the one that kept dropping slender gold leaves on the windowsill.

To everyone's utter amazement, Script improved dramatically from morning to afternoon of each succeeding day. A week soon passed, and as Saturday approached on the following week, Script could not be deterred. He was determined to take in *Presence* at Theatre Portesque. Script was amazed to hear that people all over the continent were raving about the play.

He did not know, though, that the brothers in his order were ahead of him concerning his anticipated appearance at Theatre Portesque. They informed the cast and rehearsed what would happen when Brother Writer stepped out on stage.

So, once again a Saturday night performance of *Presence* was on at Theatre Portesque. The majestic theatre was packed; there was not an empty seat in the house. Right on cue, the royal blue, front-of-the-house curtain opened fully. As on the opening night, a tall, slender young man stepped forward from the set's Storybook Barn and stood at the center of the stage.

He glanced back at the barn, then turned again to the audience, and began to sing:

"The Pasture"
I'm going out to clean the pasture spring;
I'll only stop to rake the leaves away
(And wait to watch the water clear, I may):
I sha'n't be gone long.—You come too.

Then he paused, and the crowd watched, as Brother Writer unexpectedly walked on stage. In the stillness of the theatre, each step Writer took was distinctly heard. He approached the microphone, smiled, and began to speak.

"Yes, I'd love to come along," Writer said. "And I will in a few minutes. Perhaps someone else would care to join us. First, however, I'd like to say a few words to the audience and explain our reason for the pause. We are delighted you have come to join us tonight. Actually, let me say we are thrilled by your presence at *Presence*.

"To the cast, please know how inspired we are by your brilliant performances, the singing, the dancing, the tears, and, of course, the story of *Presence* you so amiably portray. You bring to life a vitally important story, timeless yet so appropriate for the time in which we live. We're confident that tonight will prove to be another exceptional performance.

"Now, I want to speak to you about a rather personal topic. As many of you have read or heard, the playwright of *Presence* suffered a tragic accident on opening night. He was in the balcony, and so excited for the performance to begin that he rose from his seat, spun around, and raised his arms as a small sign of triumph. Unfortunately, he fainted, fell back against the balcony guardrail, and suffered a severe blow to the head.

"*Presence* was six years in the making, and the playwright hovered over every aspect of the performance. But on that opening night, he was rushed to surgery and lapsed into a deep coma. In the ensuing weeks we visited, we watched, we wondered, and we prayed. Our playwright lay before us in a coma that transported him to other realms. Where we do not know; perhaps one day he will tell us.

"Then, on Easter morning, less than two weeks ago, a phone call came through from Good Shepherd saying that the playwright of *Presence* had made a stir. Stir, indeed, then a step, and another step, and soon he was walking and talking. So it gives me great joy to tell you that tonight the playwright of *Presence* is here, present.

"Brother Script, we have a spotlight beaming down on the center of the stage, and it beams for you. I present to you, Script, the playwright of *Presence*. Script, please walk out and take a bow."

Considerably thinner than he was on opening night, Script stepped out from the wings and slowly walked into the beam of light. In the swell of thunderous applause Script stood, wiping tears from his cheeks, with his ribbon of gold.

"Speech, speech," yelled some in the crowd, but Script simply smiled and said, "Thank you, thank, you, thank you," and slowly stepped stage left, a half-dozen steps.

Then, at just the right time, the young man who had opened the play walked back to centerstage, under the beam of light, and said, "Let us begin again."

Then, as before, lines from "The Pasture" he sung:

I'm going out to clean the pasture spring;
I'll only stop to rake the leaves away
(And wait to watch the water clear, I may):
I sha'n't be gone long.—You come too.

From stage left a voice called. It was Script, who said, "Yes, I'll come along."

The young man walked over, locked his arm in Script's arm, and said, "Indeed, come along."

And off they went to clean the pasture spring!

THE END

NOTES

1 Robert Frost, *The Poetry of Robert Frost*, "The Pasture" (New York: Holt, Rinehart & Winston, 1969) 1.

2 Geoffrey Chaucer, *The Canterbury Tales* (Clayton, Del.: Prestwick House, Inc., 2009) 52.

3 Jacques Ellul, *The Presence of the Kingdom*, (Colorado Springs, Col.: Helmers & Howard, Publishers Inc., 1989) xxviii.

4 *The Poetry of Robert Frost*, "Mending Wall," 33.

5 Dante Alighieri, *The Divine Comedy*, Canto 1 (New York: Penguin Books, 2013) 5.

6 *The Canterbury Tales*, 85.

7 *The Canterbury Tales*, "The Nun's Priest's Tale," 168.

8 *The Poetry of Robert Frost*, "The Pasture."

9 *The Canterbury Tales*, "The Pardoner's Tale," 154.

10 *The Canterbury Tales*, "The Miller's Tale," 103.

11 *Inferno*, 24.

12 *The Canterbury Tales*, Prologue.

13 *Inferno*, Canto 3.

14 Ibid., Canto 17.

15 John 3:3, ESV.

16 Psalm 19:1–2, NKJV.

17 *Inferno*, Canto 3.

18 *The Canterbury Tales*, "The Miller's Tale," 98.

19 Ibid., 11.

20 *Inferno*, Canto 3.

21 Ibid.

22 Ibid.

23 *Inferno*, Canto 1.

24 Reference to William Blake's "This life's dim windows of the soul/ Distorts the heavens from pole to pole/And leads you to believe a lie/ When you see with, not through, the eye."

25 Reference to Hebrews 12:1 "Therefore, since we are surrounded by such a great cloud of witnesses . . ."

26 *Inferno*, Canto ___.

27 Ecclesiastes 9:3.

28 Ibid.

29 Story told in the Gospel of Mark, chapter 3.

30 Revelation 12:1–2, King James Version.

31 Revelation 12:3–4.

32 A prophecy of the prophet Jeremiah, quoted in St. Matthew's Gospel.

33 https://www.ling.upenn.edu/~beatrice/pangur-ban.html; http://irisharchaeology.ie/2013/10/pangur-ban/.
"The Scholar and His Cat, Pangur Bán" is perhaps the most famous surviving poem from early Ireland. Composed by an Irish monk sometime around the ninth century AD, the text compares the scholar's work with the activities of a pet cat, Pangur Bán. It is now preserved in the Reichnenau Primer at St. Paul's Abbey in the Lavanttal, Austria. Script recites the translation by Robin Flower.

34 *Inferno*, Canto 9.

35 *Inferno*, Canto 5.

36 *Inferno*, Canto 5.

37 Ezekiel 28:2.

38 *Canterbury Tales*, "The Knight's Tale."

39 The story is recorded in the Hebrew Scriptures, Book of Esther.

40 *Inferno*, Canto 12.

41 *Inferno*, Canto 3.

42 Psalm 84:10.

43 This version appeared in the Richmond *Semi-Weekly Examiner*, September 25, 1849; https://poets.org/poem/raven.

44 *The Canterbury Tales*, p.6.

45 *Inferno*, Canto 3, p.12.

46 *The Canterbury Tales*, General Prologue, Preswick House, p.21.

47 *The Canterbury Tales,* "The Knight's Tale," p. 75.

48 In a demonstration witnessed by members of Congress, American inventor Samuel F.B. Morse dispatched a telegraph message from the U.S. Capitol to Alfred Vail at a railroad station in Baltimore, Maryland. The message—"What Hath God Wrought?"—was telegraphed back to the Capitol a moment later by Vail. The question, taken from the Bible (Numbers 23:23), had been suggested to Morse by Annie Ellworth, the daughter of the commissioner of patents; https://www.history.com/this-day-in-history/what-hath-god-wrought.

49 *Great Tales and Poems of Edger Allan Poe,* "The Tell-Tale Heart" (New York, Simon and Schuster, 2007) 3.

50 *The Canterbury Tales,* "The Summoner's Tale" (New York: Barnes & Noble Classics, 2007) 669.

51 *The Canterbury Tales,* "The Knight's Tale," p. 56.

52 *The Canterbury Tales,* "The Merchant's Tale" (New York: Barnes & Noble Classics, 2007) 371.

53 *The Canterbury Tales,* "The Merchant's Tale," 379.

54 *Inferno,* Canto 30.

CPSIA information can be obtained
at www.ICGtesting.com
Printed in the USA
BVHW040252270121
598618BV00001B/4

9 781736 496701